Working Girls:
Carl Weber Presents

CH

Working Girls:
Carl Weber Presents

Katt

www.urbanbooks.net

Urban Books, LLC
97 N18th Street
Wyandanch, NY 11798

Working Girls: Carl Weber Presents

ISBN 13: 978-1-62286-983-1
ISBN 10: 1-62286-983-4

First Trade Paperback Printing August 2016
Printed in the United States of America

10 9 8 7 6 5 4 3 2 1

*This is a work of fiction. Any references or similarities
to actual events, real people, living or dead, or to real
locales are intended to give the novel a sense of reality.
Any similarity in other names, characters, places, and
incidents is entirely coincidental.*

Distributed by Kensington Publishing Corp.
Submit orders to:
Customer Service
400 Hahn Road
Westminster, MD 21157-4627
Phone: 1-800-733-3000
Fax: 1-800-659-2436

Working Girls

by

Katt

Prologue

Present . . .

The impact of the liquid slamming into her face brought her back to consciousness.

"Wake the fuck up!" an unfamiliar voice demanded as Jewels was doused with ice-cold water through the gate that separated the front seat from the back of the vehicle.

She had no idea how long she had been knocked out. The last thing she remembered was hitting the alarm and grabbing hold of the door handle on her chrome colored Maserati. After that everything else was a blur.

Jewels could tell she was lying on the floor of a van. Her shoulders were sore, her stomach was cramping, and her ankles were bleeding. Her hands were tied behind her back. Her ankles were cuffed as tight as they could be. She could hear masculine voices in front of her.

She struggled to open her eyes. When she finally did, the liquid that had been tossed in her face caused them to burn. She immediately shut her eyes, wondering what had been thrown in her face other than water. She also wondered how many hours had gone by since she was snatched. She had been knocked unconscious by a blow to the temple. Her head was killing her, and to top it off, she had to pee.

All types of thoughts were going through her head. She couldn't believe she had got caught slipping. But by who? was the million-dollar question. *Was it Kareem's peoples? The white trick's? The one she had killed after Sassy's murder? Or was it in retaliation to something Rome had done?* All these questions filled Jewels discombobulated mind. She couldn't stop wondering what was going to happen to her.

She said a quick prayer. *Please, Lord Jesus, I know that it's been a while since I've been to church, and I haven't prayed in a while, but you know my heart, so if you get me out of this fucked-up situation this one last time, I promise you that I will change my ways. Amen.*

She wondered whether Rome knew she had been snatched. She tensed when the vehicle came to a screeching halt. Her heart dropped to the pit of her stomach. She didn't know what was going on. All that could be heard was her heart pounding. Then Jewels heard a car door slam, and seconds later another car door slammed. She heard what sounded like two different voices, but she couldn't figure out what they were saying. They were yelling about something. Suddenly, the sliding side door popped open. . . .

Chapter One

Sometime during the nineties . . .

"Bitch! Didn't I tell you to mind your manners?" barked thirty-six-year-old Ice, one of St. Louis's coldest pimps, as he brought the bent-up wire hanger down with all his might on naked nineteen-year-old Melody Walker's Carnation milk–toned back.

He slicked his straight-permed reddish-brown hair back with his hand as he thrust himself deep inside of her wet box. He yanked a fistful of her hair, gripping it tightly in his left hand and putting the hanger temporarily in his mouth, then roughly began to jab his pointer finger in and out of Melody's ass, causing her head to jerk back and her body to quiver. She let out a loud whimper. But it went unheard. Ice was too busy torturing her. He was in a zone and could hear only his hips smacking up against her ass cheeks as he rammed himself vigorously inside her. He sweat profusely as he physically and sexually assaulted Melody.

"I'm sorry, Daddy!" she cried out. "I promise I won't do it again."

Ice ignored her pleas and cries. Instead, he took the hanger from between his teeth and delivered another blow to her back side. It caused her entire body to tremble. Her bottom lip shivered as if she were freezing, but that was impossible, because the heat had the room

*temperature at eighty degrees. She moaned, closed her
eyes, and bit down on her lip. It helped ease the pain.*

*"Bitch, you sure is sorry! Sorry-ass ho! You gonna
learn today, though!" Ice bellowed as he whacked
Melody's backside for a third time. He plunged his
pulsating dick as deep as he could inside of her as he
simultaneously pulled her curly fire engine–red hair
back for a second time. This time he pulled with much
more force.*

"No, Daddy, please!" Melody begged. "I'm not—"

*Her words were interrupted by the bedroom door
slamming up against the wall in the room.*

"Stop it!" a voice echoed in Ice and Melody's bedroom.

*Melody drew her attention to the open doorway.
Ice, on the other hand, rolled off of her and reached
for his trey-eight pistol. He had barely recognized the
voice when it first echoed in the room, and he didn't
bother to look at who stood in the doorway until he
spun back around with his pistol cocked.*

*"What the hell?" Ice muttered. "You little bitch!" he
cursed and shook his head in disgust. The sight of her
infuriated him. His eyes grew cold. "Take yo' ass back
to yo' room and back to bed, before I beat yo' ass!" he
bellowed, threatening her. He waved his gun in the
direction of the doorway as he spoke.*

*Melody grabbed the barrel of the gun. "Don't point
that shit at her," she spat.*

*"Bitch, you better back the fuck up!" Ice jerked his pis-
tol back and grabbed Melody by the throat. He was just
about to shove the barrel down Melody's throat when
nine-year-old Jewels yelled, "Stop hurting my mama!"*

Ice shook his head and uncocked his pistol.

*Melody gasped for air. She tried to regain her breath-
ing as she covered her nakedness with a sheet. An
embarrassed look appeared across her face.*

"I-it's okay, baby," she said, her voice cracking. "Mommy's okay," she added. "He wasn't—"

Again, she was cut off. This time, it was by Ice.

"Fuck that!" His voice boomed. "You don't have to explain shit to this li'l bitch. This my mu'fuckin' house! I pay the goddamned bills to keep the lights on and a roof over y'all funky asses' head. Ya understand?" Ice directed his words to both his bottom whore and his unwanted child by her.

"Now explain to this bitch that you like gettin' yo' ass beat like this and that mu'fuckas pay good money fo' this type shit." He wasn't asking her; he was telling her.

He wanted Melody to school their nine-year-old daughter on her own sexual fetish and the value of it in the world of prostitution. Melody wiped away the last drop of Jewels's tears, which would have joined the previous ones that stained her face. "Come here, baby." She held the sheet up with her armpits and extended her arms toward her daughter.

Jewels peered over at Ice. At nine years old, she already knew the difference between love and hate, and she knew she hated Ice. She cautiously made her way over to her mother as she rolled her eyes at him.

Melody wrapped her arms around her. She cupped Jewels's chin and raised her head. She stared into her daughter's eyes. "It's some shit out here in these streets that will scare the hell out of a weak bitch." She made sure she had Jewels's undivided attention before she continued. "But yo' mama ain't no weak bitch. And you ain't no weak bitch, and you ain't gon' be one!" Melody put an emphasis on her last statement.

Jewels's eyes widened at the sound of her mother's words. She was used to Melody being hard on her, but she had never talked to her the way she was now. She fought to hold back the tears she felt coming on as her mother continued.

"Yo' mama is one of the baddest bitches in the streets of St. Louis and is respected wherever I go. You know why?" It was more a statement than a question.

Still, Jewels shook her head no in rapid succession, as if she had been asked a question.

"Because I'm about my muthafuckin' money, and I don't take no shit from no other bitch or nigga," she said to Jewels, with conviction in her voice. "You know how I get my money? Get you all those nice things and stuff?" she asked her daughter.

Again, Jewels shook her head no.

"With this. And this!" Melody pointed to her temple and then grabbed a handful of the sheets between her legs.

A confused look appeared across Jewels's face. She was trying to process what her mother was saying, but her young mind was drawing a blank.

Ice snickered. He could see that she was struggling with what Melody had just said to her. "Your mama sells pussy!" he blurted out. "For me!" he added voluntarily.

Jewels didn't understand fully, but what little she did comprehend pierced her young, naive heart. It hurt her to hear Ice talk about her mother that way. Tears began to form in her eyes again. Before one could fall, her mother's voice dried them up.

"Don't you fuckin' cry." She gripped Jewels's face. "You hear me? Don't you fuckin' shed one tear."

Melody looked back and cut her eyes over at Ice. She rolled them hard at him.

Ice dismissed her with the wave of his pistol. He was not serious about either one of them. He leaned to the side and reached for his E-Z Wider paper and weed grinder.

She drew her attention back to Jewels. "I know it sound fucked up what yo' daddy said about me."

"Ice!" he exclaimed, jumping in and correcting her.

Melody sucked her teeth and grimaced. "Ice," she said, switching up and referring to him by his street moniker. If looks could kill, Ice would be buried in his best Sunday suit. Melody shot him a look of death, as if she were the Grim Reaper in the flesh, before she continued. "But it's the truth. That's what I do, and I'm damn good at it!" She drew her attention back to her daughter.

Jewels stared at her mother as she spoke.

"So whatever you decide you wanna be in life—I mean, whatever, whether good or bad—make sure you be the best one you can be, you hear me?"

Jewels nodded. It took all her strength not to shed a tear as her mother spoke in an authoritative tone. She knew at that moment, life as she had once known it would never be the same, and she would never see the world the way she had seen it ever again after what her mother had just said to her and what she had witnessed.

"Jewels? What the fuck are you doing up there?" The voice penetrated the bedroom door of twenty-year-old Jewels, snapping her out of her trance. She hadn't even realized she had traveled back in time. But she was not surprised. All her life she had daydreamed and reminisced about what and where she had come from. Life as the only child of a mother who was her father's ho had left memories that would haunt her and would be a part of her forever.

"I'm coming!" she replied as she shook off the memory of her parents and carefully outlined her full lips with her lip liner.

Since the day she was born, Jewels had been told she was beautiful by her mother but had never received any real major love from her father. He had always made it perfectly clear that he didn't particularly care for her.

Still, Jewels had convinced herself that she actually
was the shit. And both her father and her mother were
wrong. Beauty-wise, she believed she had exceeded even
her mother's expectations. She was nothing short of
gorgeous and everything lovely. Her skin was a flawless
café brown, and she had mountain-brown eyes. She had
a well-toned body, which came from her home workouts
four times a week. She had pothole-deep dimples, and a
perfect smile to accompany them. A new hairstyle was
her newest change in appearance. She had cut her hair,
which had gone past her shoulders and down her back,
and had styled it in a curly twist. She had been taught at
an early age that her beauty was to be used as a means
to an end, that end being financial stability and security,
safety and independence. In other words, she should not
depend on a man for anything. Which was why she took
pride in both her looks and her appearance.

To put it bluntly, Jewels was a professional escort. And
she had absolutely no problem with her title. In fact, she
loved being one. She believed it allowed her a measure
of freedom. Besides, her mother had been a whore, so
she was convinced the apple hadn't fallen too far from
the tree. It was her mother who had taught her mostly
everything she knew about a man and the power of the
"P."

Jewels was just twelve years old when she turned her
first trick, one year after she lost her virginity. Since
that day she had never had sex with anyone without
getting paid for it. She liked sex, but she loved money
even more. She loved the power that her sexual prowess
gave her. Like her mama, she did it all for the love of
the cash. She kept her mother's words at the forefront
of her mind—"Ain't nothing in this world free"—and
Jewels lived her life believing and knowing that. She was
thankful for the lessons she'd been taught by her mother

when she was just a young girl. It was because of those life skills she had instilled in her that Jewels was the strong young woman she was today.

And thanks to her mama, she had been blessed in all the right places and looked every bit of her worth. Jewels had the radiant complexion of R & B singer Mariah Carey. Just from looking at her, it was obvious that she was mixed. Although she had European features and very light skin, she had definitely inherited her mother's black genes physically. She had a very small waist, thick thighs, and a high, round ass. Now, at the tender age of twenty, she constantly stayed on her grind like a drug dealer. Like a gas station, she was available 24-7.

She worked for an escort service and independently for herself through her Web site. The thought of being a stripper had never crossed her mind. She refused to shake her ass for what she believed was a bunch of drunk-ass dudes who thought they were "making it rain" just because they threw a few one-dollar bills at a bitch onstage. Besides that, she didn't want to have to wrestle with a bunch of funky-ass bitches for those few dollars. Instead, she met with and provided sexual favors and comfort to lawyers, judges, doctors, and anybody else, for that matter, if the price was right.

As a general rule, she fucked only white and Asian men. She had learned early on in the business that they made the best tricks. She had made as much as twenty-five hundred dollars in one night with an Asian client, and all she had had to do was piss on his chest. Although it had been creepy to her, she'd been turned on by what she was paid. It had happened on her eighteenth birthday. She had made more than that in a single night, though. Ironically, that high-paying encounter hadn't been with a white or Asian john. It had been with a man of color. Which was why he was an exception to the rule.

Jewels wasn't the type to fuck with the so-called "ballas" and drug dealers. She felt they were cheap tippers and didn't know how to sample good pussy and keep it moving. They always wanted to try to lock her down and turn her into something she believed she'd never be. She wondered if they had ever heard the saying "You can't turn a ho into a housewife." Jewels was definitely not a housewife. She was a whore. Besides that, she didn't like big-dick niggas. She couldn't afford to have them wearing her prize possession out. What she had between her legs was her moneymaker, with her head game running at a close second. She couldn't front, though. She did crave her some black dick every now and then.

But she was particular about the type of black man she'd be with. Full-blooded African was her binge. She didn't want any black man who was African-American bred. She despised men of color who had been brainwashed into believing you had to act, sound, or look white to make it in this world, and she definitely couldn't stand black men who acted like niggas and ran the streets. Give her an African Mandingo straight up and down when she needed to actually feel something inside of her. It wasn't often, but she loved to be piped out by a good pipe-laying African client, while getting paid for it. The only two downsides to dealing with an African man, Jewels believed, were, one, he always wanted to lock the woman down, and two, she was always sore for a week after seeing him. She would be walking like she had been riding a horse.

One of her favorite clients was Kareem, and he was from Kenya. He worked in a brokerage firm and owned quite a bit of real estate in the greater Chicago area. He traveled nearly six hours back and forth from Chi-Town to the Lou to see her. He usually paid in advance for the privilege of spending two or three nights with her.

Although he had the perfect equipment between his legs, he had some very annoying habits. He spent at least three hours every morning in the bathroom. Jewels had no idea what he did in there all that time. Out of curiosity, one morning she'd put her ear to the bathroom door and listened.

"God bless America. These are good people!" He had kept repeating that phrase over and over again. It had sounded like he was praying.

Jewels couldn't help it. She'd had to ask him why he did that every morning. He'd told her that she had grown up in America, so she wouldn't understand, and that if she had grown up where he had, she would be doing the same thing every morning.

He had proposed to her after their first date. Jewels had told him that she wasn't about to go to no hot-ass Africa and be one of ten wives living in no damn tent with goats and shit. They didn't have high-end department stores or huge malls like the ones she loved in the Midwest over there, so she'd posed the question, where the hell was she supposed to shop? She was so oblivious to the motherland that she believed they didn't have cable. She couldn't see herself not being able to watch *The Maury Povich Show* and *The Real Housewives of Atlanta*. Those were must-see TV shows for Jewels. She was getting really tired of his ass, but the dick was just too good, and the money was even better.

With some of her older white clients, she would play the struggling college coed who was "just doing this" to help pay her way through college. She would put on a college sweatshirt with a pair of faded jeans. She would wear the bare minimum of makeup. Her hair would be pulled back in a ponytail. She looked the part. She'd had her "college tuition" paid for quite a few times. The tricks loved to save her, and she loved being saved. They always gave her a little something extra to help her get by.

It was good money for a minimal amount of work, and she did mean minimal. Some of her clients barely had two inches of dick. The white and Asian men were so small that their dicks were barely noticeable. *If I were a man, I would be embarrassed to be so unfortunate*, thought Jewels at times. Sometimes they didn't want sex. They wanted to talk about their wives or their jobs. Jewels didn't mind. It was their money.

She had come across her fair share of weirdos too. Some clients wanted to be shit on, while some of them liked to be tied up and beaten. *Whatever floats their boats*, thought Jewels. All she was concerned with was her money.

Besides the money, the best thing about being an escort was the acting part. She had to be so many different characters for her clients. She became whomever they wanted her to be. If they wanted her to be a slut, she would be a slut. If they wanted her to be a dominatrix or a struggling college student, she would be that too.

She was so used to being someone else that she sometimes completely forgot who she was. But at the end of the day, all she knew was that she was a whore and a damned good one too.

With Kareem, it was something different, though. Once a month he sent for her and paid ten large for the weekend. He paid not only for her body, but for her company as well. He treated her like she was special to him. She almost felt sorry for him because she knew she couldn't and would never give him what he really wanted—all of her.

Normally, this weekend would be one when Kareem sent for her, but when he'd called in, it was to inform the agency that he would not be sending for her this weekend. For a quick moment, she had felt some type of way. Not because she was looking forward to seeing him, but because she was looking forward to what she stood to make from their weekend rendezvous. Now here she was, about to step out for the evening with some white trick whose fetishes were some of Jewels's specialties. She knew it was going to be a long and disgusting evening, but she told herself, like always, that the ends justified the means.

Jewels stood up and took one last look in the mirror. "Let's go make this money, bitch!" she uttered, then puckered her lips and blew herself a kiss. She snatched up her MK clutch and made her way downstairs.

"You always taking fucking long, like you the shit," chided Ralph, the agency's house supervisor, who was also a flaming gay Latino man.

Jewels ignored the comment. She had been working with this particular agency for only a month, but she was already used to his snide remarks. Despite the fact that she was young, this was not her first house, so she was used to the hate, period. She knew it came with the territory. In the world of escorting and prostitution, Jewels was one of the most wanted and baddest bitches in the game. The fact that she was a freelance escort made her even more valuable to any agency she went through, so she was also used to the red carpet being laid out, meaning that she would get first dibs on big spenders.

Jewels rolled her eyes, made her way out of the lavish home, made a beeline to the awaiting silver Phantom, and climbed in. She couldn't help but chuckle when she saw Ralph standing in the doorway, with one hand on his hip, looking like Cinderella watching her step sisters go off to the ball. She gave him the middle finger as the enormous Rolls-Royce drove off. *Don't hate the player. Hate the game*, Jewels thought as she leaned back and melted into the plush leather of the luxury car.

Chapter Two

Twenty-seven-year-old Rome navigated his way through the city, toward downtown, while he nibbled on a fresh batch of catfish nuggets and a side order of fries, which sat in his lap, from one of his favorite chicken spots in town. On his right sat a cup of grape juice. He picked the drink up and took a swig as he thought about what he was going to get into today. Besides the block, he loved drama. He had been on the same block practically all his life: twenty-five of his twenty-seven years, to be exact. He could've moved, but for what? He was getting paper where he grew up. He was addicted to the drama of the streets. He couldn't sleep at night if he didn't hear gun shots and sirens outside of the bedroom window of his lavish studio apartment.

A lot of people thought that he was just some nickel-and-dime thug. He was glad that they thought that way. He capitalized on this misconception. Rome was actually one of America's worse nightmares: he was young, black, intelligent, and ignorant as all hell all at the same time. He had been exposed to the best of both worlds. His parents were the classic story of a good girl liking a bad boy.

Outside of his crew, he cared for no one and nothing other than gettin' paper in a major way. He was a strategist and a perfectionist. If something or someone stood in front of that, he moved it or them, simple as that. He stayed on point twenty-four hours a day, seven days a week, and caused havoc, if necessary. You could never tell what was going to go down when he popped up on the scene, but it was never anything good. He was just barely legal, but he'd already made a name for himself as one of the most ruthless, murderous young money getters ever to touch the streets of the Lou.

If he wasn't out making it, he was plotting and planning on taking it from somebody who had it. That was just how he came for it. But lames were making it harder for him than it used to be. He believed the game was so twisted now, as the jealous niggas would put the police on his ass within a blink of an eye. He knew that if the streets really knew how much money he was pulling in, they'd be hating and trying to get rid of him quick fast. They couldn't possibly know that despite his age, he was one of the main players in the streets. He kept it real low key and let his crew stand on the front line. He had a team of young, wild goons pitching work for him on four different blocks between East and West St. Louis. Plus, he had a few old heads moving heroin for him out of the projects. He was seeing major paper. He didn't waste his time or his money on bullshit. He didn't need a fleet of luxury cars and a neck and wrist full of diamonds. He believed that all that shit did was draw heat.

Rome wasn't too much older than some of the dudes in his crew, so he sometimes felt the need to go out there and grind and chill with them. You might catch him pulling all-nighters with the same clothes on for two days, but at the end of the day, both his and his team's pockets were fat. He didn't do drugs like that; he did a little weed here and there, but nothing harder or stronger. He got high off of chasing paper; he didn't hustle to get high. Besides, he was already a natural live wire. He didn't need anything to alter his already fucked-up state of mind.

One thing about him, about which there was absolutely no dispute, was that he was about that drama. He also played with them pistols real heavy. He had no problem with that "gun talk." He spoke that language very well. Ever since he had caught a twenty-month bid at fifteen, for a Tec-9 and letting off a round at the cops, his name had been ringing bells as a loose cannon all through the streets of the city. During his incarceration, he had added to his rap sheet. He had put in work not only on other inmates but on the staff as well. Some so-called Gs were tough only on the street, when they were around their boys or with guns, but Rome was tough, period. He was nice with his hands and had to beat up a couple of fake tough guys during his first two weeks in the juvenile detention center of St. Louis. When he got sentenced and transferred to a juvenile prison, he immediately learned that knives and razors were the guns in jail. The last eight months of his sentence at the facility were spent in the hole for stabbing a teen who owed him two bags of potato chips for the one he had sold to him.

He'd been in and out of jail since he was thirteen years old. Doing time was second nature to him, so he wasn't afraid to do it. But he had told himself that after that juvenile bid, he would not return to jail. Not if he could help it. He knew his love for guns increased his chances of incarceration, though, so he moved cautiously. There was something specifically about choppers that he loved. He always had a chopper somewhere within reach. He had been picked up and questioned by homicide detectives numerous times whenever one was involved in an incident. They knew he favored this assault weapon. But he had never been charged with shit.

When they said, "You have the right to remain silent," that was exactly what the fuck they meant. Whenever

Rome got picked up, all he said was, "Fuck y'all!" followed by "I want a lawyer." That was it, and that was all. "Dead man tell no tales" was his theory. In the streets it was rumored that Rome had at least eight bodies to his credit. He hadn't confirmed or denied it. He let them think what they wanted. He came from the code and the rules of the streets. "Real niggas didn't talk about what they did. They left all that talking and rapping to the suckas." He had been taught that bad boys moved in silence. Besides, he never knew if the Feds were listening or watching.

Rome loved taking care of his mother. His father wasn't shit.

Rome was the product of a gangsta-ass father, who just happened to be a woman beater, and a young, naive mother. His pops was nearly twice his mother's age, which meant his moms was a minor at the time he was born. His father's MO had been armed robbery, so when he'd robbed a bank and got away with it, they ate lovely, but when he hadn't, they'd been at neighbors' houses, eating what they could spare. Rome's pops hadn't been into little money schemes or hustles. He had just had a habit that would take him to his grave in the years to come. His mother, on the other hand, hadn't really been ready to be a mother, but at the time she had done what she could do. For him, being an only child and a male had had its ups and downs.

Rome hadn't been an average kid, and by the time he was in first grade, he'd been the biggest kid in his class. To be honest, he'd been the biggest kid in grades one through five, and at the time that had made him a target for all the kids with "little man" complexes, so he'd had a lot of fighting on his hands. He could remember one day in particular out of the many days kids had tried to jump him after school. He'd been in the fifth grade, on his way home from school, and these cats who always used to pick on him had come to the school just to jump him. They were all brothers, so you never got a fair fight—well, at least Rome never did—but on this day a lot would change.

Rome had gotten tired of being a punching bag and had stood his ground on this day and had decided that this day would be the last day he let anyone think he was a punk. And if that meant he would have to fight all three of them, then that was what it would be.

He saw them walking up on him. The first thing Rome did was grab the biggest one out of the bunch and beat his ass until half his crew was on Rome's ass. He kept fighting and earned enough respect from every last one of them, and from then on all his problems would be handled with his hands. He got good at it too.

But he wasn't using hands these days. He had traded in busted-up knuckles for pistols, and with those, he had earned his bones in the streets and had climbed the criminal ladder. Once he started getting money, he didn't let his mother hurt or want for shit. She didn't have to pay any bills; he took care of everything.

Rome would remember her struggling every day when he was younger. She had worked two jobs so that her only son could have the best of things. She had never graduated from high school, so she had had to work a lot of dead-end jobs.

She stayed on Rome about being in the streets so much, but she really didn't know how deep he was in them. He had thought about moving out and being on his own, but he couldn't stand the thought of leaving his mother alone.

He had been thinking about making a few major moves lately, but he hadn't really decided on when to make them happen or which moves to make. What he was sure about was that the streets weren't forever. Hustling was just a means to an end. He wanted to hustle for two or three more years and then exit the game. He believed he was nice with rap. He had dreams of being the next Jay Z or Lil Wayne. He wanted to come into the game already having money, like Young Jeezy. A lot of hard-core hip-hop listeners he respected had told him that his flow was tight.

On a more practical side, he had been thinking about investing a little money in the real estate game. He had even purchased a couple of books on the subject. But that was for later. Right now, he had more pressing issues.

This nigga must think his shit is sweet, Rome thought, seeing a familiar SUV cruise past his own ride. He couldn't believe who was in his hood. *He must got a death wish or something,* thought Rome, reflecting on an incident that had taken place earlier. This guy had robbed one of Rome's workers, knowing that he worked for Rome. *This joker has lost his damn mind,* he mused. There was no way that Rome was going to let this opportunity pass. He checked the time on his watch. *Just enough time.* He nodded right before turning around in the middle of the street. *It has to be quick, and there can be no witnesses.*

Chapter Three

Mike-G, his younger brother, Los, and his main man, Buster, were sitting around playing PlayStation while rotating a blunt of a good grade of Kush. Mike-G knew Los loved being around him. For Los, the world revolved around Mike-G. He gave Los everything he wanted and needed. Their father was doing life in the pen. Their mother had passed way from a drug overdose. At the time, Los had been only eight years old. Mike-G had been fourteen.

Ever since that day, Mike-G had been Los's father and his mother. Although he was only six years older than Los, it felt like he was much older. He made sure that Los went to school and he wouldn't hesitate to beat Los's ass if he didn't go. He didn't allow him to hustle in any way. Mike-G was like a God to Los.

"Aye, where the rest of them dutchess at?" Mike-G asked. "I'm tryin'a roll something up," he continued as he looked around the cluttered table, ready to roll up the rest of the good weed.

"Ain't no more. You want me to run and grab some from the store?" Buster asked, pausing the video game.

"Nah. I'm good. I'll go." Mike-G headed to the door.

It was a beautiful night outside. It was just barely dark out, and the temperature still hovered around a balmy seventy-five degrees. The humidity made it feel hotter than it really was. There was a minimal breeze in the air.

Mike-G jumped into his all-black Cadillac Escalade. He could've walked to the gas station; it was only one block away. He was forever stuntin' on the hoes, and he loved to be seen. He never knew when he might run into a bad bitch. He knew enough to know that bad bitches didn't fuck with niggas who walked. He swerved into the gas station and hopped out of the truck. He left the driver's door open, and the music playing on the sound system echoed throughout the entire station. It sounded like a mini club. Mike-G staggered over toward the gas-station window.

He couldn't help but shake his head every time he frequented this establishment. Arabs owned the gas station. They had had the nerve to put up a bulletproof-glass enclosure all around the front of the building. They passed items through a steel trap on the front of the window. That shit really irked Mike-G. Let him tell it, they were the same type of jokers who strapped bombs to their bodies and blew themselves the fuck up. *Now they're acting all scary and shit,* he thought and laughed to himself as he rocked back and forth.

"What do you need?" the Arab at the window asked. His tone came across as nervous.

This little raggedy-ass gas station don't have shit, anyway, thought Mike-G as he chuckled. *Them turban-wearing muthafuckas always be talking that tough-ass gangsta shit behind that glass.* In a way, though, he couldn't blame them. Anything might jump off around here. Niggas stayed shooting up the hood. But it had never crossed his mind that he wasn't exempt from what went on in the hood. Aside from the obvious, given the fact that he had haters in the Lou, he should have been more on point. The blunts he and his crew had already smoked and the liquor he had tossed back had him slippin'. Which was why he didn't see what the Arab did.

"We don't want any trouble." The Arab threw up his hands.

"Aye, man, put your fuckin' hands down. Me neither, yo," Mike-G slurred. "Aye, I just want two boxes of dutchess, a pack of Newports, and a cherry jungle juice." He noticed the Arab was fidgeting and had become more nervous. His eyes alarmed Mike-G. He knew something was wrong. "What the fuck is wrong with you, man? Just get my shit so I can pay you and leave! Damn!"

Rome was on his way to the gas station on the corner when he saw Mike-G pop up in his Escalade and roll into the gas station. He quickly ducked around the corner.

"This is perfect. Now I don't have to find his bitch ass," Rome said out loud to himself. He pulled his 9 mm chrome Glock out of his jeans and waited. He watched as Mike-G exited his truck and walked up to the gas-station window.

This nigga is a dead man, and he don't even know it, Rome thought to himself. He smiled. *This has to be my lucky day!*

The Arab's eyes bulged out of his head like two hard-boiled eggs. He had a look of terror on his face.

"Yo, what the fuck is yo' fucking problem, man?" Mike-G asked as he turned around to see what the Arab was looking at. The red beam from Rome's 9 mm was focused on the middle of Mike-G's forehead.

"What's wrong my nigga? You look like you seen a ghost," Rome said. "What you thought? Shit was sweet over here, nigga?" he added as he stared into Mike-G's eyes.

Rome loved that old-school shit by Scarface: "Always look a man in the eye before you kill him."

Mike-G noticed that innocent bystanders were scattering and were reversing out of the gas station to avoid any drama. Fear filled his insides. There was no doubt in his mind that he had been caught slipping. He had told himself as soon as he saw Rome with the gun that he wasn't going to go out like a coward. He cleared his throat before he spoke. "Rome, what's up, dawg? What type of shit is you on?" he asked.

"That real shit," Rome spat. "What was all that shit you was poppin', playa, when you robbed my li'l homies?"

A twisted and distorted frown appeared on Mike-G's face. "Man, fuck you talkin' 'bout?" he replied angrily. He was stalling for time. He knew exactly what it was about. *Damn, I shouldn't be out here like this! Now this is what I get, a fuckin' death sentence! Fuck!*

Rome chuckled. "Wrong answer, my nigga."

The barrel of Rome's gun rang out like a Roman candle on the Fourth of July.

Mike-G's brains sprayed all over the gas station's bulletproof glass. The Arab stood there, paralyzed by fear. He looked directly into Rome's face. Rome looked back at him.

"You ain't see shit! You hear me?" Rome pointed his weapon at the Arab. He knew the glass was bulletproof, so there was no sense in trying to shoot him. He figured the threat would be enough.

The Arab shook his head rapidly to confirm that he had heard Rome loud and clear. He still stood there, looking at Rome, burning the image of Rome's face into his mind. He looked up and thanked Allah that he had recently installed the bulletproof glass.

"Don't fuckin' look at me!" Rome barked. "Get on the floor and count to one thousand," he demanded.

The Arab did as he was told. Before he could reach twenty, Rome was back in his car and out of the parking lot of the gas station. He glanced at his watch, like he had done minutes before, to make sure he was still on schedule. He still had twenty-five minutes before he was to meet with his connect at the Hilton, which was only five minutes away.

He couldn't believe he had jeopardized an important meeting by detouring to take care of Mike-G. But it had all worked out. Rome couldn't let the opportunity pass, not with the game he played on the streets. If he allowed someone to play him, then he would be on the other side of the gun, and he wasn't about to let that happen.

Chapter Four

Jewels quickly sashayed through the hotel lobby after the driver let her out. She was already thirty minutes late for her client. He was a new one, but according to the DGP escort screening staff, he was filthy rich. He was paying eight hundred an hour for her services. She planned to give him at least three hours' worth of good pussy. He was in the presidential suite at the Hilton St. Louis at the Ballpark. She knocked on the door to the suite and almost ran when he opened it. He was huge, at least six feet five and well over four hundred pounds of blubber. He had the nerve not to have a shirt on when he opened the door, as if he had great pecs and six-pack abs. His gut was disgusting. Jewels couldn't help but notice the visible stretch marks on his belly. On top of that, his chest and stomach were covered with a mass of wet, curly hair. He looked and smelled like a bear.

She thought about calling the escort service back to see if they had the right guy, because this big, fat, funky-ass white man in front of her sure didn't look like no respected businessman. He didn't smell like one, either. He reeked of stale cigarettes and smelled like a wet dog.

"Jim?" she asked, smiling sweetly, hoping that he was not Jim.

"You're late. I don't like people to be late." He turned around and left her standing in the doorway.

I know this big, fat, stankin' muthafucka didn't just play me like that, she thought to herself.

She stepped in behind him and closed the door. "Yes, I am a little late, because I had car trouble. I asked the escort service to call and inform you, but I guess they didn't. I'm so sorry about that."

"Well, better late than never. Don't worry about it," he said as he sat on the bed. He looked her up and down.

She slipped out of her blazer, giving him an ample look at her full, perky breasts. They were one of her best assets. Her nipples were long and fat, and her breasts stood up and out. They were all natural. She was dressed smartly in a navy blue business suit. Her skirt was expertly cut to hang just above her knees, showing off her pretty legs but still leaving something to the imagination. She sat down and crossed her legs, allowing him to see that she wasn't wearing any panties.

"Well, Jim, time is of the essence, so if you could just tell me what you like, we can get started." She had been told by the escort service that he liked it rough, so she figured that he was just another pervert who wanted to be tied up and beaten. That was fine by her. She needed to relieve a little stress.

He just sat there staring at her for a minute. Suddenly, he jumped out of the bed. With surprising speed for a big man, he leaped across the room and slapped the dog shit out of her.

Jewels went crashing to the floor. Before she had any time to react, he was on top of her. Jewels peered up in horror. *No wonder this motherfucka pays so damn well,* she thought as the next blow he delivered knocked her temporarily unconscious.

The hot urine that splashed on her face immediately woke her back up. She regained her vision in time to see the burly man hovering over her. She could see he had a pair of brass knuckles on his right hand. Jewels lay there, playing possum. The trick kneeled down. He cocked his fist back, ready to tear into Jewels's face. That was all she needed to launch her own attack. With all her might, Jewels thrust both of her legs upward. Her feet landed perfectly between the fat, grotesque man's legs. She nearly kicked his testicles into his stomach.

"You fuckin' cunt bitch!" he bellowed.

Jewels paid him no mind. She was focused only on getting up and out of the room. She struggled to get up off the floor. Her eyes zeroed in on her emergency phone, which was across the room. Jewels made a beeline over to it and retrieved it. Her adrenaline was pumping like cheap gas while her heart did its best to jump out of her chest. She frantically looked around for her attacker. The trick still occupied the floor. He held on to a handful of his genitals as he rocked back and forth in agony.

In record-breaking speed Jewels was headed to the door, ready to make her escape. Her hands were shaking so bad, she couldn't manage to hold the phone still enough to scroll through and call for help. Besides, there were only two numbers she could call. She couldn't call the police. She could dial only the agency or her partner in crime, Sassy. Those were the only ones who knew where she was. She decided to get out of the room first and worry about contacting someone afterward. She could feel her heart rate decreasing as she reached for the door handle. She nearly stopped when there was the sudden boom.

"Where the fuck you think you're going?"

She stopped in her tracks when the trick grabbed a fistful of Jewels's hair with one hand and the back of her blouse with the other.

"Get the fuck off of me!" Jewels fought back. She managed to break free of the trick's hold. She heard and felt the back of her shirt tear, but she didn't care. All she cared about was getting out of that room and away from her crazed trick as she snatched open the door.

I just have to get out of here! Getting beat to earn some dollars ain't for me! Wait till I get my hands on fucking Ralph! Did he not do a background check on this psycho!

Chapter Five

Under any other circumstances, Rome would've been doing somersaults on the hotel bed after what he believed was a successful business meeting with his new connect. But instead, he was laid up in the hotel, thinking about what he had done moments before meeting up with his new plug. He wasn't really tripping over the fact that he had killed Mike-G. That was business. He knew his man could clean up the mess if there were immediate repercussions from Mike-G's peoples.

What had him worried was the fact that the Arab had seen the whole thing. He knew who Rome was, because Rome went to that gas station every day. Here he had just been put in a better position to expand throughout his hometown, thanks to his new connect from Chicago. But the fresh body he had caught wore heavily on him because of someone seeing the whole thing transpire. Not that he was complaining about the position he now held. He felt that he did what had to be done, according to the rules he played by, but the last thing he needed was unnecessary heat on him. Not when he was about to invest all of his and his crew's hard-earned money into his new plug. It wasn't the best connect, but it was better than having no connect at all.

For months, he and his man Red's crew had been struggling in the streets, due to the dearth of good product. Only those with the best connects, the best prices, and quality product were eating. Rome had come up on two out of the three. He had found somebody with quality product, but their numbers were above average when it came to keys of coke. Still, he was grateful for what he got and hopeful that with consistency, things would get better. He too wanted to push a Bentley, like his new connect, but he knew he had to put himself in an even better position than he was in already. If not, then he'd cross that bridge when he reached it, he told himself. He believed there was only one thing that could jeopardize all that, and that was the Arab opening his mouth. He knew he had to lay low until he figured out how to get the Arab taken care of.

Dead men tell no tales, he told himself as he pondered how he would have the matter handled.

He usually didn't drink and smoke at the same time—it was either one or the other—but tonight he wanted to get lit both to celebrate the new plug and to calm his nerves about the loose end he needed to tie up. He rolled up a Dutch cigarillo and took a blunt to the head as Chi-Raq's Pandora station blared through the room's Bluetooth. He chased the L with gulps of Grey Goose straight out of the bottle. He was feeling kind of nice.

A blunt and a half and nearly a dozen gulps of clear liquor later, Rome was faded. His eyes were Chinkier than Bruce Lee's, and his throat felt like sandpaper. Rome sluggishly climbed off the king-size bed and snatched up the ice bucket. He left the room and headed to the end of the hall, where the ice machine was.

Just as he approached it, the door next to the ice machine flung open, and out came a young, light-skinned female. She was screaming, the back of her shirt was ripped, and she was struggling to exit the room in a hurry. Her face was bloody and swollen.

"Help me please!" she yelled. She leaped next to Rome. Fear was written all over her face.

A big, fat white man came to the doorway, wearing some tight-ass white briefs and nothing else. His face was a mask of fury.

"Don't you run from me, you little black whore."

Rome dug into his jeans and removed the silencer-equipped Glock 40 he had tucked in his waistband. "Slow your roll, patnah." He pointed the gun directly at the man.

He locked eyes with the fat white man. Out of nowhere lyrics to one of Scarface's songs played in his head. *Always look a man in the eye before you kill him.* The drugs and alcohol had him in a zone.

"You better mind your fucking business, boy." The fat man attempted to step around Rome. "I'm going to kill this fucking whore."

Although the fat man's mouth was running a hundred miles an hour, his feet were in the same place. Rome didn't hear everything he had said, because his words had come out warped and choppy, but he knew he didn't really like the man's tone of voice. He especially didn't like the fact that he had called him a boy. Rome might have been under the influence, but he was coherent enough to know the fat man was not from St. Louis. His nasty Southern accent didn't help matters for him. Rome was true blue from the Lou and was proud of it. He repped St. Louis to the fullest. Which was why he didn't like out of towners. Especially white ones. Rome stared at the fat white man long and hard.

He flashed a shit-eating grin at Rome and said, "Boy, get on and mind your fucking business!"

Without hesitation or a thought, Rome squeezed the trigger in rapid succession, ending the fat white man's sentence. The bullets lifted the man off his feet and knocked him back into the room. Rome watched as the man fell backward and hit the floor with a thud.

Jewels was quiet. She didn't speak for a few minutes. She glanced at Rome out of the corner of her eye. Although he had just killed a man in cold blood, he didn't appear to be bothered by it. His demeanor was calm, and he seemed to be comfortable with what he had just done. Jewels, on the other hand, was sick to her stomach. She held on to the wall for balance as she released whatever food she had in the pit of her stomach all over the floor. She felt light-headed. All she kept thinking about was the chain of events that had led up to the present situation. She wiped the vomit residue from her mouth with the back of her hand.

"What the fuck!" she yelled.

Rome looked up and down the hotel hallway. He knew it was just a matter of time before someone stepped into the hall or off the elevator and saw them. He walked into the room and pumped three more shots into the fat man's body for a confirmation of his death, then made an attempt to close the door to the room. The fat white man's legs prevented him from doing so. He kneeled down and grabbed the dead man by his pudgy left foot, which was blocking the doorway. He held his breath to minimize the stench from the bowel movement the dead man had released upon meeting his Maker. He slammed the door shut, then turned back toward Jewels.

She had just regained some of her senses.

"Yo, we gotta bounce," Rome informed her. The sudden chain of events had somewhat sobered him up.

Before she could agree or oppose him, he had already grabbed her by the hand, and together they fled the scene. He stopped by his room, quickly snatched up the most important item there: the duffel bag containing the fifteen keys of coke he had just received. As luck would have it, the elevator arrived and opened three seconds after Rome pressed the elevator button. He pulled Jewels in the elevator, put his back against the wall, and glanced over at her.

She looked a hot mess. Her makeup was practically smeared all over her face. It had dried up and had mixed with the dried blood from her nose and mouth. The two top buttons of her blouse had popped off, and there was that big-ass rip on the back, and her skirt was wrinkled and had shifted.

"Yo, you gotta tighten up, baby," he told her. "You gonna get us knocked," he added. Rome shook his head in disgust.

Why the fuck did I get involved in that shit? he asked himself and cursed silently. He watched as Jewels tried to fix herself up. She was still somewhat in shock.

"Here. Put this on." He took his fitted off and handed it to her. The last thing they needed was for someone to see her face looking the way it did and to get suspicious. He was all too ready to get out of the elevator and the hotel. He peered up at the numbers as they counted down.

Jewels eyed him. Her mind was racing all over the place at a million miles a minute. She couldn't believe she had just witnessed a violent crime and had become an accessory to a murder. *This has to be a fucking nightmare or a practical joke,* she thought. If it weren't for bad luck, she wouldn't have any at all, she believed. *Why me, God?* she questioned. It was just days before her birthday, and now she was in a predicament that could possibly have her spending it in jail. The thought of that caused Jewels's stomach to tighten. The dinging sound of the elevator caused her to jump and snap out of her daze.

When they exited the elevator, Rome put his arm around Jewels's waist and gripped it tightly. She flinched.

Her nostrils tingled from the weed and the alcohol that Rome reeked of.

"Keep cool," he whispered. He kept his arm wrapped around her and pulled her close to prevent someone from seeing the rip in her shirt.

Jewels nodded.

No one paid them any mind. They blended in with the other patrons as Rome navigated her through the lobby and into the parking garage. Flashing lights could be seen as he hit the alarm on his keychain.

"Get in!" he ordered Jewels as he jumped in the driver's side of his white Denali truck.

Minutes later, Rome was weaving in and out of the downtown traffic. He didn't slow down until he had gotten outside city limits.

Jewels sat across from him, still trying to process what had just taken place back at the hotel. Bits and pieces flashed through her mind. From the moment the trick named Jim opened the door, she had had a bad feeling about the evening. She knew she should have canceled when she got the feeling. She had always followed her gut, but this time she had let greed supersede what she trusted, and now she was in an SUV with someone who she believed was a stoned cold-blooded killer. There was no doubt in Jewels's mind that he had killed before and that he wouldn't hesitate to kill again.

"Did you have to fucking kill him?" Jewels said, lashing out, breaking the dead silence.

"Nah. I could've let him kill your ass," he retorted, taking his eyes off of the traffic to glance at her. He laughed at his own joke.

"You're a fucking animal. How can you laugh after what you just did?" Jewels snapped, horrified.

He pulled over to the side of the street.

"Get your yellow, stuck-up ass out of my muthafuckin' truck."

A surprised look appeared across her face. "Where the hell am I supposed to go? I don't live out this way." She was shocked that he was actually trying to put her out on the street.

"I don't give a fuck about all of that. All I know is that I just saved your life and probably put the rest of mine in jeopardy, and I don't know your ass, and you got the nerve to call me a muthafuckin' animal. Yeah, you're right. I am an animal. Now, get your ass up out of my truck." He popped the locks on his SUV and waited for her to get out.

For some strange reason, she was afraid of him. But at the same time, for some strange reason, she was aroused by him.

"I'm sorry," she said sincerely. "I'm just scared. Could you please drop me off at home?"

Rome stared at her long and hard before he responded. "Let's start with your name," he replied.

Jewels contemplated giving him a fake name, but considering that he had just literally saved her life, she kept it real. Besides, no one really knew her real name, anyway, because she went by the name Lite in her profession.

Rome couldn't recall hearing the name Jewels before. He nodded. "I'm Rome," he offered.

"Short for Jerome or Romeo?" Jewels forced a smile. She was trying to lighten the tension between them.

"Short for Rome," he replied dryly.

Jewels got the hint. She sat back and folded her arms.

Rome snorted. "Where you stay at, yo?" He whipped back into traffic.

"South Side. In the new condos," she answered.

Rome cut his eyes over at her. He knew the area all too
well. It was nearly forty-five minutes across town. Away
from the hood. The only blacks who lived in that part
of town were either married to upper-class Caucasians,
were biracial, were athletes, or were niggas who were
seeing major paper and wanted to move out of the hood.
Although Jewels could pass for a half-breed, he didn't
think she fell under that umbrella. If he had to bet money
on how she had come to reside in the upscale area, he
would bet that she belonged to one of the bossed-up
pimps. *But who, though?* he wondered. He knew all the
major money players in the Lou and knew which chicks
belonged to whom. He often used females to get to his
enemies, so he always liked to know who was connected
to whom in case of an emergency.

He took another look at Jewels. Her face didn't register
with him at all. He had a thing for light-skinned women,
so he was sure that they didn't travel in the same cir-
cles. As bad as she was, he knew he wouldn't have ever
forgotten her. *Even with her face all beat up, she is still
badder than the average chick running around St. Louis,*
thought Rome. As he racked his brain, another option
came to him. One he had never even given a thought, but
it made sense.

"Fuck was you doing in the room with that cracker
alone like that fo', anyway, huh? They don't screen them
muthafuckas?" he asked. He came across as a concerned
parent. "As fine as you are, your man don't provide you
with no security?" He had complimented her in an odd
way. He wasn't into hookers, but he couldn't front. She
was one of the baddest chicks he had ever laid eyes on,
and he had laid eyes on many.

Jewels took offense at his comment. She batted her
eyes and clenched her jaw to keep from snapping. "My

man? Security? Who the fuck you think you talkin' to nigga?" Jewels wanted to say. But she didn't think that would be good for her health, or her life, for that matter. She had just seen him kill for less, so instead, she humbled herself. "Can we please just not talk?"

She closed her eyes. The reality of all that had happened started to set in. *I wouldn't even be in this predicament if Kareem hadn't fucking canceled on me!* she thought. She wanted to place blame on somebody for the fucked-up things that kept happening to her. Jewels felt drained. She also didn't want to tell him what she did for a living. Usually, she didn't care if people knew what she did. It was easier that way, because she didn't have to beat around the bush. It was either they wanted her services or they didn't. Simple as that.

She preferred dealing with tricks, although in her heart she despised them. She considered them weak. She loved the control that she had over men. The way they turned into putty in her hands, and the way they got all excited at the sight of her tight body. She had been walking all over men since she was thirteen years old. She had always been lucky . . . up until now. She had never been raped, beaten up, or robbed. Her mother had taught her well, and she had always been an excellent judge of character. She had never really given much thought to the reality of the danger of her profession. She had totally misjudged that crazy muthafucka tonight. He could've killed her. She wouldn't make that mistake again.

She had heard all the horror stories of streetwalkers being raped, robbed, and killed. She considered herself to be a notch above a "streetwalker." She wasn't out there sucking dick in the back of cars for twenty-five dollars. She was definitely a whore, but she did have standards and principles.

"Yeah, okay." Rome shook his head and let out a light chuckle.

Jewels rolled her eyes. They rode in silence, but Jewels was pissed. She didn't like to be judged, especially wrongly . . . somewhat. She felt that was exactly what Rome was doing. It took all her willpower not to explode on him. She believed her life depended on it.

Rome was not like the average man Jewels came in contact with. He was not a trick, and he sure as hell wasn't weak, either, so she could not control him or the situation. She analyzed men for a living and sized them up on a regular basis just for GP. Rome was like no other man she had ever encountered. The man exuded danger. He reminded her of her own father. It wasn't that he looked dangerous, like Ice did. She found him to be nice on the eyes even though looks weren't her thing. He was dark-skinned, with the most perfect set of white teeth that she had ever seen. She could tell he wasn't that much older than she was, but like her, he had seen some things at a young age that had made him mature for his age. She noticed his strong jawline and his deep dimples whenever he opened his mouth to talk with his baritone voice. He had a short, nappy Afro, but even that worked for him, she thought. His razor-sharp lines gave it sex appeal. He was of average height, above six feet. She estimated that he weighed about 190 pounds, even though he appeared bigger, because he was muscular. His chest protruded, and his shoulders were broad.

Jewels stole occasional glances at his massive choco-late arms. She could feel her inner thighs moisten. *What the fuck? Why is my pussy getting wet?* She couldn't believe she was getting turned on. That was something that rarely happened. She crossed her legs to keep from fidgeting in the seat. She stared out the passenger-side window to take her mind off her thoughts about Rome. She felt like a little girl, and she hadn't felt that way in a long time. The feeling caused her thoughts of Rome to switch to those of her father.

"Why you sitting over there looking all scared and shit?" Ice looked over at ten-year-old Jewels and grimaced. "I'm not going to hurt you," he added.

Jewels sat in the passenger seat, with her hands folded in her lap. She turned to face her father. "I'm not scared of you," she retorted.

And she wasn't. Their eyes met.

Ice let out a light chuckle. "Good. 'Cause I don't want you to be scared of no mu'fuckin' nigga, includin' me. You hear me?" Ice stated.

Jewels didn't respond. Instead, she turned and continued looking out at the streets.

"Did you hear what the fuck I said?" Ice's sudden harsh tone startled her. The bass of his voice vibrated through her young body.

"I heard you!" Jewels snapped back. She didn't bother to turn and face him this time.

"Act like it, then!" he shot back as he turned the corner.

Jewels snarled and mumbled under her breath. She hated Ice with a passion. She had actually had thoughts of killing him. She hated the way he treated her mother. She couldn't believe her mother had left her alone with him. It was the first time she had ever been anywhere with Ice by herself but her mother had insisted. Usually, Jewels would go out with Melody while she worked. Which was why the streets that Ice traveled down were all too familiar to her.

Jewels stared out of Ice's navy-colored Lexus. She recognized the faces of the young and older prostitutes, pimps and hustlers. These were the same faces she saw whenever the bus or taxi dropped her and her mother off. Jewels actually looked forward to visiting the area her mother worked. It was the only time she got to play with other kids. Most of the older hookers had sons and daughters her age or a little older. She normally stayed at one of their houses until her mother was ready to go home. She was glad something had come up and Ice had to take her to where she knew her mother would be. She couldn't wait to get out of the car and away from him. She wouldn't have to wait too much longer.

"I know that bitch ain't." Ice's Lexus accelerated up the block.

His sudden outburst caused Jewels to jump.

Jewels was so used to hearing her father call or refer to her mother as a bitch that she immediately started looking around for Melody when he said it. Her mother was nowhere in sight though. Jewels peered over at Ice. His attention was focused on whatever had caused his mood to change. Jewels followed his eyes. Her eyes widened at the sight of the milk-white Cadillac that had pulled alongside the curb. She had seen the car many times and knew the person driving it. Her mother had introduced her to them. She also knew the woman who was leaning over into the passenger-side window. Her fishnet stocking–covered legs were crossed sassily, and she clearly seemed to be enjoying the conversation. Ice's Lexus came to a screeching halt. Jewels head jerked back from the sudden stop. He threw his car in park.

"Stay here," Ice ordered, his voice booming, as he reached under the driver's seat, retrieved his revolver, and grabbed hold of the door handle.

Before Jewels could respond, he was out of the car. She watched as her father made a beeline over to the woman, whom she knew as Lacy. She had seen the surprise on Lacy's face, and then her face was flooded with fear when she saw Ice get out of the Lexus that had pulled up behind the Cadillac. She was already sitting erect and had backed away from the Cadillac's window.

Jewels leaned over and turned the key in the ignition, then leaned back over to her side and cracked the passenger's window. It rolled down just enough for to hear what all was taking place outside of her father's Lexus.

"Ice? Daddy, is that you?" Lacy asked, her voice quivering with fear.

As he was coming toward the car, Ice pointed at her. "Bitch, no. It's Ronald McDonald. Bring your monkey ass over here!" Ice growled.

Jewels watched as Lacy climbed out of the Cadillac and scurried over to Ice. Ice grabbed her by the cheeks and squeezed hard. Jewels could literally see the veins in his hands from the death grip he had on Lacy's face from where she sat.

"Bitch, you got all this free time to be socializing? That means you got my bread all the way straight. So where it at?"

Jewels watched in awe as Lacy reached into her clutch, which was dangling from her shoulder. Seconds later, she revealed a monstrous knot of cash. Ice snatched the bankroll out of her hand.

"Now, get yo' funky ass back to work. I'll deal with you in a minute." Ice shoved Lacy by the face. She nearly tripped and fell over her own feet. She recovered her balance just in time. Then she did as instructed and did it quickly. She wasted no time fading into the background and waited nervously for what would come next.

Jewels's eyes followed as Ice went to the driver's side of the car. He placed his right hand on top of the Caddy.

"*What you think this is?*" *he asked the man behind the wheel.*

Jewels couldn't hear what the driver was saying, but her father's response gave her a good idea.

"*Don't 'What's up?' me, Slim. What the fuck you think you doin'?*" *Ice asked him.*

Before Slim could open his mouth to answer, Ice answered the question for him. "*Disrespectin' me. And you of all people should know that I don't like being disrespected. But apparently, you don't.*"

Jewels couldn't believe her eyes. Ice drew his .38 revolver. He reached into the Caddy and grabbed the man known as Slim by the head and nearly snatched it off his shoulders. Everybody within range, including Jewels, watched as Ice brought his pistol down onto the side of Slim's face repeatedly.

"*Let me catch you talking to one of mine again and you'll be tryin' your pimp game in hell, li'l nigga,*" *Ice thundered. He released Slim's head. As he walked away, he took his gun and put a bullet in a back tire of the Caddy. The sudden explosion of the shot caused everybody to take cover and Slim to pull off frantically. Just when Jewels thought Ice was done, she saw him turn in the direction of Lacy.*

His eyes met those of Lacy. He walked over to her and backhanded her across the face. Spit and blood flew out of her mouth.

"*I should have you bloody and naked, lying in the middle of the street, with yo' dumb ass,*" *Ice said.*

"*No, Daddy. It wasn't like—*"

Lacy was met with another hard slap to the face.

"*Bitch, I don't want no excuses. I want you to get this money right and stop wasting time out here, you hear me?*"

Lacy's head shook up and down like a bobblehead doll.

"Good. Now, go make Daddy some money."

Jewels sat there with a confused look on her face.

Lacy lit up like a Christmas tree. A huge smile appeared across her face. Her once fearful mood had now been replaced with happiness and love. It was the same way she had seen her mother react to her father after he had hurt or disrespected them. Jewels did not understand it. She sat erect as Ice made his way back to the car.

Truth be told, she didn't feel any sympathy toward Lacy. Her mother had taught her that for every action, there was a reaction, and that everybody chose their own path. Since Lacy had made the decision to be a prostitute, she should follow the rules and regulations that came along with it. Every whore had made the choice to live that lifestyle, according to Melody.

"Why that window down?" was the first thing Ice said to Jewels as soon as he hopped back in the car.

Jewels didn't know whether to lie or tell the truth. She remained silent.

"So, you was listening to all that shit?"

Jewels nodded.

"Good. Because you got to see what a weak bitch looks like up close and personal," Ice stated as they drove by Lacy. "She ain't nothing like yo' mama. Nah." Ice shook his head and smiled at the thought of Melody. "Yo' mama one of a kind, loyal and true to this shit. That ho Lacy, any nigga spittin' the right game at her could scoop her young, dumb ass up when I turn my back. She ain't got no street smarts and when you ain't got that, you ain't got shit out here!" Ice's words lingered in the air. "Always remember that," he added abruptly as he pulled over and double-parked.

Jewels nodded for a second time. For the first time, she had really listened to Ice. He talked like her mother but rougher and rawer. It made sense. And the way he spoke about her mother, convinced Jewels that he actually did love her. When Jewels looked up, she saw her mother approaching her father's car. The clicking sound of the Lexus's doors was Jewels's cue. She opened the car door and started to climb out.

"Hey."

The grip of Ice's hand stopped Jewels in her tracks. She turned back and looked at him.

"You gonna be one of a kind too!" Ice shot her a wink, followed by a loving smile. "Remember I told you that." He released her arm.

Jewels didn't know what to say, so she didn't say anything. She exited her father's car and was met with a big hug from Melody. She couldn't help but look back at her father one last time before he pulled off. She had no way of knowing it would be the last time she would see him alive.

She would never forget how the young pimp Slim had taken him away from her and her mother. Her trip down memory lane as she reminisced about the first connection she and her father had made was cut short by the sound of a voice, followed by the touch of her arm. Jewels jerked back.

"Whoa!" Rome threw his hands up submissively. "You good over there?" Rome questioned.

She stared at him, wide eyed. His voice had startled her, and it had brought her back to reality. A sense of embarrassment swept through her.

He was staring at her.

She cleared her throat. "Yes, I'm fine. Why are you staring at me?"

Rome shook his head in disbelief. "Because I told you we were here three times, and you still ain't said shit." He chuckled.

Jewels looked around and then forward. She hadn't even noticed they had stopped. She wondered how long he had been watching her. He was pulled in front of the gated community she lived in.

"Excuse me. It's been a really long night," she offered as an explanation for why she had zoned out. What else could she say? She knew she couldn't tell a total stranger, a killer at that, that he had just made her pussy throb and get wet. She was convinced the chances of them ever seeing each other again were slim to none, and she felt that was for the best. "I just wanna put all this behind me."

Before Rome could say anything, Jewels's phone rang. She looked down at it in her lap. She hadn't realized she had five missed calls from the agency and double that number from Sassy. There was no doubt in her mind that they knew about the trick back at the hotel. But how? she wondered. She looked over at Rome.

"Go ahead." He shrugged.

Jewels grimaced. She unlocked the screen on her phone and took a deep breath before answering. "Hey, girl," she greeted Sassy. Her voice cracked a little, but she doubted Sassy would notice.

Sassy asked her if she was okay. Jewels could tell by Sassy's tone that she had heard about the hotel incident.

"Yeah, I'm okay. Why you ask? I didn't even know you was calling my phone," she admitted.

In her peripheral vision, Jewels could see that Rome was both watching and listening as Sassy wasted no time telling her what she knew. She could practically feel his heat on the side of her face.

"What? Dead? The news? That's crazy," Jewels said, putting on her best Academy Award performance and pretending to be surprised.

She repeated Sassy's words for Rome's satisfaction. She knew how the game was played. Her life depended on how the incident was reported.

"No! I didn't do it, bitch! Is that what they're saying?" A mixture of fear and nervousness filled her body. "So, what are they saying happened?"

Sassy said something.

"Nothing? So, why the fuck you scare me like that? And no, I don't," a relieved Jewels lied.

Rome felt somewhat relieved as well, but he knew they weren't, or rather he wasn't, out of the woods yet. His initial thought seemed more promising than ever now. He continued to listen to Jewels's conversation.

"The fat muthafucka started trippin'," she went on. "He beat the fuck outta me, and I got the hell up out of there."

She waited for Lacy to reply. She could tell she believed her and was genuinely concerned. After all, Sassy was her road dawg and her only friend.

"Thanks for checking on me. I'm taking it down. I'm beat." She needed to end the call with Sassy. "Okay, tomorrow I'll be ready, but I'm not fucking with that agency no more," she added.

Sassy spoke.

"I knew you were gonna say that. Bye, girl." She disconnected the call. For the first time in hours, Jewels smiled. She knew if she was done with a spot, so was Sassy. That was just how they rolled.

"So wassup?" Rome asked.

"If you're asking whether any photos flashed of us or any warrants were put out for our arrest, the answer is no," she answered. "They have no leads, according to my girl. But she said that they said something about him having outstanding gambling and loan-sharking debts and that they think it may be in relation to that." She played back to him what Sassy had said to her.

Rome grabbed his chin. "Cool, cool," he repeated.

"Well, this is where we say our good-byes," Jewels told him. "Thanks." She paused. "For everything." She didn't feel the same way she had felt when she first got in the Denali. Bottom line, had he not killed the fat white man, she might possibly be on the news instead of him.

She waited for Rome to say something. She could tell that he was pondering whether to say something. She wanted him to say something, anything, but he didn't say a word. Jewels let out a light sigh, then reached for the door handle, opened the car door, and put one foot on the ground.

"Hold up for a second." His tone was forceful but unsure.

She was nearly half way out of the truck. She didn't know whether he had had a change of heart or not. Her first impulse was to take flight, but her gut did not alarm her of any imminent danger.

Jewels turned to face him.

Rome brushed the top of his head with his hand. "I know this shit gonna sound crazy, but I need somewhere outside of my normal surroundings where I can lay low at," he blurted out. "Just until I get the official four-one-one on that hotel shit," Rome added. That was partially true.

Rome needed to be sure that the situation didn't come back to bite him on the ass, but he was more concerned with the earlier body, Mike-G's. He knew different types of heat came with anybody finding out it was he who had pushed him. Not only was he thinking about the reper- cussions from Mike-G's little brother if he found out, but he was also considering how credible a witness the Arab would be. If he wanted to remain a free and healthy man, he knew he had to handle both of those situations before they caught up to him. Which was why he needed a safe place to clear his head and think of the best way to handle both matters.

Jewels's face became distorted. Did this MF just ask to use my place as a hideout spot? she thought. Jewels couldn't believe her ears. "Um, l-lay low?" Jewels stumbled over her words. "Look, I appreciate you—"

"I'll pay you." Rome's words stopped Jewels in midsentence. He had spoken the magic words and didn't even know it.

Jewels studied him. Aside from the obvious, Jewels had already determined that Rome was not someone who stressed over money. Everything about him told her that he was no stranger to it. What she did pick up on was that his money was most likely obtained through illegal means, particularly drugs. She wanted no parts of that world. She wasn't about that life. Still, with all that had happened, she couldn't deny the fact that she was still alive because of him, and he needed to lay low because of her. It also didn't hurt that he had offered to pay. She was no fool. The day had been blown. Not only had she gotten her ass kicked and almost gotten killed, but she also hadn't made any money, and that was a problem. She couldn't recall the last time a day had gone by without her making some type of money. She glanced at the time on her phone. It read 11:34 p.m.. *The night is not over with yet,* she thought. She considered Rome's request. She looked at him before looking right and left at nothing specific, then directed her attention back to him.

"How much?" she asked. "And for how long?" she quickly added.

Rome took a long shot in the dark, and it seemed as if it might pay off. He believed he had more than enough in his pocket to convince her to let him stay. With it being Wednesday, he knew he needed to survive through the weekend. He shot out what he felt was a reasonable number for the amount of days he needed to stay.

"Five stacks for the rest of the week, up front."

Jewels hadn't even computed how many days it tallied up to. She was focused on the amount that Rome had just offered her in one lump sum. She thought about the offer.

Rome grimaced. "Look, I promise you won't even know I'm there," he said, thinking that would help with her decision making.

Jewels went with her gut feeling. "Just until Monday?" She wanted to be sure. Had it not been for the fact that she really could use the money, she wouldn't even consider his request so seriously.

"Or sooner." Rome lit up. He couldn't believe she had agreed. He began reaching into his pants pocket. Jewels's eyes zeroed right in on the knot of hundred-dollar bills Rome pulled out.

She counted with him as he peeled off fifty bills from the wad of cash. That didn't even seem to put a dent in his bankroll. Jewels climbed back into the Denali.

"Pull in there." She pointed.

"Okay. Here you go." Rome went to hand her the money but stopped as Jewels extended her hand.

"But all I ask is one thing," Rome said. He fanned the money in Jewels's direction as he spoke.

Jewels eyes went up in her head. She knew there had to be a catch. It was too good to be true, she thought. "What's that?" she asked dryly.

"Nobody can know I'm here. Not even your partner who called you." He put an emphasis on his words.

Jewels nodded in agreement. *Believe me, we're on the same page*, she thought to herself as Rome handed her the money and then threw the SUV back in drive and pulled into her complex.

Rome pulled into the spot marked eighty-three and killed the engine.

Jewels hopped out and made her way to her place in the complex. Rome followed her. She hurried up the stairs and reached her door in record time. Quickly, she searched her bag for her keys. She didn't want any peering eyes noticing her guest. She got the keys out, placed the house key in the keyhole, unlocked the door, and stepped inside.

"Welcome." She waved her hand as she stood in the doorway, waiting for Rome to enter.

She owned the three-bedroom condo that she lived in. Ice had been smarter than he appeared. Jewels remembered thinking that when she found out that he had transferred the property's title to her name so that he would not have to file it on his taxes. She hadn't found out that she owned the condo until years later, after his death. She loved her spot. It was huge and had been fully rehabbed with updated everything. She had a huge walk-in closet, which had once been the fourth bedroom. Her bathroom in her master bedroom was as big as the second bedroom and had a Jacuzzi tub and a separate shower. The third bedroom she had turned into her home office. The contractors she had hired had laid her spot out just the way she had envisioned it. Her kitchen was equipped with all Kenmore stainless-steel appliances and granite countertops. She had huge bamboo cabinets with glass doors, a granite-top island in the middle of the space, and large diamond-shaped marble tile on the kitchen floor. She had dropped nearly ten grand for the contemporary burnt-orange-colored soft-leather furniture.

A peculiar look appeared on Rome's face as he did a quick scan of the condo. He was actually impressed. It was evident to Rome that Jewels was in her early to midtwenties, and that was what impressed him. He didn't know any woman her age who had her shit together like she did.

Where he came from, females her age were generally on Section 8, were sack chasers, or were chicks who let dope boys use their cribs as stash spots.

"So, you can use this room while you're here."

When Rome turned in her direction, he saw Jewels standing in the doorway of a bedroom. He made his way over to where she stood, and peered in. *Nice,* he thought. *This'll do just fine.*

The room had a queen-size bed, part of a bone-white bedroom set, and a forty-two-inch flat-screen television.

"Appreciate it." Rome walked past her and entered the room. He went straight to the bed and fell back onto it.

Jewels rolled her eyes up at the ceiling and twisted her face. She had never let a man cross her threshold to stay the night, either for business or pleasure, let alone spend a few days. *You sure you're okay with this?* she questioned herself for the second time.

Rome leaned up just in time to catch the look of disdain plastered across her face. "You sure you're cool with this?" She was making him unsure about being there. The last thing he needed was to be around an unstable and unpredictable chick right now.

I hope I don't have to slump this chick, Rome thought.

"Yes, I'm okay," Jewels replied in a reassuring tone. Even though she was a little uneasy, she had made a deal and needed the money. As far as she was concerned, he was not getting it back, whether he left now or later.

Jewels hesitated before she spoke again. "It's just that I've never had a man in here." She couldn't believe she had just told him that.

A peculiar look flashed across Rome's face. *Is she fucking serious?* he thought to himself. *Does she really expect me to believe that?* "Yeah, okay," he wanted to say.

"Oh," was all he said instead, and then he began unloosening his black Pradas.

Jewels could tell he didn't believe her. Other than the fact that he had rescued her and killed someone over her, she didn't know him from a can of paint, but for some reason, it bothered her that he thought she was lying. She knew it was time for her to go to her own bedroom, before she said something that she'd regret and that pissed him off. It was apparent that he was a killer, and even though she wasn't afraid to die, she wasn't ready to die tonight. She had already escaped death and seen enough of it for one day.

"If you need anything, please help yourself. Your money includes total access to the refrigerator," she told him. She caught his head nod before she closed the guest-room door behind her. *Bitch, let it go,* she told herself, but she couldn't. She opened the guest-room door. "Just so you know, I don't have to lie to you or any other nigga about who or what I do under my roof," Jewels spat, then closed the door behind her again.

Rome sat there for a second. His chuckle and the shaking of his head were a delayed reaction to Jewels's words. He didn't know what she was talking about at first. Then it dawned on him that she had noticed he didn't believe her about never having a man in her home. Rome stood up, made his way over to the guest-room door, and locked it. He pulled out the remaining weed he had from the hotel, along with a pack of E-Z Wider paper, and twisted up a fat one. *I know her ass don't smoke,* he figured. He cracked the one window in the room and posted up near it. He didn't want to do anything that would jeopardize his opportunity to lay low at Jewels's crib. He couldn't believe how things had worked out in an ironic way. He didn't care about killing the fat white trick. He was sure that it couldn't be traced back to him. After all, he wasn't even a registered guest at the hotel, at least not under his real name, anyway.

He lit the spliff and peered out into the darkness. *You gotta fix this shit, Rome,* he said to himself as he took a deep drag of the potent cannabis and exhaled out the window. Any way you looked at it, laying low was the only move he could make right now, even if it meant being with a chick he didn't know.

Chapter Six

The vibration of the window glass and the sound of music drew Jewels's attention to her living-room window. She pulled her drapes back just enough to see out, even though she had an idea who was disturbing the peace. She shook her head and smiled. Sassy had just pulled up, bumping Beyoncé, with her convertible top down. Jewels thought her friend looked like a million dollars in that ride. She was in a white 2012 BMW 645i, with a peanut butter–colored leather interior, sitting on twenty-three-inch chrome wheels.

When her phone rang, she already knew who it was.

"Bitch, I'm outside. Come on out," was what Jewels heard.

"I'm not ready yet. Give me a few minutes."

"I knew it!" Sassy declared. "I'm coming in."

Before Jewels could protest, Sassy had already hung up.

She could literally feel Rome's eyes piercing her back. Maybe this wasn't such a great idea, after all, she thought for a second.

"She's coming in," Jewels informed him.

Rome nodded and got up off the plush couch. "Just make sure she don't be roaming around and come across me. Remember our deal," he reminded her. He went into the guest bedroom and locked the door just as he heard the doorbell ring.

Jewels waited a few seconds before she opened the door to let Sassy in.

"Damn. You slow as fuck!" Sassy complained.

Jewels ignored her comment and gave her a quick hug. "You look good, girl," Jewels complimented her.

"As I should." Sassy spun around. Her smooth-looking dark brown skin glowed as she flashed Jewels her million-dollar smile.

She knew she was the shit and made sure she looked the part on a daily basis. Sassy ran her fingers through her natural, long, straight, Asian-looking black hair.

"You are the most conceited bitch I know," Jewels said as she turned and made her way back to her bedroom to finish getting dressed.

"Whatever." Sassy rolled her deep brown, almond-shaped eyes and closed the door behind her.

"Damn. When and where did you get this table from in your hallway?" Sassy called out to her. She knew it wasn't there the last time she was over, which was last week.

"A few days ago," Jewels answered. "But why are you inspecting my damn crib? Bring yo' ass in here while I finish getting ready." Jewels stuck her head in the hallway. She wanted to make sure Sassy didn't start floating through her place and stumble across Rome.

"How much that shit cost?" Sassy asked plopping on her bed. "It looks expensive. Plus, I know how you like nice shit," she added.

Jewels smiled. Her friend knew her all too well. "Cost me almost four grand," she replied.

"Daaamn!" Sassy said in her best Ice Cube and Chris Tucker impersonation. Her thick perfectly arched eyebrows rose up. She even added the lean with it from the movie *Friday*.

Jewels burst into laughter. She loved Sassy like a sister. She could do no wrong in Jewels's eyes. Sassy was her road dawg, and they had a bond that no one else would understand. She was what you called a lethal weapon.

She was exotic looking, with a big-ass apple-bottom booty and some big-ass double D tits. Shamirah Davis, aka Sassy, was only eighteen but had a mentality far beyond her years. But like the saying went, "Never trust a big butt and a smile." They had chicks like Sassy in mind when they said that. She also had a cold heart.

They had both been through a lot in their young lives, but Sassy had been through a little more than Jewels, and it had shaped her into the coldhearted chick she was today. She was originally from the Lou, but after her mother got killed, Sassy was forced to go live with her uncle, his girlfriend, and their six-year-old son in a two-bedroom Section 8 apartment in Gary, Indiana. She was nine at the time. Her uncle's girlfriend made it perfectly clear that she didn't really want Sassy there and that Sassy should not ask her for a damn thing. It was evident that her uncle and his girlfriend got high. Her uncle began raping her on her tenth birthday. He used to force her to have sex with him. She was sure that her uncle's girlfriend knew what was going on and simply didn't care. Sassy had no one to turn to or tell what was going on with her, so for years she dealt with it. By the time she was twelve, her uncle didn't have to force her or ask her anymore. She enjoyed having sex. When his guilt finally got the best of him and he stopped sleeping with her, he had already created a little monster.

Sassy had started planning her revenge and escape the first day her uncle laid a hand on her. Sassy began forcing herself on his son. In a sick way, in her mind it was payback for what her uncle had done to her. He had taken her innocence, so she took his son's. Then, when the time was right, she decided to blackmail him. She threatened to report him to child welfare services and to tell the cops that he had been molesting and raping her for years. Her uncle wasted no time giving her some hush

money. She knew at that very moment what she could
get from men and how to get it. She knew that, like her
own mother, she would hustle men for life. Her motto
was, "The only thing a man is good for is a quick fuck and
a quick buck." With the thousand dollars she got out of
him, she purchased a bus ticket and returned to St. Louis.
That was when her and Jewels's paths crossed again—on
different terms and under different circumstances.

The two of them had first met during the time when
Jewels had gone to work with her mother back in the day.
Their mothers had been close, so it was only right that
they would become close as well.

Jewels's mother had met Sassy's mother, Noel, back
when she used to run with that crowd. They had turned
tricks and done cons and other capers together when they
first started out in the game, but then they had gone their
separate ways. Five years later, they had reunited one
day, when Melody was coming out of a motel out East.
Noel had had a child by then, just like Melody. She had
also had a drug habit. She was addicted to crack. But the
drug didn't affect her half-black and half-Latino features.
She was still beautiful, just like Jewels's mom. Everyone
thought she was the finest crackhead on the block.

One day Jewels's mother saw her standing on the
corner, begging for food and money for drugs. That day
Melody fed Noel and copped her some drugs to get high.
The next day, when Noel woke up, Melody told her it
would be the last time she starved and got high, and it
was all the way up until the day she was killed. She was
dragged down the block, while hanging on to a fleeing
trick's arm, and he drove her right into a fire hydrant. It
was the day both Jewels and Sassy had lost their mothers.
It was Jewels's mother who had killed the white man who
had killed Noel. The shot from her .22 to his temple had
cost her the rest of her life in prison. Jewels and Sassy
had been as thick as thieves ever since.

Jewels couldn't stop laughing at Sassy's Ice Cube and Chris Tucker reaction. "You a mess, girl." She peered back at Sassy through her bedroom mirror as she enhanced her eyelashes with her MAC eyelash brush. She believed she had done a good job of covering up the bruises and marks she had on her face compliments of the dead white trick.

"No, you the mess," Sassy shot back. "What the fuck happened yesterday?" Her tone became serious. "I thought you was a part of that shit—well not a part of it— but all I kept saying was, 'Please don't let them say they found a dead woman's body.' I would've lost my fucking mind if that would've happened," Sassy said, rambling. Her voice was loud.

It made Jewels nervous. She wondered whether Rome could hear her from where he was. She knew she had to shut Sassy up. When she turned around, she saw that Sassy was wiping tears from her eyes. It had never dawned on her how Sassy would be affected by what she had seen on the news. She knew Sassy had known where she was and who she was with. Just like she knew how overprotective Sassy could be toward her. On more than one occasion, Sassy had let it be known that she would kill for and over Jewels. There was an older streetwalker who could confirm that Sassy didn't play when it came to Jewels. She had a keloid scar running from the side of her left ear down to her jawline as a reminder of the day she had disrespected Jewels in public, in front of a bunch of escorts and other streetwalkers at a local playa's ball.

"I told you, I don't know anything about what happened to that fat fuck. I was already gone, after he beat the shit out of me." She walked over to Sassy and wrapped her arms around her. "But I'm okay. Thanks for being concerned." She kissed her on the head.

Sassy peered up at her. "Okay, enough of this mushy shit. Let's go fuck up some commas!" She pushed Jewels off of her and sprung up from the bed.

Jewels chuckled. "You are some type of crazy! I'm ready." She snatched up her Gucci shades and her matching clutch.

Moments later, they were hopping in Sassy's BMW.

Rome watched from the living-room window as Jewels and Sassy sashayed to the car. "Damn!" He admired Jewels's beauty.

She bad as shit, he thought to himself as she flung her hair over her shoulder with a swing of her head right before she stepped into the dropped top. It was the first time he had seen her dressed up. Rome blinked, shook his head rapidly, and released the curtain he had peeled back slightly. *Later for that broad,* he told himself. *Stay focused, Rome.*

He unlocked his iPhone 6 Plus, scrolled through his call log, and placed a call.

The caller picked up on the first ring and spoke.

"Yeah, I'm straight, but we gotta talk," Rome began.

"Yeah. You good, though?"

"Yeah. Let's meet in about an hour. I'll text you where."

"A'ight."

The phone went dead and left Rome with his thoughts. *I just hope this bitch ain't one of them hungry sack chasers. I don't want to put a bullet in her head too.*

Chapter Seven

Los paced back and forth in the one-bedroom apartment, while Buster rolled up a blunt of Kush.

"Why the fuck ain't nobody talkin'?" Los said in a booming voice. He was still heated behind the news of his brother's murder a few days ago. But he was more heated behind the fact that neither he nor his deceased brother's right-hand man could find out who was behind it and why.

"Li'l bro, don't worry," Buster said as he dried the blunt with his torch cigarette lighter. "We gonna find out who did that shit. And when we do"—he paused to lick the Swisher Sweets filled with weed—"we gonna handle that." He put the blunt in his mouth and lit it. "You know the streets talk. Just 'cause they silent now don't mean they gonna be forever." He took three pulls of the L, then passed it to Los.

"You right," Los agreed. He plopped down on the sofa and took a long drag of the bud.

"On everything I love, I'ma make whoever did this regret that shit," he declared in between pulls.

Buster nodded. He knew Los meant every word he was saying. He was only eighteen, but he was a young cannon. The only person in the world who could ever keep a tight leash on him was Mike-G, and he was no longer here. There was no doubt in Buster's mind that it was just a matter of time before Los went on a rampage. He felt he owed it to his ex-partner to watch and have Los's back, right, wrong or indifferent.

After all, had it not been for Mike-G, Buster wouldn't even be alive. The scar Buster that bore on the right side of his neck and that ended just shy of his Adam's apple was a constant reminder of how Mike-G had helped him cheat death after a robbery went wrong and he was left in a pool of his own blood in an alley on the East Side. It was Mike-G who had found him and had taken him to a hood doctor to patch him up. It was also Mike-G who had ridden on the dudes with him who were responsible for slicing his throat and robbing him for an ounce of coke. Since then, Buster had been a loyal soldier to Mike-G.

"We on the same page, li'l bro." Buster accepted the blunt from Los and inhaled a mouthful of smoke. He leaned his head back, puckered his lips, and let out a cloud of rings, then added, "If it's the last thing we do."

"Facts," Los agreed. "Whoever violated gonna be put in the motherfuckin' dirt, believe that," Los added. He slammed his fist into his palm.

"Don't worry about it," Buster replied. "Like I said, when the streets start talkin', we gonna be listening."

"You right," Los told Buster.

"Yeah, we'll be listening," Buster repeated as he let out a gust of smoke. "But for now we make sure he goes out the right way."

"Yeah. I'ma set everything up." Los took back the blunt from Buster.

"Man, I can't help but wonder how in the world he didn't see that shit coming. He always was on point. Fuck! I'ma make sure whoever did it will suffer worse than a trapped mouse."

Chapter Eight

Plaza Frontenac, a mall, was where you could find Jewels and Sassy whenever they weren't with a client. Sometimes you could find them at this premiere luxury-shopping location with a client as well, if they got lucky, which they often did. But today they were spending their own money.

The heads of men of all colors turned and their necks spun as Jewels's and Sassy's hips swayed from side to side through the high-end mall and their outfits clung to their bodies. Jewels's ass cheeks looked like two soccer balls bouncing up and down as her Gucci flip-flops echoed throughout the mall while she strutted. Sassy's, on the other hand, looked as if two midgets were in a wrestling match. Even gay men and women with their girlfriends cut their eyes over in the direction of the two of them in passing. They knew all eyes were on them. It was nothing new. They couldn't help but laugh when a Spanish guy was unsuccessful at trying to sneak a look at them while walking beside his girl. All they could hear was, "You want her, go be with her, *puta!*" right before his girl stormed off.

Out of spite, Jewels was tempted to press him but decided against it after she did her usual quick assessment of him. Physically, he was attractive, but that meant nothing to her. You couldn't deposit looks into a bank account, and nothing about him made her think, feel, or believe he had money. He was dressed in Polo from head to toe: tee, shorts, and kicks. Normally, that look would make for a promising potential client, but Jewels could spot bootleg a mile away, and everything he had on was a knockoff. Jewels continued ripping the mall's runway with her partner in crime until they reached their first destination.

"Welcome back, Ms. Jewels, Ms. Sassy," said one of Louis Vuitton's security guards as he greeted them at the door with a nod.

"Hey, Andre," Jewels and Sassy replied in unison, returning the greeting with a smile and addressing him by his first name.

Andre inconspicuously eyed Jewels as she walked through the store like she owned the place. She could see him out the corner of her right eye. Jewels knew he was digging her. *Too bad he can't afford me,* she thought.

"Another cute face with broke pockets," Sassy said to her.

Jewels looked back at Andre, who apparently hadn't heard Sassy. He flashed her his best smile.

She playfully punched Sassy in the arm. "Be nice." She grimaced.

"What?" a laughing Sassy retorted.

Jewels rolled her eyes and waved Sassy off. "I can't with you." Jewels chuckled.

With all the waves and smiles Jewels received from other employees, one would easily figure out that she and Sassy frequented the establishment. Jewels was more known than Sassy. She practically lived in the store. She always got a kick out of a line in a popular rap song that the artist 2 Chainz recited: "When I die, bury me inside the Louis store."

For the next five hours, they hit up every high-end store from Gucci to Tiffany. Seven stores and swipes later, and minus a combined total of thirty stacks, Jewels and Sassy strolled out of the mall the way they had come in—with all eyes on them. The shopping spree had done Jewels some good. Up until then, she had still been a little on edge about what had kicked off at the hotel.

"Girl, you balled out," Sassy told her as they strutted through the parking lot with designer-store drawstring bags dangling from their wrists.

"I need all this stuff," Jewels said in her own defense. "You know my birthday is coming up soon," she reminded her.

"Really, bitch?" Sassy cut her eyes over at Jewels. "You really needed an eight-thousand-dollar diamond bracelet?"

Jewels laughed louder than normal as she pretended not to see the two gangbanging-looking black guys sporting red bandannas wrapped and tied around their wrists who were trying to get her and Sassy's attention. Sassy moved in closer and matched Jewels's stride. She leaned in and licked the outer part of Jewels's ear, then sucked on it.

"She's spoken for," Sassy announced just as they passed the two dudes, and then she planted a seductive kiss on Jewels's cheek.

One of the thugs threw up his hand in submission while the other gave a thumbs-up and smiled. Sassy and Jewels chuckled and giggled all the way to the car.

Today was a better day, thought Jewels. This was just what she had needed, something to take her mind off of yesterday and her new guest back at her place. She had just blown nearly twenty grand on herself without blinking. Now, her mind was on making it back to her condo. As if her thoughts had been heard, her cell phone rang just as she climbed into the passenger's seat of Sassy's BMW. She smiled as she peered at her 6 Plus screen.

"Hello," she cooed into the phone.

Sassy noticed the sudden change in her tone and demeanor.

"Okay," was all Jewels said before hanging up.

"Bitch, who was that? Got you acting all sultry and shit over there." Sassy chuckled as she questioned her friend.

"That was someone who's going to reimburse me for some of the money I just spent," offered Jewels

"Well, I hope he got some deep pockets, 'cause our shopping sprees ain't cheap."

"Now, you know better than to ask that shit!" Jewels laughed.

"Yo, I wanna ask you a question about the other night."

Jewels thought she had already satisfied Sassy's curiosity. "What? I thought you got over that shit. Don't tell me you ain't get enough mush!" Jewels let out a nervous laugh.

"Nah, it ain't like that. I just thought you would call Ralph."

"What makes you think I didn't?"

"I called him right after I spoke to you and he ain't hear from yo' ass."

Jewels's eyebrows rose. "Bitch, you a fucking investigator now!" She laughed, hoping the questioning would come to an end. "Well, if you must know, bitch, I didn't call Ralph, 'cause I think he set me the fuck up. I'm thinking that agency shit is not for me, anyway. I could have been killed. Can you not see these fucking bruises on my face? I think you should leave it too. You got enough clients on your own, and so do I."

"You right we should. And I sure as hell don't want to be caught in a situation like that. Besides, we the baddest bitches they got!" Sassy raised her hand for a high five. "And since you mentioned it, you covered those bruises pretty well, or else I would not be seen with your ass!"

Jewels was happy that conversation had ended. She was already keeping a secret house guest, and not telling Sassy about it didn't sit well with her. But she knew it had to be that way. All she could do now was wait until her guest left, and then she'd tell Sassy the real deal.

Chapter Nine

"What's good with you?" Rome said, greeting his right-hand man, Red. The two exchanged a brotherly hug and a handshake.

He and Red had been getting money and putting in work together for over ten years, since they were both thirteen years old. Red had earned his name not from his light-skinned complexion but from how red he turned whenever he got mad and was about to seriously hurt somebody.

"How the money looking out there today?" Rome asked.

"Nigga, it's slow as fuck ever since I handled that Arab shit," Red replied. "And da boys is running wild out there, yo. I was about to take it in early, but I had to see what was good with you," he added.

"Okay. I feel you." Rome nodded. "And I appreciate you takin' care of that for me," Rome said, thanking him.

"Come on, bruh. You know I got your back always," Red replied.

"No doubt, baby boy." Rome flashed his signature grin. "But I'ma still lay low at the chick crib for a few more days. No need to make it any hotter than it already is. Plus, I still wanna see if them fuck boys figure out anything," he remarked.

"Yeah, I been keepin' my ear to the streets to see if Los and Buster up on anything. So far nothing," Red reported. "But what's up with you and ole girl?" Red wanted to know.

Rome's facial expression became stoic. "Absolutely nothing, my dude. That's the furthest thing from my mind." He left it at that.

"I feel you, but let me tell you about this fuck shit that kicked off after I took care of the Arab," his partner said. "While you all up in uppity land, at the little classy chick's condo."

"Go 'head and tell me." Rome chuckled.

"Check this. It was me, Kev, Reel, and Deuce. We went to check out these chicks out East. You know me being who I be, I had the strap on extra. We sitting in this bitch's crib, getting fucked up, and her nigga walked in showing time, so Reel, punk ass, is trying to cop a plea on some ole sucka shit to this bitch-ass nigga, while me, Kev, and Deuce's ass is going at it with dude's boys. Yo, I was so fucked up. Ole boy almost got the one up, but before I knew it, I felt for his strap, and there it was, right where Daddy had it. I think I blew half that nigga's head off. When his boys heard the nine pop, they hauled ass for the door, and I was trying to finish every last one of them pussies."

"No doubt." Rome nodded. "But what was that nigga doing?"

"That bitch-ass nigga still had his tail between his legs."

"I told you not to fuck with that nigga. I told you he was bitch, man. The only reason niggas show him any type of love is that they know what you would do to them over your team."

"Nigga, whatever."

"That's real, my nigga. They don't know like I know that you're the glue that holds all that shit together."

"Appreciate it." He gave Rome dap again. "But on some real, what's up with that new connect? Last time we met up, you didn't put much out there. Besides, there was other pressing business to handle."

A huge grin appeared across Rome's face. "We good with that," he informed him.

"Yeah? What's the numbers looking like?"

"Right now he chargin' me twenty a brick, but it's gonna change as we grow and build a relationship with ole boy. That's still hella better than the twenty-six we was paying, and it's a better quality, straight from Chi-Town."

"Word? That's what's up! If it's as raw as you saying, I'ma cook the fuck outta that shit. Been waiting for this." He rubbed his hands together.

"Yeah, we about to be all the way good," Rome confirmed. "I'ma shoot back through later and drop the first two joints off for you to chef up. I just came to grab the bread so I can hit this African motherfucka off so he don't be deep in our pockets. And check you and bring you up to speed on my end. Couldn't tell that shit over the jack, ya dig?"

"I already know, bruh." Red handed him a Polo Sport bag full of cash. "That's sixty-two in there."

"A'ight. After I get at dude, I'll hit you in the a.m."

"Bet."

Rome and Red gave each other parting fist bumps. Rome looked at his watch. He had just about figured out Jewels's schedule and movements. He did his best to stay out of her way and to be seen or heard as little as possible. He knew she would not be home for another two hours at least. He wanted to be back at her crib and in the bedroom before she returned.

"Be safe, my boy." Rome hiked the Polo bag over his shoulder.

"You too, bruh," Red returned.

Then Rome exited the way he had entered.

Chapter Ten

Morning...

To the average chick, turning twenty-five had some meaning, but to Jewels, it was just another day and another reason to get money. For as long as she could remember, ever since she had started escorting, she had worked on and through her birthday. For some reason, she made the most money and got the best gifts on that day, and today would be no different.

Kareem had arranged for a limo to pick her up and bring her to his hotel. But first, he had surprised her with a shopping spree for her birthday. She was surprised because he had been a little tight pocket lately, and ever since he had canceled on her that day, she had not been so sure about continuing to deal with him as regularly as she used to. But he had made up for it in a major way, thought Jewels.

It had been a couple of days that Rome had been at her crib, and things had been smooth sailing. At first she had been a little skeptical about leaving him alone at her place, but her fear and concern had been put at ease when she'd gotten back from the mall with Sassy and had found her place intact, with nothing out of place. She had thought it would be difficult having him there, but it had wound up being some of the easiest money she had ever made. It had taken a lot for her to give him her pass code to the front gate and a spare key to get back in, but he had reminded her of their agree-

ment. She had given in, with the intent of changing both
the code and the locks once he was gone. But, with
all that had happened, it felt kind of good to have a
man around the house. She had never gotten the full
scoop on who the fat white trick really was. For all she
knew, he could've been in the Mafia or something and
they were out there, trying to track her down. At least
with Rome there, she knew she had a fighting chance if
that was the case.

At times, it is if he isn't even here, thought Jewels. As
far as she knew, he had left the house only twice in the
three days he had been there. Where he went was of
no concern to her. The fact that he could go unnoticed
and unheard added to Jewels's comfort level. He was
unnoticed at all times.

Rome was in the shower when Jewels was heading
out. For some reason, she felt the need to tell him she
was leaving, but she shook it off. As she made her way to
the front door, she noticed the dozens of balloons that
partially covered her living-room ceiling, and the card
that was wrapped up in the dangling strings.

She stared at them oddly. He must've accepted them
while I was in the shower, she thought to herself, believing
that Kareem had sent the balloons, along with the card,
for her birthday. *This nigga be OD'ing!* She laughed as
she thought of Kareem as she walked over to retrieve the
card. Once she had grabbed the envelope, she squeezed it
to see if any money was in it. She smiled when she felt the
bulge at the crease in the card inside the envelope.

She unraveled the card and made a beeline to the
awaiting limo. Once she was secure inside the car, Jewels
tore open the envelope. Surprised would be an understatement. Five one-hundred-dollar bills fell out of the
card when she opened it. But that wasn't what surprised
her. The person from whom the card—and, apparently,

the balloons—had come was not who she had expected. She couldn't believe it. The words on the card made her smile.

Overheard today was your born day and just wanted to give you a token of my appreciation and say thank you. I know it's not much, but you can never have too much. A little something to enjoy your special day.

Jewels was speechless. She hadn't even realized that she was still smiling until the driver said, "Maybe this can add to your smile."

When she raised her head, the driver handed her a much thicker envelope, which read FROM ME TO YOU. Kareem had also gotten her a birthday card. His contained a larger amount of money than the one she had just opened from Rome. Still, she couldn't stop thinking about the fact that she had received a card and money from Rome at all.

It took her less than an hour to blow the five grand Kareem had given her in the card to spend. A pair of Vera Wangs and a MK bag later, she exited the mall and headed back to the awaiting limo. Kareem had already hinted that he was horny and that he wanted to fuck, so she knew she had to put in work as soon as she walked through the door for the five-thousand-dollar birthday present and whatever else he was going to give her afterward.

"What the hell happened to your face?" was the question Jewels was met with, delivered by a voice with a deep African accent, when she entered the plush hotel room of Kareem Musa. No amount of makeup could hide the bruises now. In a few days they had turned purplish, which made it more difficult to cover them up. This was the first time he had seen her since he canceled their appointment and she was attacked. She let out a gust of hot air and rolled her eyes as she walked past him.

"It's your fucking fault," she wanted to blurt out. Instead, she remained silent and decided to make him pay for her pain and suffering.

"Tell me. And look at me," he insisted as he shut the door behind her.

Jewels could hear the concern in his tone. When she turned to face him, the look on his face confirmed it.

"You really wanna know?" Her tone was dry.

"Yes. That is why I asked. Now tell me, please." He had moved in and grabbed her gently by the sides of her arms. She was tempted to pull away. She hated when he acted like he was her man and got all mushy on her. She didn't show it, though. She stayed in character.

"Your replacement." She stared him square in the eyes. She could see them fill with surprise. She knew he knew what she had meant. She watched as his eyes softened.

"What do you mean?" He wanted to know what had happened.

Jewels took a deep breath. "When you canceled on me, I had to take another client. I couldn't afford to miss an entire day. So, I went out on a date."

She smiled on the inside as Kareem's jaw tightened while he listened.

"He was supposed to be some respectable, rich white man, but he was a fucking pig and a monster!" Jewels's voice increased in volume in between her sniffles. "He beat me like I was nothing!" she cried out.

"I'm sorry." Kareem wrapped his arms around her. "What was his name?" he asked.

The question caught Jewels by surprise. She shook her head on his chest. "Just let it go. I don't even want to think about it," she offered, instead of giving him a name.

And it was the truth. She did not want to talk about the dead fat white man. She wondered what Kareem would have done had she given him a name. As far as she was concerned, he was a square and was not about that street life. She knew his rules didn't apply to her world.

"Okay, my love." Kareem grabbed her by the hand and escorted her to the bedroom. He wasted no time sexing her. She hadn't been in the room for three minutes before he had his dick out, a condom on, had her bent over, with her pants down to her ankles, and was ramming himself deep inside of her.

Damn. This nigga wasn't lying. He horny as shit, she thought as he pounded away.

Kareem gripped her hips and thrust himself repeatedly into her wet box. She looked back at him and started throwing it back. That was all it took for Kareem to explode. He doubled over, out of breath, and rested his midsection on her back.

"I need that!" he announced with his deep, thick African accent.

Jewels flashed a fake smile.

He raised himself from on top of her and escorted her to the king-size bed. Jewels noticed his dick was still semierect. He was the only man she knew who could nut and have his dick spring back into action if it received a certain kind of attention. Jewels knew that was why he was guiding her to the bed. She pushed him onto the bed and attacked the helmet of his dick with a vengeance. Seconds later, Kareem was back pounding on top of Jewels, who was now lying on her back. Nearly an hour went by. Jewels woke up to the hotel room phone ringing, but the person had the wrong number. She hadn't even realized she had dozed off. Kareem was nowhere in sight. She looked over and saw a note lying next to her, on the pillow.

Meet me downstairs at five, it read.

She looked down at her watch. With forty-five minutes to spare, she got up, hopped in the shower, and quickly got dressed. She threw on a long white Chanel T-shirt and some black leggings. She slipped into some black-and-white Chanel flat sandals, grabbed her clutch, and walked out of the room. She called Kareem to check his whereabouts, and he told her to meet him in the lobby in fifteen minutes.

She went down to the lobby and milled around, but Kareem did not appear. She looked down at her watch and noticed that it had been thirty minutes since Kareem had told her to meet him downstairs. *Where in the hell is he?* she thought. *I know he not on his bullshit again.* Just then a text came through from him, apologizing for not being able to make it when he had said he would. He said that his meeting was being held over, and told her to grab his American Express card out of his luggage and go have fun. She was pissed until she read the second part of that text. A huge smile appeared on her face. She responded by saying, It's okay, baby. Just call me when you are ready.

She went back up to the room and grabbed his card and then went back down to the lobby and waited for the driver in the lounge area of the hotel. She ordered a glass of white zinfandel, then pulled out her cell and searched for Sassy's number. She grimaced when Sassy's phone went to voice mail for the umpteenth time. *What the fuck is up with this bitch?* thought Jewels as she drank her white wine in one gulp. She ordered another. When she looked back up, there was another glass of wine on the bar in front of her.

When she looked around, she saw an Asian-looking man sitting at the end of the bar, nodding his head at her. She looked at him, smiled, and he smiled back. Jewels gave him a quick look over. He wasn't one of those little, short, thin-haired Asian men; he was fine. He looked like he had a little black in him. He looked like he had money, because he was nicely polished. He finished his drink, walked over to her, and asked her name. He introduced himself as Patrick.

Patrick? she thought. She was expecting to hear Chung Fu, Li Ho Ma, or some shit like that. Her phone started to vibrate. She looked down and saw it was the driver, letting her know that he was out front. She grabbed her bag off the bar, finished off her drink, gave a polite head nod, and began to leave. He insisted that she take his number and asked her if he could see her again, when she had more time.

"Not making any promises," she replied.

Jewels strolled away as if she was the shit. There was no doubt in her mind that he was watching her ass in those leggings. She stuck her ass out and swung it from left to right as she headed for the hotel lobby's exit.

Outside, she stepped into the black Maybach that awaited her. She felt like a million bucks in the beautiful luxury car. *This how you spend your birthday,* she thought and smiled on the inside. *Shopping sprees and big tips,* she told herself. She was living the lavish life, and this was all she wanted. Just as she finished balling out in downtown St. Louis, Kareem texted her. He was ready for her to return to the hotel room.

When she reached the room, she had to keep her composure. Kareem had it all laid out for her. She was met with a trail of rose petals that began at the suite's entrance. There were birthday balloons with her name on them everywhere. They covered the entire ceiling of the suite. He had a chef in the room, who was cooking shrimp fettuccini, crab legs, T-bone steaks, and chef salad. He knew that she loved seafood and steaks. He had two candles burning on the nicely set table and some Maxwell playing in the background. He had gone all out. Jewels was used to the royal treatment, but Kareem had her really feeling like a queen.

He had a sexy black dress lying across the back of a chair. He instructed her to put it on. She could not believe her eyes. No man had ever treated her so nice before. She had to get her composure together, because she did not want to seem as if she wasn't used to this. And she definitely didn't want to give Kareem the impression that this moved him out of the client zone into a more personal one. She made her way to the bathroom to change into the dress that he had bought for her. Afterward, they slow danced around the hotel suite and then sat down to eat dinner.

Later he excused himself from the table and asked her to go freshen up and join him in the master suite. Jewels strolled to the master suite like she was walking on clouds, because that was how she felt when she opened the door. She was surprised to see Kareem lying buck naked in the bed with two other women, one white, the other Latina. He wanted a threesome, hell, a foursome.

His dime, his time, thought Jewels as she entered the room. *Besides, after all this shit, he deserves whatever,* she concluded.

She knew Kareem was trying to read her face and was seeking approval. She flashed him an approving smile, agreeing to join him and the two chicks lying beside him.

Jewels stripped down to her birthday suit and made her way to the bed. She crawled over to Kareem like a tiger. She slithered up his large, masculine legs until she reached his dick, which stood straight up. Jewels began to lick his dick up and down, while the two women were engrossed in a lip lock. She started to suck on his balls while stroking his dick.

"Yes," he cooed.

Jewels rose up and sat her ass firmly on top of the head of his dick and slowly rubbed it across her hole until it was juicy wet. She then turned around and dropped down on his dick until it felt like a hand in a glove. She started riding his dick from the front, and he loved it. They both exploded at the same time.

The girls walked over to him, and one started licking him between his ass cheeks. *Of course, it is the white bitch licking his asshole*, thought Jewels. Most of the clients she dealt with enjoyed their asses being licked, but that was not Jewels's specialty, so she decided to take notes from the white chick, especially after seeing Kareem's reaction.

Hours went by. Jewels was in sex heaven. Between receiving double head from the white and Latina chicks and riding Kareem's dick while the two girls took turns riding his face, Jewels was exhausted. She got up in the middle of the sexual excursion and left them to do their thing. She went into the bathroom to freshen up. When she came back out and began to dress, Kareem didn't want her to leave. He kept begging her to stay the night with him. She shot him a lie about having to check on Sassy, and he bought it, knowing how close the two were. He climbed off the bed and walked Jewels to the door. The two women smiled seductively and waved good-bye to her. When they reached the door, Kareem revealed his hands from behind his back.

"Happy birthday," he said. He handed her two stacks and a jewelry box from Tiffany & Co.

Jewels lit up. Not at the present, but at the money. That was exactly what she had needed. She opened up the box, and inside it was a beautiful diamond necklace.

"Thank you." She kissed him on the cheek.

This will match my bracelet perfectly, she thought.

"You're welcome." He planted a kiss on her forehead. "Anything for you, love."

Jewels smiled as she reached for the handle on the door to the suite.

Moments later, she was laid back in the Maybach, replaying the events of the day, the best birthday she'd ever had.

Chapter Eleven

The sound of rapid fire penetrating the bedroom window caused Rome to roll out of bed and onto the floor. It sounded like the Fourth of July outside, despite the fact it was the middle of winter. Fortunately for him, he slept with his weapon under his pillow. His first reaction was to hit the floor and grab for his burner, all the while thinking to himself, I know these niggas didn't bring this shit here.

He rose up from off the floor, gun in hand. His vision was distorted by shattered glass flying everywhere. He steadied his breathing and took aim at the first thing he saw moving. He zeroed in on the figure. He couldn't believe his eyes when he saw the shooter. He knew it had to be someone close to him, because not many people knew where he laid his head. He had a suspicion the shooter wanted his spot. Rome cocked his hammer back. Not today, chump, *he thought as he tightened his grip on his pistol. Before he could let off a round from his nine, out of nowhere a bullet tore through his chest.*

Rome sprang up in a cold sweat. He wiped the perspiration from his face and brow. He couldn't believe he had just had that nightmare. It had been nearly ten years since he had relived the day he cheated death when a fellow street colleague got the drop on him and shot him in the chest when they were teens. Rome had been left for dead but, miraculously, had survived, only to end his ex-friend's life when he recovered. The last time he had had that dream, something bad in his life had followed.

Rome hopped out of the bed and made his way over to his pants. He retrieved the ringing cell phone, which had jolted him out of his sleep. A wet spot in the shape of his silhouette had soiled the sheets.

"Hello?" he answered, but the caller had already hung up.

He called back the number, and someone picked up.

"Wassup, homie? Talk to me."

The person on the other end of the line said something.

A frown appeared across Rome's face. "Word up, my G?" he asked in disbelief after receiving the unwanted news. "I can't believe this shit," he cursed. "So when you think that'll be?" he then asked. "Not trying to rush the process or anything. Safety first, ya dig?" he added.

The person said something back.

"Oh, a'ight. Well, just keep trying to walk that down, bruh." Rome nodded.

He was surprised by what Red had shared with him. According to him, the threat to Rome's freedom and possibly his life was harder to track down and take care of than either of the two had realized. He knew before he could return to the streets as normal, he needed one other thing handled.

"Cool," Rome replied after listening to Red. He ended the call after being reassured that another week would not go by without all loose ends being tied up.

Damn. Why can't this nigga find these motherfuckers! Maybe I should just go back and act like it ain't nothing. Fuck. Just when things were looking good.

Chapter Twelve

Jewels was starving, but still, she patiently waited for Sassy to bring her ass to lunch. The only reason she did was that she did not want to hear her homegirl's mouth. The two of them had been playing phone and text tag all morning and it was getting annoying, but Sassy had finally agreed to meet over lunch so that they could catch up. They hadn't seen each other since they burned the money down together nearly a week ago. They normally didn't go three days without catching up on the latest in each other's lives. Jewels caught movement in the direction of the entrance to the restaurant. She let out a deep sigh when she saw that it wasn't Sassy.

Jewels was someone who was always on time and never fed into the CP time mantra. If you told her 1:00 p.m., that was the exact time she would be there, not thirty minutes late, like Sassy currently had her waiting. But it was all good since she was sitting in an upscale downtown eatery, sipping a fruity alcoholic beverage, as she checked her social media sites to pass the time. Her entertainment was interrupted by a text from Sassy, stating she was walking up the block.

The life that Jewels lived was nothing that could be considered normal, but she did what she needed to do to pay her bills and live the type of lifestyle she so loved. She had been raised to be a survivor, and that was exactly what she was. She did not have many friends, because unless you came from it, you simply wouldn't understand what it was that she did for a living. And Jewels was not in the habit or business of lying to people, so her work enabled her to keep her distance from most. Only Sassy knew what the real deal was since she lived an identical lifestyle. The only difference was that where Jewels drew the line, Sassy crossed it. She had an insatiable appetite for dope boys, who were the opposite of Jewels's clients. Let Sassy tell it, and Jewels's life was dull and boring, but in fact, it was just the opposite. Jewels was just about to text her again when she glanced at the time and noticed ten more minutes had passed and still no Sassy.

Just as she scrolled through her phone and found her friend's name, Sassy appeared, looking like the bona fide diva she was. Her hair was "blowing in the wind" fabulous as she walked through the revolving glass doors. She was draped in all black, like she had just attended a funeral. She sported a black leather sports jacket with matching skintight black leather pants. Her black Louboutin heels added to her short height, giving her an extra three inches, as she clicked clacked on the marble tile as she strutted through the small bistro. All Jewels could do was smile at her friend. She could not front. Sassy looked like a million dollars, but she could never give her conceited ass the satisfaction of acknowledging this.

"Did you miss me, bitch?" Sassy asked playfully, pulling one of the extra chairs at the table out for her Gucci bag.

Jewels chuckled. *Two peas in a pod,* she thought. The other extra chair was occupied by Jewels's bag. "Took your ass long enough to get here," she replied dryly.

"I apologize, but you know my young stallion can't get enough of this," she cooed with a wink. "He worked my ass overtime. But he paid for it, though," she added.

"Uh–huh. Whatever." Jewels rolled her eyes.

"Real talk." Sassy put an emphasis on her sincerity. "I have been trying to catch up with you but our schedules were not aligning," she said in her own defense.

"Yeah, you right," Jewels agreed. "But I am sure it could have been planned sooner if you weren't so caught up with your young thug."

"Ummm, young stallion, bitch!" Sassy said, correcting her.

The two of them both broke out into laughter as they proceeded to study the menu.

When the waiter returned to the table, Jewels was the first to order. "I'll have the salmon Caesar salad, with a Grey Goose and tonic with two limes please."

Sassy followed her. "And can I have the chicken teriyaki with brown rice and a refill of this bistro punch? It's so good."

After jotting down their order, the waiter disappeared into the back, and Jewels and Sassy people watched in between looking at their phones. Sassy clearly was more occupied with everything else and for a moment, Jewels was a bit envious, but at the same time, she watched her friend in admiration, so it was okay. Besides, it wasn't like Jewels didn't have other options. Men had recklessly eyeballed her and tried to get her attention even before Sassy had arrived at the restaurant. Her first two drinks had actually been sent over to her by two different gentlemen at the bar.

Even though Sassy was her girl, looking at her was a reminder of the life Jewels courageously lived, and it was one that was indeed complicated. In her opinion, it took a strong type of person to understand why she lived the life she lived. It took an even stronger person to live with herself while living the life she did. And as far as Jewels was concerned, both she and Sassy were that type of strong bitch.

She had decided a long time ago that life was about choices, and you were going to either talk about making moves or actually make them. Never one to settle, Jewels felt this was the perfect arrangement. She had been raised and taught by the best. Her mother had always told her that a fair exchange was no robbery. Jewels had taken that to heart and had run with it. She specialized in providing a service where both parties were happy. Men got to fuck a bad bitch with no strings attached, and she got paid for letting them. In her and Sassy's mind, this was a true win-win lifestyle for them.

The waiter returned to the table with their drinks.

Once he was gone, Sassy took a large sip from her glass.

"So what has been up?" Jewels asked.

"Nada. I have been maintaining. I have a new client, fine as hell, but a little on the weird side."

"Why you say that?"

"Well, he likes to hold a teddy bear and suck his thumb when I'm rocking the mic." Sassy giggled at the thought.

Jewels nearly spit her drink out as she busted out laughing.

"Well, that's nothing compared to the nasty mutha-fucka who likes for me to pee on his dick and after I do, you know, this weirdo actually cums," Sassy continued.

"Eeew. Okay. I'ma need you to stop before I can't eat." Jewels held her stomach and frowned.

"Bitch, please. All them nasty motherfuckas you gotta deal with, it's a miracle you don't be having nightmares and shit every night." Sassy chuckled.

Had anybody else said that to her, Jewels would've taken offense, but she knew her girl meant no harm or disrespect. Ironically, that was what their conversations consisted of mostly whenever they got together. Besides, what Sassy had said was nothing but the truth. It was a blessing that Jewels was not haunted by some of the things she had been paid to do and, most recently, by the fate of the fat white man. Nope, Jewels slept like a baby and counted her money in her sleep. That was the game she played, and whoever tried to play it was subjected to what came with it. At least that was how she saw things.

"Touché," Jewels agreed with a smile.

"Yeah, I thought so." Sassy returned her smile. "Besides, to pee on a nigga for five stacks . . . Shit, he can get TLC's 'Waterfalls.'" She doubled over at her own joke.

Jewels joined her again in laughter. "Are you serious? No sex? Just straight urine?" she asked.

"Yup. Serious as a heart attack," Sassy confirmed. "I just drink five gallons of water whenever I am planning to see him. His favorite color is red, so I make sure I have on some red lingerie while I do a striptease, and before I remove my thigh-high stockings, he's begging and pleading for me to wet him."

The waiter returned with their food and placed their respective plates in front of them. They each flashed fake smiles and stopped speaking. Once the waiter was out of earshot, they resumed their conversation.

Jewels broke the silence. "That's crazy."

"Yeah, tell me about it."

"Sassy, could you pass the salt, please?"

"Sure. Here you go."

"And the pepper too, please. Thank you."

"Damn. Anything else?" Sassy complained jokingly.

"Shut the hell up."

"I'm serious. But what's up with you, anyway?" Sassy said, changing the subject.

Jewels's whole demeanor changed. She was caught off guard by Sassy's question. "What do you mean?" she asked defensively.

"Damn. What the hell is wrong with you?" Sassy asked. She had noticed the change in Jewels.

Bitch, you're overreacting, Jewels told herself. "Nothing." She managed to get the word out without her voice cracking.

"Oh." Sassy looked at her oddly. "Sound like you was hiding some shit," she asserted.

Jewels knew she had to keep her cool. Sassy had known her long enough to know if something was wrong. She knew Sassy was studying her.

"Bitch, you know everything there is to know about me," she said with a light chuckle. "I don't have nearly as much excitement in my life as you do," she added.

"Yeah, right. I heard different."

Jewels could have sworn her heart skipped a beat. "What is that supposed to mean?" She wanted to know.

"Look at you." Sassy laughed. "Thinking somebody got something on your ass. I was just messing with you. Relax," Sassy told her.

Jewels shook her head. Sassy was right. She needed to relax. *How the hell could she know anything?* Jewels thought, reasoning with herself.

"Girl, I don't know what the hell's wrong with me. I think it's because it's close to my monthly." Jewels blamed her actions on an imaginary menstrual.

"Sound like you need some dick." Sassy chuckled. "What's up with Africa?" she then asked.

Jewels rolled her eyes. She knew who Sassy was referring to. It was the name she had given Kareem. "Same ole, same ole. Still head over heels for my ass," she offered.

She was glad they had moved on to a specific person. She didn't think her nerves could take it anymore. For a minute, it had felt as if Sassy could see right through her. She hated hiding from Sassy the fact that she had a killer staying at her house. Jewels was sure if she told her,

Sassy would understand and wouldn't say anything, but she couldn't take that chance.

"You might as well marry that nigga and retire," Sassy joked.

Jewels found no humor in that and didn't crack so much as a smile.

"I'm playing. I'm playing," Sassy sang.

"Anyway, what you trying to do from here?" It was Jewels who now changed the subject. "I was thinking about heading over to the mall. Nordstrom has a new shipment of shoes I want to check out," she informed Sassy.

"Girl, I would love to go, but young stallion will be here in"—Sassy looked at her phone and scrolled through the text she had just received from her expected ride—"ten minutes to pick me up," she said.

"Well, damn. You didn't plan on us really hanging out too long, huh?" Jewels sounded pissed.

"Girl, you know it's not even like that, but it's just something about that young nigga that I cannot get enough off. He just turns me the fuck on." Sassy closed her eyes and did a quick reminiscence of her last sex scene with her young street client.

"Whatever, bitch!" Jewels sucked her teeth.

"Don't get mad 'cause you ain't got nobody."

Jewels flipped her the bird. "You know what? Go ahead. I ain't even mad at you. If the shoe were on the other foot, I'd do the same thing. Handle your business. Make sure you call me," Jewels said in an understanding tone.

"Thanks, girl. I'll make it up to you." Sassy stood and gathered her things. She scurried over to the side of the table on which Jewels sat, and threw her arms around her neck. "I'll call you later." She corrected herself when she continued, "No. Matter of fact, I'll call you tomorrow." She laughed as she said it.

Again, Jewels shook her head. "Just make sure you call me."

Just then a milk-white Mercedes CL600 pulled up along the curb outside the restaurant.

There was no doubt in Jewels's mind that this was Sassy's ride. *He must really be getting it,* thought Jewels, realizing that she had never seen Sassy's young stallion pick her up in the same ride twice. She also realized that this was actually the first time she had gotten a good look at him. On a scale of one to ten, she gave him a ten for the car and a six in the looks department. Not that it mattered. Apparently, he was also a ten in the pockets, the way he broke Sassy off on the regular. No matter what the case was, as odd as it sounded, with all that she did for money, Jewels just couldn't see degrading herself by dealing with hustlers.

Sassy waved good-bye as she ran to the door. Once outside, she hopped in the front passenger's seat of the Benz. The young stallion also waved and shot Jewel a flirtatious wink just before he peeled off into the ongoing traffic.

Jewels rolled her eyes. "Not in this lifetime, motherfucka," she mumbled under her breath before finishing off her drink.

Chapter Thirteen

Sassy had been looking forward to this day, but she had never expected for it to turn out the way it was just presented to her when she was picked up. When she cut her lunch date short with Jewels, she had been under the impression that it was for a quickie with her young street stallion and a couple of dollars. She had been working on him for months now, getting all she could get while the getting was still good. She had thought that once they hooked up from the restaurant, they would hit up a mall or two, they'd grab a bite to eat, and then they'd have great sex for a nice piece of change, which would end with her pockets being fatter.

She was surprised when she found out he had other plans. Surprised that he asked her to spend the weekend with him. She had never stayed longer than half the evening. He blamed it on living with his brother. But he had told her his brother no longer lived there. And now she was charged up and ready for action. Tonight she had every intent on coming up with a shitload of money, and she would be receiving the fuck of her life, as she always did whenever she linked up with her young stallion. He always showed her a time to remember whenever she was with him.

The main object, hands down, was money with Sassy, but she was in dire need of having her pipes cleaned, let her tell it. The thought of them both caused her pussy to twitch. It was a no-brainer which one made her pussy throb the hardest, though. Niggas always were scream-ing it was money over bitches, and Sassy was not one to object, because she lived by the rule of money over nig-gas.

The red Christian Dior dress fit like a glove, accentu-ated her round ass, and showed just enough cleavage to make any man or woman want more. Sassy sat on the chaise lounge in her bedroom, lotioning her legs before slipping her feet into the stiletto heels she had recently purchased. Sassy then walked into the bathroom and looked at herself one last time before applying gloss to her lips. Her young stallion was sitting in an SUV, waiting for her outside her place, as she threw some things in her Gucci bag and changed into her evening wear.

Once downstairs she was greeted by a guy with a linebacker build and a Rick Ross–shaped beard. He wore a black suit and tie. It didn't take a rocket scientist to see that he had been to prison. Aside from the obvious bulging muscles, probably built in jail, the tattoos on the side of his face were a dead giveaway for Sassy. She liked how her young boy was a boss. *Too bad it's all about the Benjamins,* she thought, believing that if things were different, things between them could be too.

The reality of it was that Sassy was a whore, and he was a dope-boy trick that she happened to like. Still she liked how he set the red carpet out for her whenever he wanted to see her. The driver smiled and nodded as he opened the car door for her. She climbed into the backseat of the pearl-white SUV. She was greeted by her young stallion, who looked good enough to eat. She was immediately intoxicated by his cologne. The two locked eyes as they embraced one another and kissed.

"Mmm . . . baby. I missed you," Sassy cooed. It had been only an hour since he dropped her off to get ready.

"Oh, yeah?" Los flashed his million-dollar smile.

"Yes, Daddy," she purred.

"How much?" he asked, flirting.

"I will show you later on tonight." She winked.

He picked up the bottle of champagne that was sitting in the ice bucket and filled two flutes with bubbly. He passed the first glass to Sassy. "I was looking forward to seeing you tonight. You really have had me jonesin' fo' that pussy for the past few weeks, you know that?" he stated and asked all in the same breath.

Sassy cheesed and nodded like a bashful schoolgirl. She was in character.

"You missed this dick?" he asked, grabbing a fistful of his jeans. "Or this money?" He then patted the bulge in the front pocket of the jeans.

Sassy moved in closer. She put her hands between his legs and began stroking his semi-hardness through his jeans with her left hand and placed her right hand on his pocket.

"Both," she cooed. She licked the outer part of his ear.

"Good answer," he replied.

They continued to engage in small talk until they arrived at their destination, which was unknown to Sassy. All she did know was that it was going to be expensive. When the driver opened the door for them to exit the SUV, Sassy looked at the front of the restaurant and saw the sign and the huge glass window and began to smile. She had wanted to eat at this particular place for a few months but it was by reservation only and she had been unsuccessful at nabbing one.

"Oh, my goodness!" she said as she smiled.

"What, babe?" Los flashed her a smile.

"This is hot!" she exclaimed.

Sassy took hold of his hand as they walked toward the door. Once inside, they were immediately seated in an exclusive area to the left, which had only a few tables and chairs. It was almost as if the establishment had its own personal VIP area.

After the two were seated, the waitress, who resembled a walkway model, poured champagne and placed two menus on the table for the couple.

"Welcome back, Mr. Gross," greeted the waitress, who was named Estella.

Sassy looked around and had to do a double take. She didn't know who the waitress was addressing. Her date didn't strike her as the type of man who frequented this establishment, but it was evident that he did.

"I will be serving you guys this evening," Estella said, and then she began to run down the menu. "Tonight's chef's selections are our lobster and crab étouffée with jasmine rice and our grilled lobster stuffed with prawns and scallops and served with a wild rice pilaf and grilled asparagus," Her tone was pleasant.

Los nodded for Sassy to order first as he continued to look at the menu.

She ordered the grilled lobster, one of the chef's selections, while Los went with a medium well-done porterhouse, asparagus, and a baked potato.

"Excellence choices." The waitress smiled. She gathered the menus and then vanished into the back of the restaurant.

"So, baby, what is the occasion?" Sassy asked.

"I don't need one to show you that I fucks with you hard body," he said with a wink.

"Truuue," Sassy sang. *If he only knew*, thought Sassy.

The two dined on their meals as they conversed between laughs and flirts. They were on their third bottle of champagne, and both of them were feeling good. Sassy rubbed his inner thigh under the table. She could feel his dick stiffening from her touch. She flashed him a smile, then picked up her flute with her free hand and tossed the remainder of the champagne back. They finished up with dessert and then walked out of the establishment and over to where Los's car and driver awaited.

On the ride to his house, Los definitely had plans for Sassy. He had been enjoying the view as her ass jiggled in the dress. He was going to have so much fun removing it once they were inside his penthouse.

Once inside he immediately went to his room, where he retrieved two blunts from the safe he kept under his desk and lit them. He took a pull from the first one, and as the smoke filled his lungs, the intoxication was immediate. Before exiting the room, he made sure to leave the safe door cracked. Soon enough, he would be able to confirm his suspicions.

Sassy walked over to him, took the other blunt, and took a small pull before letting out a slight cough as they both made their way back to the living room.

"You ain't ready for this!" Los told her. "This that fire right here. You used to that mid from those corner boys you used to fucking with," he added.

"What?" she asked and then rolled her eyes as she proceeded to hit the blunt again. The weed caused her to have that same cough again.

"See? I told you, shorty." Los laughed.

"I'm not choking from the weed. I'm choking because of that bullshit you just said," she muttered, correcting him. "I don't fuck with no corner boys. Unless you're one," she said, challenging him. "I only fuck with bosses and do boss shit, because I'm a boss bitch," she pointed out.

Sassy knew what he was insinuating but she wasn't going to let it ruin the evening, since as far as he knew from what she had told him, she dealt only with those about that dough. She walked over to his wet bar and poured two glasses of cognac and handed him one.

"Thanks, love." Los took the drink and tossed it back.

"You're welcome, boo!"

"Don't call me boo."

Sassy knew he hated the term *boo*, but since he wanted to start, she was gonna play along with him. "Aaaw, poor baby. What's wrong?" she asked in a baby voice as she removed her stiletto heels.

Los finished the remainder of the blunt and removed his shirt and tie. He walked up to Sassy and palmed her ass and tongued her down before she could refuse. The two went to town right there in the living room removing all their clothes and both kissing and sucking on all exposed body parts.

"Oh, baby," Sassy cooed as his mouth found her caramel breasts. She straddled him and began to grab his hair, needing to hold on to something, but his Caesar cut was not complying.

He sucked her nipples steady and slow, awaiting the moment for them to get wet and stiff and also sensitive to the touch. He slowly dropped his hand to one nipple and thumbed it in a slow motion, which he could tell was driving her wild, as he felt her pelvis thrust. Sassy was so swollen, she felt she was going to burst any minute, because she was so turned on by his touch. She was anticipating his next move so much that she could hardly breathe. He touched her inner thigh sending chills up and down her spine. His tongue continued to explore her body as he made his way below her navel, and she arched her back, waiting for his next move. His mouth finally found its treasure and was relentless with giving pleasure.

Sassy was in a pure utopia as his tongue explored her clitoris and her love canal. Sassy could barely control herself as she felt her body arching more, and for the first time, she called out his street moniker, knowing at the exact minute that wasn't even his name. She did not care, though. She just did not want the feeling to stop. She begged as she cried out his name. He was devouring her pearl tongue, and she was loving every minute of it. Her sweet box craved his tongue as her body hungered for his touch. Sassy was seconds away from begging him to stop as he met her with his tongue. He played with her tongue as she grabbed his wand and milked the throbbing member with her perfectly manicured hands. The feeling was much too intense for both of them. He was too good, and she couldn't stop. He jerked and thrust as he gyrated and released himself into her hands. He knew exactly what he was doing to her, and he wanted to see how she would respond. She licked her fingers as she got up and walked to his bedroom.

Los got up and took the last swig of cognac in his glass and proceeded to pour another as he heard water running in the direction of his bedroom. He thought the two of them would shower together, only to be surprised when he walked over and saw Sassy standing in the bathroom doorway, soaking wet. He immediately made a beeline over to where she stood. He picked her up and carried her to the bed. He guided his dick and entered her sweet box, managing to touch her walls and make her moan in delight. His member fit perfectly inside her warm, tight glove, and with each stroke she got wetter as he picked up the pace.

Yes, I'm definitely gonna get my money's worth and then some if this ho ain't genuine! Los thought.

The two continued their love making for another two hours, before passing out from pure exhaustion.

Chapter Fourteen

Rome had been laying low at Jewels's condo for longer than he had expected. He wound up breaking Jewels off with another stack for the extended time he had to be there. The two coexisted under the same roof without exchanging any words other than a courteous good morning or hello. For the most part, he had stayed in the guest bedroom and out of Jewels's way, but she had seen him coming in and out of the shower a few times. She didn't know why, but her inner thighs got wet every time she caught a glimpse of his body, which was strange, because aside from his physical features and his boss demeanor, she was not attracted to him.

Still, for the past couple of nights, she had found Rome invading her dreams. At first, she had thought it was due to the shock of what had transpired back at the hotel, but the ending of the dream had convinced her that was not the case. It always started out about the murder of the trick, who would have possibly killed her had Rome not killed him first, but it always ended with her and Rome having sex . . . for free.

One early morning, around 4:00 a.m., Jewels had gotten up to get a bottle of water. Half asleep, she had climbed out of bed and had slipped into her slippers, with next to nothing on. She had had no idea she would run into Rome, who was tiptoeing to the guest room, dripping wet, after forgetting his towel. Jewels had tried not to look but couldn't help taking in an eyeful. She even found herself staring a little bit too long. It was Rome's snicker that snapped her out of it. She had been with many men, but none of them had been put together like Rome. Kareem was the only one who came close. What pissed her off was that she was sure that he paid her absolutely no attention at all. When their eyes met, he had a blank stare on his face, as if he was unfazed by her standing in front of him in her bra and boy shorts–cut panties. That was a first for her. She was used to getting all the attention. She felt some kind of way because he wasn't even looking in her direction.

After that encounter, she had purposely let herself be seen naked a few times by Rome. Each time, he had barely glanced her way. She had even worn her sexiest lingerie, which left very little to the imagination, and still he had paid her no attention. She was on the verge of asking him if he was gay. She had heard about a new trend called "homo thugs." She had seen it on *Jerry Springer.*

Homo thugs were these hard-core-looking-ass niggas with braids, gold teeth, and all that other gangster shit. They looked the part, but there was a catch to it. Underneath all of that gangster shit, they like what she liked—dick. She hoped that wasn't the case with him. *That would be a waste*, she thought to herself.

Rome had kind of enjoyed the past few days at the condo. He had felt relaxed and peaceful. He had called his man to see how the situation was looking after he pushed Mike-G's wig back. He wasn't concerned with the Arab anymore. Red had taken care of that. Red had let Rome know that the block was definitely hot right now for him. Rumors and speculation had already began to surface and float around in the streets. The homicide squad had been through the hood several times, asking questions.

They had been to Rome's mother's house three times already. Rome wasn't really worried. He knew one of the local snitches probably had dropped his name for a quick fix after catching wind of just one rumor about what had happened to Mike-G. He had played the "cat and mouse" game a few times with the homicide detectives. Now that the Arab had been taken care of, it would only be a short time before he could show his face in the hood.

He was trying to stay focused but Jewels was making it difficult for him. She walked around him buck-ass naked. His dick jumped every time he caught a glimpse of her nakedness. But it stood erect when he caught her bending over the sink in her bathroom as he walked past. He couldn't help but stop and take in her beauty. Her skin was perfect and flawless. It looked creamy and silky. Her waist was so small that it almost didn't look like it belonged to her. Her thick thighs and hips flared out- ward. Rome noticed she had no cellulite, stretch marks, or wrinkles on her ass. Her stomach was flat and tight.

Now he leaned against the wall and watched as she applied makeup to her face. He could see her grape-sized nipples and the small patch of silky hairs over the top of her pussy from the reflection in the mirror. Rome was tempted to walk through the cracked door and roll up behind her but sided against it. The last thing he needed was for her to flip out and kick him out. He couldn't afford to take that chance. He still needed a few more days to get things situated in the streets before he could return to them. His eyes widened when he saw Jewels hike one leg up on a stool and begin shaving between her legs. It gave him a full view of her inner thighs.

"Fuck!" he cursed under his breath.

Damn, that pussy looks so soft and juicy, he thought. *I'm not really into eating pussy, but he wouldn't mind sucking hers*, he told himself.

Even her little feet were pedicured and perfect. She had the type of look that made a man want to kiss and suck on every part of her body. He had her all wrong, he thought. Not only was she a bad bitch, but aside from her profession, he believed she was also good peoples. Being around her had allowed him to see that she wasn't stuck-up and high maintenance. She was funny, and a nigga could sit down and have a conversation with her. He also could tell she was smart.

He was used to dealing with straight hood rats and women with three or four kids by three or four different niggas. Chicks with stretch marks and baby fat all over their asses. It really didn't matter to Rome. He enjoyed the pleasures of a woman when the opportunity presented itself, but he had no real preference. But he knew Jewels was different than what he had had in the past. True, he knew she was an escort and, for the most part, made her money from the exchange of sex, but she didn't put him in the state of mind of a streetwalker or a whore.

He wondered how she had gotten into the lifestyle. She could have any man she wanted, he concluded, as he continued to watch Jewels shave. He envisioned himself propping her up on the bathroom counter and sexing her until she was exhausted. It had been a minute since he had sexed a female. Watching her made him horny. Rome didn't realize he had slipped into a daydream. The sound of the blow-dryer brought him back. When he focused in, he could have sworn that he saw Jewels looking back at him through the mirror. He quickly leaned back and faded into the background. "Shit." He shook his head.

He hoped she hadn't seen him and thought he was on some creep shit. He backpedaled to the guest room, hoping she didn't come out and confront him. She didn't. He knew his stay was coming to an end, and he was tempted to double back and walk in on Jewels in the bathroom, but he wasn't no sucka or no trick and didn't want to come across as one. He was convinced she was not a kept woman. Anybody with a pair of eyes could see she made good money, because her condo was plush. Rome closed the bedroom door and fell onto the bed. He let out a gust of hot air.

I gotta get the fuck outta here, he thought. He knew if he stayed any longer, he would find himself thinking about Jewels more than he should be. As he pulled out his phone, he could hear Jewels's footsteps approaching his door. He could tell she had stopped in front of the door by the shadow at the bottom of it. Rome waited before dialing his boy. Five seconds went by before she had finally walked off. Rome wondered what that was all about. He shrugged and continued with placing his call.

Jewels hadn't been able to help bursting into a light chuckle when she watched Rome scurry away from the cracked bathroom door. What he couldn't have known was that she had left the door open, hoping he would notice her. It had taken all her willpower and strength not to laugh while she teased him as he watched. It had not been her intent to let on that she saw him through the mirror, but she could tell he'd seen her peering at him for a brief second. As she had made her way to her bedroom, she'd stopped at the guest bedroom Rome was occupying. Her body told her to enter the room and let him put out the fire she possessed between her legs. It wasn't often she got turned on by a man, but lately, Rome had managed to do just that without doing anything in particular. Jewels stood in front of the door, contemplating. Her mind won the battle and convinced her not to grab the door handle. She inhaled and grimaced, then made her way back to her bedroom. "What the hell is wrong with you?" she asked herself out loud.

She knew this was not like her. When it came to sex, it was always business and never about pleasure or personal matters. She had always taken care of herself when it came to that. Besides that, Rome was not the type of guy she had ever gone for. But there was just something about him she couldn't shake. Jewels entered her bedroom and went straight for her top drawer. She slid her assorted panties and thongs to the side and retrieved the seven-inch dildo they hid. She removed the towel she was wrapped up in and slid up on her bed. She spread her legs wide and inserted the tip of the dildo inside of her. She closed her eyes, tossed her head back, and bit down on her bottom lip. An image of Rome appeared in her head as she took all seven inches inside of her, causing her beautifully manicured toenails to curl.

Oh, yes. Do me like that. . . . Make me cum all over you. . . .

Chapter Fifteen

Meanwhile across town at around the same time . . .

Sassy awakened to the sound of Los's loud snoring. Her head was hurting from the alcohol and weed mixture. Her mouth felt like a cotton ball in the Sahara Desert. She got up and walked to the kitchen and grabbed a water from his well-stocked refrigerator and walked back to the bedroom. Her attention was drawn to her left. She had a nose for money, and it was as if the scent of it had just breezed past her nostrils. Sassy stopped and doubled back. When she looked down, she noticed, as she had the last few times she had been there, that the door to the safe on the floor was ajar. *This nigga is so messy,* she concluded.

The average person might have been nervous and skeptical, but Sassy had balls like a man, let her tell it. She had already told herself that if the safe was open again whenever she returned, she would dip into the money again, only this time she would take more than just a bill or two. And that was exactly what she planned to do. She tiptoed closer to the safe and took a look inside it. *Holy shit*! she declared. There were nothing but hundred-dollar bills in the partially cracked safe. There appeared to be a lot more bills in it than there'd been last time she was there. They were neatly stacked inside the metal box. Sassy had never seen so much money at one time.

She cautiously looked around, then grimaced and shook her head. *Bitch, make sure you know what you're doing,* she reasoned with herself. She bent down and ran her fingers over a few bills. She guessed that there were over fifty Gs in the safe. She turned quickly to see if Los was awake. Sassy noticed his eyes were closed and his snoring was still loud. She grabbed a handful of bills and quietly hurried into the bathroom to put them in her clutch, which was on the bathroom counter. She returned to the safe to make sure that everything by it was just as it had been when she first approached it. To play it off more, she went to the living room and retrieved her undergarments and put them back on, then grabbed two water bottles from the fridge, went back to the bedroom, and climbed back into bed.

"Baby," she called as she placed tiny kisses on Los's neck.

Los's eyes slowly opened. He stretch and yawned.

"Hey, gorgeous. You ready for round two?" he asked as he grabbed his manhood.

Sassy flashed him half a smile.

Truth be told, all she wanted at that moment was to get dressed and go home. As far as she was concerned, she had got what she had come for, and so had he, so their business for the time being was coming to an end. Besides, her intuition was getting the best of her. It would not allow her to continue to be in his presence after she had stolen from him this time around and had done it for no other reason than the money was there.

Ironically, she didn't need the money. She had more than she knew what to do with. *The two racks I got from him is a new Hermès bag, at minimum,* she thought. She told herself he wouldn't miss it. But for some reason, she felt different than she had all the other times she had stolen from Los, and she did not like the feeling. She had gotten away with it the other two times and wanted that to be the case this time.

Sassy's thoughts were invaded by Los's movement as he climbed off the bed. He ignored Sassy's attempt to hold him hostage in the bed.

Los went into the bathroom, suppressing his first desire, and made his way to the shower to wash off the previous night's sex. But then, while the shower was running, he stepped into the other room, the one where his safe was. It took only a glance for him to know what the deal was. He went back into the bathroom and jumped in the shower. He needed to clear his head so he could better deal with the situation at hand. He had thought Sassy wasn't like the hoes he usually dealt with.

After his shower, he returned to the bedroom to find his bed made and the pillows fluffed. He paid this no mind, though. He had other things on his mind. He quickly dressed in a tank and basketball shorts and exited the room with his phone in tow. His fingers wasted no time sending out a text.

We have a problem. I'ma start the solving process, but I'm going to need you to finish it.

Within a minute there was a reply, which read, No doubt!

Los was met with the aroma of bacon frying as soon as he entered the kitchen. He closed his phone and walked toward Sassy, who was frying turkey bacon, scrambling cheese eggs, and making wheat toast to serve on the side. He was still feeling some type of way, but for the moment his hunger distracted him, enabling him to ignore his emotions. He greeted her with a peck on the forehead. He sat down at the dining-room table and waited to be served. Sassy presented him with the cooked breakfast, orange juice, and a blunt she had rolled for him. He ate in silence while sending texts and reading e-mails from his phone. Sassy wondered what was wrong. Normally, he was more affectionate and attentive, but he didn't seem quite like himself, and her paranoia immediately set in.

"I'm gonna go after I'm done eating," she informed Los.

She was considering leaving without being paid, but she didn't want to make any move that would draw suspicion. She sat there and played with her eggs as she said something else to Los. She didn't even hear Buster enter the penthouse. One minute he was not there; the next minute there he was. When she caught sight of him, she instantly tried to cover herself with her hands. She was still in her bra and panties. She proceeded to get up in order to go hide in Los's bedroom.

"Didn't know you were expecting company." She stared at Los. "I'll just get my things and catch a cab or something," she offered.

"No need to run off. Buster has seen what you got before."

Sassy did not like the look plastered on Los's face as he spoke. Her gut feeling was throwing all types of daggers at her stomach.

This nigga knows. A sense of fear swept through her body. For a brief second, she was tempted to come clean and confess, but then she thought better of it. She believed it would only make matters worse. Besides, she was not really sure if she was just overreacting or if Los really knew anything.

"Yeah, I know, but I still feel funny, you know?" She conjured up a smile as best she could.

"No worries, boo!" Los now had a smug look on his face.

Sassy felt even more uneasy now. Before she knew it and had time even to shield herself, Los smacked the shit out of her. The blows dropped her to the floor. Sassy was in shock and began to cry.

"Yeah, bitch!" Los said in a booming voice. "What the fuck you thought? Shit was sweet?" he yelled as he hauled off and kicked Sassy in the midsection. "You fucking thieving whore!" he bellowed

Sassy just sat on the floor, doubled over from the kick and holding her cheek with one hand and her stomach with the other, attempting to alleviate the sting coming from her face.

"I am sorry!" she cried. "I'll give it back!"

"Save all that pleadin' and beggin' shit, bitch!" Los barked as he walked over to her and stood over her. He kicked her again in the stomach, then grabbed a handful of her hair and slammed her head on the floor. Sassy kicked, scratched, and clawed but was unsuccessful at stopping Los's attack on her. She let out wails and cries of pain, but Los kept up his assault.

No one could hear her because of the soundproof walls and door. He became more enraged with each blow. Then, out of nowhere, he did the unexpected. He turned her on her stomach and pulled her panties down. He dropped to his knees and rammed his dick deep inside her ass. Had the crib not been soundproof, Sassy's cries would've been heard throughout the city. She let out such a loud cry of pain that it could have shattered the windows. He pumped her ass four good times before dragging her over to the side of the couch in the living room. Sassy lay there, paralyzed by pain and fear.

What would Jewels do in this situation? she wondered as her bottom lip quivered and her body trembled. *If I can just make it to my phone,* she thought. But that was wishful thinking. The spit that landed just below her right eye brought her back to the imminent danger she was presently faced with.

"Bitch, all you had to do was ask, and I probably would've broken your dumb ass off. But you wanna be on some sneaky thief shit." He grabbed a fistful of her hair. "You dumb-ass bitch! I thought you was stealing from me the last time. This time I knew exactly what to do. I bet if I look in your bag right fucking now, that bill I marked will be there. Stupid fucking bitch!" Los kicked her again, only this time in the face. "To think I was ready to make you . . ." Los raised his fist to land a much-deserved blow to her face.

"Yo, come on. That's enough," Buster said, intervening, holding Los's arm.

Los spun in his direction. He could see Buster's stone face and demeanor. Although Los was the boss now that his brother was dead, Los still knew better than to go up against Buster. His reputation exceeded him. He had put more work in the streets than a slave in a cotton field. Buster had been his brother's gunman, and now he was his. The last thing he wanted to do was put himself on the other side of Buster's barrel. He had the utmost respect for Buster, and his response demonstrated as much.

"My bad about this situation with that fucking thieving bitch," Los replied. Not only did he respect Buster, but Buster was Los's old head. The one from his neighborhood who had made it easy and safe for cats like him and his brother to eat and live in the streets. "Shit just got out of hand. Next time I won't let it get this far," he promised.

"Don't worry about it. Let's just clean this mess up," Buster replied. "And how about you just make sure there isn't a next time?" he added in a cold tone.

Los couldn't argue with him on that. Because of his temper, a girl was dead, and had it not been for Buster taking care of it, Los could be sitting in jail. "You right," he told Buster. "But the good thing is, ain't nobody gonna miss this bitch," Los asserted.

Buster shook his head. "It ain't about that," Buster reminded him. "We got other shit to handle. We don't got time for this type of shit, li'l bro."

Los nodded in agreement. "I feel you, bro. After this I'ma tighten up," Los assured him. "This bitch is all yours," he then said. He wiped his mouth to remove the residue of spit that dripped from it after he had hog spit in Sassy's face. "Do what you do best. I'ma go handle what I'm supposed to be handling." Los stepped over Sassy's limp body.

A sinister smirk appeared on Buster's face. He sat the large suitcase he was holding on top of the dining-room table and opened it. Sassy had noticed him standing there with the suitcase in hand. She hadn't given it any thought until he pulled out the contents inside it. Her eyes widened with fear when Buster spun around to face her.

Oh, God, please hear me right now. I don't want to die like this. Please don't let this happen to me. Please . . . take care of Jewels. . . . Sassy closed her eyes and knew that this was just part of the game she played and that there was no getting out of it.

Chapter Sixteen

The following morning, Jewels woke to the smell of breakfast cooking. The aroma of eggs, sausages, and pancake syrup hit her nose as soon as she entered her kitchen. She couldn't believe her eyes. Rome stood over her stove, in a wife beater and navy and white Adidas sweatpants, scrambling some cheese eggs, while the sausage grease popped and the pancakes were waiting to be flipped. She could see the dented muscles all over his back. She inhaled, then exhaled lightly. She tightened up at the right time. Detecting her sudden presence, Rome spun to face her.

"Hey, you hungry?" Rome greeted.

Jewels nodded. It had been a long time since she'd had a home-cooked meal. The closest she got to homemade food was at a Waffle House, when she found the time to visit one. Fast food during the day and fancy restaurants at night was how she'd gotten used to living. The one thing she was missing in her life was a man. Not to take care of her, but just for his presence. She realized she was more like her mama than she had thought. It had taken her a long time to figure out what Ice had meant to her mother. She saw the same qualities in Rome.

Growing up, all she had ever known about Ice was that he had everything a man could ever wish for—a beautiful place to call home, a growing empire, fancy cars, and money coming out his ass. And he'd had his share of females through the years. But no matter how many women he had, Jewels remembered that her mother was always his number one, and he took care of his number one.

"Here. Have a seat." He pulled out a chair at the table for her.

Jewels felt like a high school girl. She was both surprised by and impressed with his gesture. The days he had spent under her roof were enough to convince her that she had him pegged all wrong, and this was just one more thing to prove that. She had seen him only as a hard-core street dude, the type that Sassy went for, but the fact of the matter was that he was no different than her. Someone who had made the best out of the hand they were dealt. She believed they both were hustlers of two different products, but nonetheless, they both sold something in exchanged for financial gain in order to survive. She had learned a lot about Rome, as well as about herself, while he stayed with her. She had actually enjoyed him being there, in more ways than one. She smiled at the thought.

"Well, I guess I'm going to have to repay you for this big breakfast, then, because I haven't been treated like this in a while," she said.

"You don't have to do that. You don't owe me anything. I should be thanking you," Rome replied. "It's the least I could do. I did it out of the kindness of my heart." He smiled.

Jewels returned his smile. For the first time, she smelled the oil he wore. It was a refreshing scent, one like none she had ever smelled. She knew it was an oil because she had smelled the same fragrance when he'd burned the oil in her oil burner in the bedroom he occupied. It was also a scent she had thought about while lying in her bed at night, pleasuring herself.

Bitch, get it together, Jewels told herself. *Money over niggas. Remember that.*

"Well, thank you," she replied, shaking off the spell she had almost succumb to from his smell.

"No need to thank me," Rome offered. He set a plate in front of Jewels, along with a cup of the coffee he had brewed from the grounds he'd found in the cabinet. He then snatched up his plate and made his way back over to the table and pulled out a chair. After he sat, Jewels watched as he bowed his head and closed his eyes to say grace.

You can't be serious, Jewels thought in disbelief. She never would have thought that Rome was someone who said grace over his food. She had taken him for a "sit down and dig straight in" type of dude. She appreciated seeing this. Melody had stressed to her the importance of thanking God for the food He provided, no matter what was going on in her life, where she was, or how little it was.

When Rome opened his eyes, he saw Jewels staring at him.

"Wassup?"

"What?" Jewels shook her head.

"You were looking at me."

She hadn't even realized it. "I'm sorry," she said, apologizing.

Rome laughed. "You good." He took a monstrous bite of the sausage, egg, and cheese sandwich he had put together on a soft buttered and toasted roll.

For the next few minutes, they ate in silence. Rome was the first to finish. He saw that Jewels didn't have much left on her plate. He stood to clear his plate and carried it over to the sink.

"I'm done," Jewels announced, and he returned and took her plate over to the sink.

She watched as he loaded her dishwasher with the dirty dishes. *He has to be the only dude in the streets who moves like this.* Jewels was convinced of this.

"I know you said I didn't have to, but thanks again. That was really nice of you." She walked over to Rome and extended her hand. He dried his right hand on the bottom of his wife beater and took her hand.

"Oh!" he exclaimed, remembering the last token of his appreciation that he had for her. He stuck his hand in his sweatpants pocket. "This is for you. For the extra days." He handed her a stack of one-hundred-dollar bills wrapped in a twenty-five-hundred-dollar wrapper.

Jewels smiled with her eyes. "You don't have to give me anything extra." She held out her hand and pushed the stack back in Rome's direction.

"Nah. You straight," he insisted. "I'd be insulted if you didn't." He pushed it back toward her.

You don't have to tell me twice. Jewels laughed inside. "Thanks."

"No prob." He smiled. "Well, I gotta get outta here, but take my number down," he then said.

"Okay." Jewels didn't hesitate to pull out her phone, but in the back of her mind, she wondered if she would ever even dial it or need it for anything.

Rome took her phone, punched his number in, and dialed his own phone.

"Got you," he told her. He handed Jewels back her phone. Then out of nowhere, he threw his arms around her and said, "Be safe, baby girl." Then he released her.

"You too," she cooed. She was still trying to process how good his arms had felt around her.

"You a'ight?" He chuckled. He stared at her oddly.

She joined him in his laughter. "Yes, I'm fine."

He gave her a thumbs-up. "I'ma grab my bag, and then I'ma be out."

Jewels nodded.

Within minutes, Rome was headed to the front door, with his duffel bag hiked over his shoulder. Jewels walked him to the door.

"Feel free to use that number whenever. I'm single and nobody answers that line but me." He wanted her to know that.

"I'll keep that in mind." She smiled.

There was an awkward silence, but Rome broke it.

"Thanks again, lady. You definitely good peoples," Rome told her.

"Appreciate that," she shot back.

He walked out, and then she closed the door behind him, the man who had been her temporary roommate and had saved her life.

Rome sat in his SUV for a moment, staring back at the place he had grown fond of in the week and a half he had stayed there. In that short period of time, he had gotten to see another side of the female he had perceived as stuck-up and self-centered. He wasn't too knowledge-able about the game she played in, but he knew when somebody had hustle in them. Aside from having a pretty face and a banging body, she had struck him as a money-getter chick after he had observed her in her own surroundings. *Tighten up, nigga*, Rome chastised himself. He snapped out of the daze he was in. He smiled at the fact that it was not the first time Jewels had been the cause of him drifting off. *If only things were different, things could be different*, he thought. *Wishful thinking about what could be,* he observed silently as he started the ignition on his SUV.

Chapter Seventeen

A few days later . . .

The sound of her buzzer startled Jewels. Since Rome had left, she had been a little jumpy. She had gotten used to having a male presence around her place. She had been tempted to make up a bogus reason or an excuse to convince him to stay a few more days, but in the end she had sided against it. When they'd parted ways with a hug, Jewels remembered feeling weird, but not in a bad way. It had almost felt as if he didn't want to leave or let her go. She had sat and thought about it the whole day, until Kareem had called her and invited her out to be his escort at an event he was attending in the city. Jewels hadn't realized she had dozed off while watching *The Man in 3B,* a movie she had been dying to see all week. The buzzer rang for a second time.

"I bet you it's this bitch, Sassy," Jewels cursed under her breath.

It had been a week since she had last heard from or seen Sassy. She had been trying to reach her ever since they had parted ways at that downtown restaurant.

"Stop playing on my damn buzzer," she blared through the intercom.

A male voice came across the intercom. "Excuse me?"

"Oh, I'm sorry. Who is this?" she said apologetically.

"Postal service."

"Who are you looking for?" she questioned. She hadn't ordered anything, and she was not expecting anything.

"Uh, a Ms. Jew—" he began, but before he could finish, she hit the buzzer.

Jewels cautiously looked out the window as the mail carrier drove through the gate. When she opened the door, he handed her a certified letter that required her signature. She couldn't believe her eyes when she read the return address. The name Melody Walker meant everything to her. She hadn't seen it or spoken it in quite some time, she realized.

Damn, she is good. I've never heard of someone sending a certified letter from where she is at. She must have the guards hooked, but she always did have that effect on men, thought Jewels as she opened the letter from her mother.

My precious Jewels,

I don't have to ask how you're doing, just like you don't have to ask me, because bitches like us only do one way, up! It has been so many years since I last saw you. It would be really good to see a familiar face. I would love for you to come and visit me for Mother's Day next weekend. I sent this letter certified to ensure that you would receive it in time. I know you're probably wondering how I managed to pull this off. Let's just say, you get it from yo' mama! (smile).

Anyway, if you're reading this, then I see you finally took my advice and moved into the condo Ice left you. Use that as an opportunity to stack your paper and get the fuck out of St. Louis. I've met some good people that have some great opportunities out in New Jersey, New York, South Carolina, and Miami. If you ever wanna relocate to any of those places, just let me know and I'll put you in touch with the right people. Not gonna make this a long and drawn-out missive. Just know I will always love you, because you are my only child. That is a dangerous life to live. You are all that I have. Do not give anyone a reason to take you from me. I expect to see you next weekend.

Love,

Mom

Jewels smiled as she read the letter over and over again. She hadn't realized it had been that long since she'd last seen her mother. She had been so busy on a paper chase that two years seemed like a week. There was nothing to think about. Next week Jewels would be going to see her mother.

Jewels's gut kicked in and told her something was wrong. *Why, after all this time, would my mom want me to visit? She knows that place is not my style. There is only one way to find out what is up.*

Chapter Eighteen

Men with assorted weapons lined the walls. Rome looked around. He made eye contact with each man posted up, then drew his attention back to the person he was there to see. *Who the fuck this nigga think he is? The African Pablo Escobar or something?* thought Rome as he did so.

"Yo, Africa," Rome called out to his connect. That was what he'd been told to call the man responsible for putting him in a better position in the drug game. He really didn't care what he'd been told to call him. The only thing Rome cared about was getting better prices so he, Red, and their crew could turn it up in the streets. The competition was saturated for many different reasons. In Rome's case, the prices he was paying prevented him from taking their operation to the next level. "Man, you killin' me with these numbers," he admitted.

"What do you mean?" Rome's connect replied, his voice booming. "I give you the best coke money can buy," he bragged. "What is the problem? You are a drug dealer, aren't you?" Africa continued in a condescending tone. It was apparent he had taken offense at what Rome had said.

Rome's face twisted up. *Who the fuck this nigga think he talkin' to?* he asked himself. His chest swelled. Although he was in a room full of armed African soldiers, he refused to back down.

Rome tried to reason with his connect. "Man, it ain't the quality of the product. No doubt, your shit. You got that A-one, but you killin' me on the prices. I can't compete with the dudes that got A-one too, who got them birds for cheaper than what I'm movin' mine for. I know you can understand that."

"Nobody has better product than me," Africa replied arrogantly.

Rome took a shot in the dark and pressed his luck. "Yo, how do I know you not the one supplying my competition with the same product and better prices?" He looked Africa square in the eyes. He searched for any hesitation or doubt in his eyes. He knew he was risking it all with his accusation.

Red had always told him, his mouth would be the death of him, and he knew his tongue had just thrown him in a potential frying pan. He expected the best and prepared for the worst. He was willing to handle what came behind him speaking his peace. He expected bullets to be flying over the disrespect he had just spat at his connect. Rome had just accused him of not playing fair. According to the rules he followed and the laws he lived by, those words were punishable by death if not proven correct. Instead of being met with lead, he was met with questionable words.

"How dare you accuse me of something like that!" his connect started off with. "For weeks now, I've been taking care of you. Who sells and what somebody sells it for are not my concern. My only concern is what I sell it for. You have a choice. Either pay the price or not. You can take it or leave it. Now, what you going to do?" Rome's connect matched his stare.

Rome laughed on the inside. He knew his connect had no idea just how loose a cannon he was. *Yeah, okay,*

Kunta, he thought. Rome knew now was not the time or the place. But he'd never forget this day. He took his time before he spoke. He did a quick scan of the room. He might have made some stupid moves in the past, but he was no fool. *Live to fight another day*, he reasoned with himself.

"No doubt, Africa. We good," Rome said as he offered a gentlemanly handshake.

Rome was far from stupid, and fucking up his only connect over some over rated price he didn't like would undoubtedly be a reckless move. Although the price was not to his liking, he was sticking with it for now, but as soon as he found another, Africa would no longer be needed.

Chapter Nineteen

Jewels was just a kid when her mother was convicted for killing a trick. Her mother was sentenced to life without any possibility for parole. She was charged with first-degree murder. Jewels remembered being taken to the huge courthouse building by Sassy's mother. It was the last time she would see her mother as an innocent child. During the trial she didn't even recognize her mother, because she looked so different dressed in loose-fitting clothes. She looked like a schoolteacher, thought Jewels. Her mother's words to her that day after the judge sentenced her had stuck with Jewels. *You take care of yourself out there. Don't be no weak bitch!*

Her father was dead, and her mother was going to prison, so Jewels was pretty much on her own. She took her mother's words to heart and did just that: took care of herself and never showed any signs of weakness.

Ever since Jewels had gotten that letter from her, Melody had been weighing heavily on her mind. She couldn't stop thinking about how things had been before she went away. How they had fed the whole community during the holidays, how she had helped her mom plan the dinners and the parties for the top pimps and hoes to show how her dad was ballin'. While she herself had been living the life, Jewels had never met or come across anyone more thorough than her mother. It seemed that ever since she had read that letter, something about her mother and her childhood had surfaced in her mind every day.

Before she knew it, it was Sunday. Visiting hours at the prison were from eight until three. It was already nine in the morning, and she had a three-hour drive. She didn't want to look too fly, so she decided to dress down and put on an Adidas jogging suit and some Adidas sneakers. She put on a baseball cap and let her hair hang out. She grabbed her bag and hopped in the awaiting car from the service she'd hired. The car jumped onto the highway and made it to the prison in two and a half hours.

The sign read ST. LOUIS CORRECTIONAL FACILITY FOR WOMEN THREE MILES AHEAD. Jewels's driver navigated the Lincoln down I-70 until he reached the exit ramp that led to the prison for women. At the front gate to the prison, the driver brought the car to a stop, jumped out, and made his way to one of the back doors of the vehicle. He gave Jewels a helping hand as she stepped out of the car. All eyes were on her as she was let off in front of the front gate of the institution.

"You can just find a park spot, and I will text you when I'm done," she told the driver, and then she walked toward the entrance. She now realized why so much time had gone by since the last time she had visited this human warehouse. A butch-looking officer degradingly searched and groped her before she was allowed admittance. She was glad she had left her bag in the car, because they were ripping those bags up as they searched through them. *I pay too much for my shit*, she thought. They told her that she would go back with the next group and that she should have a seat.

For some reason, Jewels was a little nervous to see her mother. Out of nowhere her hands started shaking. *Bitch, it's your mother, the woman who raised you, not the first lady,* she joked to herself. Jewels shook it off. She waited for about an hour before they finally let her see her mother. She was the last glass partition on the end.

Jewels walked slowly toward her. It felt like the hall just kept getting longer and longer to her.

There she was, looking better than she had looked in years. She had put on a few pounds, but she wore it well. Her hair was cut short, unlike the last time Jewels had seen her. It had once been down to her ass. She looked like a goddess to Jewels. She could actually see herself in her mother. She definitely had gotten both her body and her beautiful features from Melody.

"Look at you," was what Jewels's ears were met with when she picked up the phone hanging to her right. "You look like me when I was your age," Melody added.

Jewels smiled. "No. Better!" she shot back jokingly.

"All right now." Melody chuckled.

For a moment, it felt like old times. Despite the circumstances, they shared a mother-daughter moment.

"You don't look so bad yourself," Jewels offered. "Considering that beige is not your color," she said, adding a little humor.

Melody smiled. "I'll take that as a compliment."

"It was." Jewels chuckled. "Your locks got longer since the last I seen you," she observed.

"Yeah. I gotta wash and grease them, though," Melody replied. She grabbed a handful of her dreadlocks and smelled them.

Jewels smiled. She did the same thing with her natural hair whenever she felt it wasn't up to par, even if it was tight. "Is everything okay?" she asked, wasting no time. Ever since she had gotten her mother's letter, she hadn't been able to sleep. It was not like Melody just to write and send a random letter. Even though she seemed to be in good spirits both in the letter and in person, Jewels knew there was something her mother was not telling her.

Melody took a deep breath. She could tell her daughter was searching for answers in her eyes. She stared at her daughter proudly. She didn't need glasses to see that Jewels was at the top of her game. The fact that she always dressed down each time she came to visit Melody told her what type of woman her daughter was. It showed her that Jewels was a confident woman and that clothes did not make her. She made them.

"I'm dying," Melody blurted out.

At first, Jewels thought her ears were playing tricks on her. A look of shock and disbelief instantly appeared on her face. Before she could even respond or comment, Melody spoke again. "They say I have HIV. Shit. I'm not even surprised. But that's the bed I made a lot of years ago, and now I have to lie in it," she explained. "On another note, I sent you another letter. It has some important contacts in it. Use them if you ever need to. A lot of good peoples in there," she said, abruptly changing the subject.

Jewels was still speechless. A lump formed in her throat. She was trying to conjure up some comforting or consoling words for her mother but found it difficult. She didn't want to display any type of weakness in front of her. Her mother hadn't made her feel this way since she was a little girl. She couldn't believe she had just dropped that bomb on her and then had moved on, like she hadn't even mentioned it. Jewels wanted to cry but knew she couldn't. Instead, she fought and suppressed her tears. So many questions floated through her mind. She cleared the lump from her throat.

Her mother stared at her, waiting for her to say something.

Jewels finally spoke. "How long do you have?"

"Shit, I don't know." Melody shrugged. "Tomorrow, next week, a month, ten years. That's not the point," she said. "I told you because I felt you needed to know. I didn't want you to get a phone call saying I was dead from HIV. I would rather you hear it from me beforehand."

Jewels was silent as her mother spoke. She didn't know what to say. She actually wanted to scream and cry. She knew she couldn't. The last thing she wanted to do was disrespect her mother by showing what her mother viewed as weakness. The two locked eyes.

"So, you're not going to say anything?" Melody asked.

Jewels took a deep breath and sighed. "What's there to say?" She grimaced.

Melody ran her hand down her face, then across her short dreadlocks.

Jewels watched as her mother fidgeted on the metal stool. Her mother started looking everywhere but at her, from the ceiling to the floor. She even picked at her nails and peeked at other inmates' visitors. Then the strangest thing happened.

"Ma?"

"Just go!" Melody waved Jewels off.

"What?" a confused Jewels questioned.

"You heard me!" One tear could be seen escaping from Melody's eye. "Get the fuck out of here!" Melody stood and banged her fist as hard as she could on the Plexiglas. The boom echoed on the other side of the glass. Jewels was surprised at how loudly and with what force she had banged on it. She was sure the COs would drag her away for being out of order. Before Jewels could say a word or the COs made a move, her mother stormed off, leaving the telephone receiver dangling.

Jewels stood there and watched as her mother disappeared through the steel-gray doors. It wasn't until an officer tapped her on the shoulder that reality set in. Jewels exited the visiting room and then the facility. She slipped on her Dior shades and pulled out her phone to text the driver. Once she spotted the car, she scurried over to it. The driver saw her approaching and hopped out to get the door for her. Jewels flung herself in the backseat, and moments later she was heading back home. She couldn't help but replay the tape in an effort to figure out what had just happened with her mother.

Surprised would be an understatement for what Jewels felt. Her mother's outburst was not the cause for the way she was feeling, though. She had seen her mother become explosive on more than one occasion before she went off to prison, so the fact that she had a temper wasn't a shock. What Jewels hadn't expected at all was that tear. In all the years she'd had with her mother, Jewels had never seen her mother shed one tear, until today.

Melody had never broken down in front of her, or in front of anyone else, for that matter, as far as Jewels knew. As a kid, she used to think that God had removed the ability to cry from her mother. Had she not felt it growing up from her mother, she never would have thought that her mother loved her, because Melody was not an affectionate woman or the type who released her emotions by shedding tears.

The thought that today might be the last day she ever saw her mother again saddened Jewels. And for the first time in a long time, she wept. *Why would she do this to me?* she wondered.

Deep down Jewels knew why, but she just didn't want it to be true. Knowing what her mother was, and recognizing that weakness was something her mother never showed, made it possible for Jewels to accept the fact that they would never see each other again. And it gave her some comfort.

As the car drove and the tears flowed, Jewels pulled out her phone. She wiped her tears and cleared her throat. If there was anyone who could reverse her feelings, it was Sassy. She wouldn't relate the incident to Sassy, but she could find comfort in talking to her until they saw each other later. Jewels dialed Sassy and then put the phone to her ear, waiting for a snappy greeting, but there was no answer. She opted not to leave a message and to try again later.

Damn. Since when she don't pick up her phone?

Chapter Twenty

"I was a little skeptical at first, but I'm glad you finally came to your senses about making moves on them pussy-ass niggas," Red admitted.

"I don't know what I was thinking by leaving that shit alone." Rome shifted in his seat. "Whenever and wherever we see them niggas, it's going down," he added.

"True," Red agreed. "Now all we gotta do is track down these fools."

"We will," Rome asserted.

"Yeah. I got niggas on the lookout." He paused. "Niggas know Los, and the other cat was never too far behind, since Mike-G was no longer in the picture," Red told Rome.

"Who? That joker named Buster?" Rome asked.

"Yeah. According to ole girl, he always around." Red remembered what the young chick he was sexing had told him about Los and his brother's man, Buster.

They were from two sides of the town, so they were not familiar with him. His chick knew more about Los than Buster, but she had stressed how close the three were when Mike-G was still alive, and how Buster and Los had gotten closer since his death.

"I don't give a fuck where them fuck boys at. As long as they not in our way," Rome stated.

Red shook his head. "Man, they could pose a potential threat."

"Bro, any nigga threatening this shit here gonna get put in the fuckin' dirt," Rome stressed. "Now, stop worrying about them jokers, and worry about counting this paper," he added. "Here."

Red caught the stack of bills Rome threw to him.

"Count that. I'ma count this one," Rome told his right-hand man. "Don't forget to separate all that shit, either. You know how Africa be complainin' like a bitch." Rome grimaced.

Red chuckled.

"I'm dead-ass serious, my nigga. He like a little bitch. If we ain't need him, I'd dead his dumb ass with the quickness." Rome meant every word.

"I know, homie, but we need 'im," Red reminded him.

"No doubt. I hate getting stuck with all those singles and fives my damn self. That shit be too bulky. We'll just dump that shit in one if these strip clubs or something."

Red nodded. He was always up for a turn-up night.

"Where that paper at I told you to go get from them dudes across town?"

"I got it. It's in the back, already stacked and counted up."

"How much was it?"

"All together, it was about thirty Gs."

"All right. Let me get that."

Red went and retrieved the book bag with the money.

"Ever since we knocked off Mike-G's li'l bro, shit been picking up," Rome said.

"I was thinking the same thing," Red revealed.

"We still got to be careful, though. You know it's a lot of hatin'-ass niggas that been hearing how we came up. You been seeing that shit on the news, how they been finding dudes bodies." It was more of a statement than a question. "And you been hearing about dudes from up top getting set up and robbed. Trust me, it ain't just these dudes we gotta watch out for. It's these chicks too. Bet money that out of all that shit that's been happening in the surrounding area, some, if not all, them shits involves a chick. That's why we got to be on point at all times, 'cause like dudes, bitches can get cold hearts too. Plus, you best believe that the word is out that we getting paper. Especially after we break out with them new whips, they gonna be on our dicks, beggin'," Rome pointed out.

"You ain't never lied, bro."

They both laughed.

"Fuck 'em!" Rome exclaimed. "Let's count this paper and keep stackin'." Rome thumbed through the stack of one-hundred-dollar bills from the pile of money in front of him.

Chapter Twenty-one

The next morning . . .

"Yes, this is she. Who is this?" Jewels said to the unknown caller.

The caller spoke.

"Yes, I do. What is this all about?"

The mention of Sassy's real name and the line of questioning alarmed Jewels. A bad feeling swept through her body.

Please, God, no! she prayed to herself, not wanting to believe what she believed the caller was going to tell her.

Her prayer was two weeks too late. The St. Louis local morgue had confirmed her biggest fear. Sassy's body had been found in a Dumpster, mutilated. She had been brutally murdered, according to the man on the other end of the phone. Jewels felt a little light-headed. Her head started to spin. She suppressed her anger and her other emotions while on the phone, but inside she was hurting and was angry over the loss of her best friend, her sister from another mother.

No! Why? she questioned silently. Her ears tried to reject what the coroner was saying to her. She could not believe her friend was dead.

Jewels was asked to come and identify the body. She agreed. Before she hung up the phone, she asked how long Sassy had been dead. The coroner's answer caused all sorts of thoughts to run through her mind. Her estimated time of death was the last time Jewels had seen her, and Jewels knew with whom. The image of his face appeared in her mind as clear as a bright, sunny day. She didn't know him, but she knew of him and what he was about. Jewels remembered Sassy mentioning him more than any of her other clients from the streets, which was why Jewels was immediately able to put a name to the face.

Sassy used to always brag about how she had a young stallion in the bed who broke her off proper all the time. She had also expressed how he would get rough with her and possessive. *I told her about that type of nigga*, Jewels thought as she reviewed in her mind the countless conversations between them about the risks and dangers of such clients. But Sassy had never listened to her, and now she was dead, possibly at the hands of the type of nigga Jewels had warned her about. Jewels shook her head.

Sassy was her only friend. The two of them had been through thick and thin. The paths that they both chose at a young age had formed a bond between the two of them, and they had been down for each other ever since. They had watched out for each other and had trusted only each other. Now she had no one. Jewels thought back to how Sassy had first got turned out.

She remembered Sassy telling her the story about how a major street player by the name of Big John had turned and strung her out. He was the biggest, most notorious pimp in all of St. Louis. He was also a known killer. Word was that he would kill your grandmother if you owed him money, no matter if you were male or female, family or friend. He ran the streets on both sides of the river. He was big, black, ugly, and powerful, with some long money.

It was rumored that he had married Sassy because she witnessed over twenty something murders he had committed, and he'd thought that if he married her, she could never testify against him. He owned a lounge bar, out of which he ran a back-door prostitution ring, a spot over in East St. Louis. He was pimping most of the young girls out of the club. Hell, he had eventually ended up pimping Sassy's ass, too, and had turned her into his number one ho, because she was pretty and well shaped, so she made the most money. She was his snitcher ho: she kept a look out on all his other hoes, because some of them would try to cuff his money. Big John would beat her ass for anything, but she was still his top moneymaker, and he never treated her differently, even though she was wifey legally. He had Sassy's ass sprung out on crack just so she would be able to service a trick, and eventually, she was hooked on the shit. She literally traveled down the same path as her mother had with drugs. And just like Jewels's mother had cleaned Sassy's mother up, Jewels did the same for Sassy.

Jewels reminisced about all the nights she and Sassy had hit the streets. Sassy had been cool to her, and she had loved her like a sister. She smiled as she reflected on how Sassy had always looked good and had always been well dressed, wearing fly shit and carrying nice bags. Sassy reminded her so much of herself. She laughed as Sassy's voice played in her head. Sassy would always brag about how she had dudes to support her expensive spending habits. She would always say, "You have to use what you got to get what you want." She had loved money and had been obsessed with it, just like Jewels. They'd been two peas in a pod.

Jewels sniffled. Although tears didn't spill out of her eyes, she was crying on the inside for her girl. She didn't

know for sure, but her gut told her that the young stallion Sassy had been referring to, who went by the name
Los, was behind her murder. She didn't know how to
prove it or even where to find him, but at that moment,
Jewels made a pact with herself that she wouldn't stop
until she figured out one or the other, if not both. And
when she did, she vowed to make him pay somehow or
someway.

Rest easy, baby girl, Jewel thought, wishing her
deceased friend eternal peace. *And I promise I will find
out who did this to you and will make them regret it*, she
promised.

The sound of her "Boss Bitch" ring tone drew her
attention to her phone. She couldn't believe the name
and the number that came across her screen. Is this a
sign? she wondered.

Jewels answered the phone. "Hey." The surprise
phone call was welcomed. "Can we meet somewhere?"
she wasted no time asking.

This can't be a coincidence, she reasoned.

"Meet?"

The caller hesitated at first, but after some persuasion,
Jewels was given an address.

"I'm not familiar with the area, but if you tell me the
address again, I can meet you there." She snatched up
the pen and pad on the table.

"Better yet, I'll come to you. Yeah, I don't want you to
feel uncomfortable."

"Oh, okay. I'd appreciate that. I'll be here." She hung up
the phone after thanking the caller for offering to come
and get her. She made her way back into her bedroom,
then slipped something on and waited until her guest
arrived.

An hour passed, and Jewels became anxious. Suddenly,
her intercom buzzed. She was expecting only one person,

so she pressed the button to allow entry. Jewels went to the door and waited.

At first Rome had been hesitant about coming, but Jewels hadn't sounded like herself over the phone. He felt he owed her since she had let him lay low at her crib for over a week. As he approached her door, he saw her standing there, looking like an angel. She had on a robe, but it didn't matter, because he knew what was under it.

"Hey," Jewels said and greeted him with a hug.

She smells so good. Get it together! he ordered himself.

"Hey, you. Everything good? I wasn't expecting this," he said.

"Come in so we can talk." He walked by her, and Jewels closed the door behind him. For the first time, she allowed her emotions to take over.

Rome heard the door shut; then he heard a sound that surprised the shit out of him. Jewels was crying. He didn't know what to do. He just stood there and stared at her.

Jewels attempted to wipe her tears away, but new ones appeared just as quick.

Rome stepped to her. He was scared of what would happen, but he figured she needed it. He pulled her into his arms and held her as she wept, all the while brushing her hair back with his hand.

After a few minutes Jewels moved out of his arms and looked up at him. "He killed her."

Rome was confused. He didn't know who she was talking about. "Who? Killed who?"

"He killed her. My best friend. The only person who had my back, no matter what. He killed Sassy," Jewels explained.

Rome thought for a second, then remembered who she was speaking of. *The chick that was here when I stayed here*, he thought.

"I want to hire you. I want him killed." Jewels was serious. There were no more tears streaming down her face anymore.

"Whoa . . . That's not how it works, baby girl." Rome took a seat on the sofa in the living room.

"I know it sounds crazy, but you're the only person I know that can do it. I'll pay you whatever you want. Just tell me you'll do it."

Rome stared into her eyes. There was only coldness, and no regret, in her glare. "First, tell me how you know she was killed by the person you think."

Jewels took a seat next to Rome, and for the next hour, she spilled everything she knew about Sassy's killer and why she thought she'd been killed. She only hoped that her plea wouldn't fall on deaf ears.

Chapter Twenty-two

Later on that evening . . .

Rome sat around a square-shaped table with Red at their detail shop, also known as the chop block, a place where you could bring stolen cars and get money for them. Their establishment was growing by the day. There was always one hustler after another bringing in hot cars to swap parts for some fast cash. He still couldn't believe the coincidence when he found out why Jewels wanted to meet with him.

Rome had called the meeting with Red to discuss his latest quest, minus the event that was causing him to move faster than expected. After all, they were going to hit him anyway so getting a jump on things might have its benefits. Red didn't have to know the reason why he wanted to make the move now.

In the past, Red had been against some of Rome's methods when handling certain things, but the love was bulletproof, and eventually, he started backing Rome on anything that came their way. Rome was not sure that would be the case now, even though the two were as thick as thieves. After Rome's mother died, he and Red had grown closer. Rome had put him in charge of looking over the streets. He had taken Red in as his own and had embraced him like a brother. He and Red had butted heads numerous times, but that was as far as it had ever got. Nothing had ever escalated into anything more.

After hearing Red's opposition to moving now, Rome spoke his mind. "I'm me, and you know I do whatever I got my heart set on doing, Red. I'm gonna hit that nigga, and that's that. Ain't no nigga untouchable, Red. You just gotta know how to maneuver around their position."

Red took a seat in the chair beside Rome and dropped his blunt ashes in the ashtray. "No offense, but me and the homies tried to get at him and his mans and couldn't get a steady trace of these dudes. That's why we decided to let it be for now, remember?"

"Bruh, I got all of that. Fuck waiting for the right time. We gonna make it the right time," Rome said with force.

Red shook his head. "Man, them jokers ain't as soft or small time as you think. You try to make a move on cats like them, there's bound to be some repercussions," Red pointed out. "You better make sure you send them six feet under, or it's our asses. Just be prepared for whatever we got coming to us. It's all a part of the game. You live by the gun, best believe you gonna die by the gun." Red swore he saw fire in Rome's eyes. He was tired of trying to talk sense into his hardheaded friend about moving too fast.

"Man, fuck that! That's the plan. I'ma send that nigga to be with his muthafuckin' Maker and family."

"All right," Red sighed. "I tried to talk you out of it, but I see it's no use. Just remember, moving too fast can cause a bigger mess than we need right now. At least let me get some things in order before we do this. I gotta make sure that when the heat comes down, niggas are prepared. You feel me?" He lit another another blunt and took a long drag.

This nigga, he thought as he let out a mouthful of weed smoke.

Chapter Twenty-three

"Hello, my love." Kareem met her at the door.

He extended his arms, and Jewels stepped into them. He gave her a bear hug, then released her, grabbed her by the hand, and closed the door behind them.

"I have something for you." He looked back at her.

Jewels looked up at him and smiled. *It better be that stack of cash that got me to agree to this shit,* she thought.

Kareem led her to the master bathroom, where he had a hot bubble bath waiting for her in his built-in Jacuzzi. "For you." He smiled.

Though she preferred money, a nice hot bubble bath was just what her body needed, thought Jewels. Normally, she didn't like him pampering her like they were a couple, but tonight she felt different. She wanted to play the role. She bit down on her bottom lip, just the way she knew he liked, and grabbed hold of her spaghetti straps. She released them. Her dress slithered down her curves and onto the floor. There was nothing left to take off, so she stepped into the awaiting bubble bath.

The hot water massaged her body as she positioned her back up against the hot tub. She watched as Kareem removed his wife beater and loosened the drawstring to his linen pajamas. His semierect was larger than her average client's full erection, thought Jewels as her eyes traveled down and zeroed in between his legs once he was undressed. She stared at him seductively as he climbed into the hot tub. He wasted no time exploring her body.

He massaged Jewels's clit with his pointer and middle fingers. She threw her head back and closed her eyes. Between the water and his fingers, Jewels was in heaven. Her mind began to drift to when she first met Kareem.

It was Labor Day weekend. Sassy picked Jewels up about four in the afternoon on a chilly Sunday. They were bored out of our minds, so they decided to go to the St. Louis Rams' first home game of the season. They were playing the Dallas Cowboys, and it just so happened that there was a professional fight going on at the Ambassador that same night. They knew that there would be men with money from all over the Lou and the surrounding areas this weekend and that there would be parties everywhere. They wanted to be where the action was. It was a good thing that they went after different types of men, so it didn't seem like they were in competition with each other.

It was chilly outside, but Jewels made sure she was looking good. They moved like they were the queens of the Lou. Male bodies were everywhere. Surprisingly, there were more men of color than Jewels had expected. That was not her cup of tea, but she couldn't deny that the place smelled like money. She scanned the room without looking obvious. She surveyed the room's occupants, ranking them from low to high in her mind. Then there he stood. He looked all right in terms of his face, but most importantly, he was sitting in some three-thousand-dollar seats, so she knew he was work-ing with something.

He couldn't take his eyes off of her. Finally, he got up enough nerve to step to her. He reached his hand out for her to shake it and said in his deep homeland accent, "My name is Kareem Musa. And yours?"

Jewels told him her name. She checked him out as they chitchatted for a minute. He was well dressed.

She noticed how his suit fit like a glove, and he sported a Windsor knot tie. The Salvatore Ferragamo shoes he rocked told her all she really needed and wanted to know about him. His hair and goatee were freshly trimmed. He looked like he had been beat up a lot: he had no scars, but his skin was rough. His face was strong and masculine.

They exchanged numbers, and Jewels promised to give him a call soon. She didn't want to lock herself in until she had explored all her options, though. Ultimately, despite all that money in the building, they made no money that night. Jewels put the evening behind her and moved on.

Three days later, Kareem started blowing her phone up. It was a Wednesday evening, and she was tired as hell from working all day. For some reason, she had been the pick of the day and had gone out on four gigs, at four hours a session. Just as she laid her head down on the pillow, her cell phone started vibrating. She contemplated not answering it but picked up, anyway.

A male voice was on the other end. "This is Kareem Musa," he announced. Jewels chuckled over the fact that he had said his whole name again. "I have been trying to get at you before I leave St. Louis to go back home. Do you have any plans tonight?" he asked.

"Kareem?" she asked, pretending not to know. She knew it was him because she had locked his number in and couldn't forget how he presented his first and last name at all times.

"Oh, my apology." His accent was just like Eddie Murphy's in Coming to America. "Kareem Musa. We met a few days ago at the Rams' football game."

"Oh, hey," she answered, with no interest in her voice.

He chuckled. "So, what's up, baby? Can we get together tonight, before I leave town?"

"Well, I'm kind of tired tonight. Let's get together tomorrow night." She was toying with him.

"I told you I am leaving town." His voice had a little more bass to it now.

She could tell he wasn't trying to hear that shit. She felt it was cute. He kept trying and trying to convince her to go out with him. When he mentioned where they would go, she was sold. Brio, an Italian restaurant, in Frontenac for dinner. She loved that place. They agreed on a time to meet.

Jewels was dressed to kill. She accessorized with a silver dome-shaped ring, her iced-out Rolex watch, rocks in her ears, and a thin platinum necklace with a dangling diamond that matched her earrings. Her hair was up in a ponytail, with some Chinese-cut bangs. She checked herself out in the mirror, grabbed her MK bag, headed out, and jumped in the awaiting car.

After the car picked her up, it returned to Kareem's hotel, where he was waiting outside. She gave him credit for not just showing up at her house in the car. They made it to the restaurant thirty minutes late, but after he checked in with the host, they were seated at their table. Jewels was impressed. Especially when he held a brief conversation in Italian with the maître d'. They were in a private section of the restaurant. The entire time, he had a huge smile on his face, looking like a teenager on his first real date. He did not look as good to Jewels now as he had when they first met. But his status and his full pockets made up for it.

He stood up to pull her chair out when she excused herself to go to the restroom. Upon her return, he did the same and whispered little sweet things to Jewels. She wasn't used to hearing such words of adoration from a black man. They talked for a little while, getting to know each other. He was good at conversation and kept her attention. Jewels noticed he stuttered a little when he used certain words, but other than that, he was cool. She asked him what he did for a living, and he said that he was a businessman. She wanted to ask what type of business but left it at that. He must've been a boxer and was punched in the face too many times, she thought to herself. He seemed to be the romantic type. Which wasn't her type, for sure. But he did have money, and that was all that mattered.

He ordered a bottle of pinot grigio and continued to talk about everything under the sun. She could tell that he would be very generous with his cash, because he stressed his love for women and said that they should always be treated as a queen. After they finished their entrées, Jewels nearly drank the whole bottle of pinot grigio by herself. She was feeling nice by the time they left the five-star restaurant. He was staying at the Ritz-Carlton in Clayton. When Jewels suggested they go back there, he didn't seem surprised. She could tell he was expecting to hear that, and of course, he agreed. She liked clients like that, who let her lead.

Jewels wasted no time in showing her appreciation. As soon as they hit the penthouse suite, she was all over him. Jewels pushed Kareem down on the bed and unzipped his slacks and released his dick through the opening. She wanted to see what he was working with. He passed with flying colors. Jewels wrapped her lips around the helmet of his pulsating "eight and some change" shaft. She just sucked the tip of his head. She peered up at him while she held his pre-cum in her mouth. As soon as their eyes locked, in one gulp she swallowed it.

She removed his shirt and started licking him up and down his chest and then began to suck his nipples. He moaned as she began to lick his neck, and he tensed when she inserted her tongue inside his ear. Suddenly, he rose up and clapped his hands together. The room lights went dim, and soft music filled the air. The move turned Jewels off immediately. He had set the mood for romance, but for her, this was business. Still, she knew she had to play the role that was being scripted for her.

She slithered out of her one-piece dress, revealing her sexy black-lace lingerie set. It was cut on top so that her titties protruded and in the ass part so that her cheeks could hang out. She took his hands and rubbed them all over her breasts. She started licking his lips and slowly stuck her tongue in his mouth, and he started sucking it. She grabbed his hand and moved his fingers up and down her ass crack. He never stopped her. She realized he was just as freaky as she was. He said it turned him on. He added in between moans that he loved the booty hole. It was nice and wet for him, and she was willing to please her client at all costs. He slid inside Jewels's brown eye rough and raw. She grunted at first contact, but after a while, she handled it like the real bitch she believed herself to be. In no time, it was as if he was sexing her pussy. Jewels's asshole was wide open and wetter than ever. She actually climaxed three times from the anal sex.

Afterward, he begged her to stay, but she left. That day she received the biggest tip she had gotten in her entire career. It was the first time she had been completely satisfied with her tip and the sex at the same time.

A few days later, Kareem texted her and invited her to his private party at this new club in downtown St. Louis. The club had been open for only three weeks. He had reasons to celebrate, because he had just gotten back from Las Vegas and had made a lot of money off *a Mayweather fight. Jewels later overheard him telling someone on the phone that he had hit for a quarter million.*

She called Sassy and invited her to go to the party with her. Of course Sassy was down for anything that brought the ballers out. It was the beginning of winter, so it was somewhat chilly outside. Sassy wore Dior winter-white leather shorts with a matching leather vest and Dior winter-white leather knee boots to complete the match. Jewels had on a sexy, body-fitting, soft black-leather catsuit and some black diamond-studded Gucci stilettos, and carried a black Gucci clutch to match. She had kept it simple with the jewelry and had thrown on some diamond studs.

They made it to the club around midnight. The line was down the street and wrapped around the corner when they pulled up. Jewels called Kareem so that they could bypass the line but got no answer. She instantly became pissed. There were certain things she and Sassy did not do, and standing in lines was one of them. They pulled up to the front door for valet parking, and Sassy gave the valet the keys to her Mercedes, then looked at him with a straight face and said, "You better take care of my baby."

All eyes were on them as they proceeded to the front of the line like celebrities, walking past bitches who rolled their eyes. When they got to the front door, Jewels whispered something in the bouncer's ear. She knew him from the boutique she frequented. He did some part-time security in the strip mall where the boutique was located. It was no secret that he wanted her. The next thing they knew, he removed the rope and they were wearing wrist bands to get into the VIP section.

"What the fuck did you say to him?" Sassy asked once they were out of earshot of the bouncer and inside the club.

"I gave him my number and told him to use it later if he remembers it and wants you to suck his dick," Jewels replied with a straight face.

"Shut the fuck up!" Sassy broke into laughter.

But Jewels's facial expression never changed.

Seeing that she was serious, Sassy pushed her. "You dirty bitch!"

That made Jewels smile.

As they looked around the club, they saw it was filled with money getters and sack chasers. Jewels had already peeped out the valet parking lot to see if there were any potential clients in the house. The assorted Benzes, Beemers, Audis, and tricked-out old schools had told her all she needed to know. As far as she was concerned, Kareem had stood her up, since he hadn't answered her calls, so she was going to make the best of the situation. She and Sassy levitated through the club, bopping their heads and snapping their fingers to the jamming sounds. It was packed, and it was off the chain. Jewels recognized a few athletes, entertainers, and known street ballers in the spot.

As they headed to the ladies' room to check their makeup and hair, Jewels noticed someone eyeing her to her left. She made eye contact with the guy who was checking her out. Judging by his bronze-toned complexion, his wavy jet-black hair, and the way he was dressed, Jewels knew he was of Indian descent. He was fine and smelled good. But Jewels kept on walking. As she walked past him, he grabbed hold of her hand and gave her his business card. She glanced at it quickly. It read ALI KHAN, REAL ESTATE INVESTOR AND PROPERTY DEVELOPMENT. Jewels could read only his name and title because she was distracted by the two shiny rocks in his ears. She knew they had to be at least four or five carats each. And then there was the diamond-faced Rolex peeking out from under his sleeve. There was no doubt in her mind that Kareem was somewhere and was watching her every move. Without blinking, she tossed the card on the floor. There was no way she was going to blow her definite for a possible, even if she was pissed at him.

Finally, they reached the VIP section, which was where Kareem and his crew were. Jewels rolled her eyes at him, while Sassy bogarted her way into the VIP section and made herself comfortable in between two of Kareem's friends. She wasted no time scoping the club out, just in case things didn't go right with one of the Africans. Kareem and his boys were looking like a million bucks up in that spot, and they for sure didn't go unnoticed. Jewels could see that Kareem was in boss mode. It was evident that he and his boys were the ones who were large and in charge that night.

Kareem waved his hand in the air for the waiter to come over to their section. He ordered eight more bottles of Cristal, then pointed to Jewels and Sassy. Jewels ordered a bottle of Patrón for herself and Sassy. They partied all night long. The DJ was on point. Four shots of Patrón later, Sassy was giving one of Kareem's peoples a lap dance. Jewels knew she had to be drunk. She would have never given him the time of day if she were sober, and Jewels knew it. He was not her type at all.

Kareem wasn't paying Jewels much attention, so she decided to do her own thing and dance by herself. Besides, she didn't care. She knew at the end of the night he would be leaving with her. After all, he was paying for her time. As the night came to an end, Sassy wound up dissing Kareem's friends and linked up with one of

East St. Louis's top dope boys. Jewels left the club and went back to Kareem's hotel room at the Four Seasons.

They barely made it to the room, since Kareem spent the elevator ride sucking her tits. They finally made it up to the presidential suite. They got straight to the point, no foreplay and no teasing. Kareem was very touchy-feely tough, almost too touchy-feely. Jewels wasn't surprised when he confessed to being an ass man. But she could tell he was surprised and turned on when she let him stick his dick in her ass on the first night. He played with Jewels's asshole with his fingers for a little just to get her wet. Then he gently eased his long, massive dick inside of her brown eye. They fucked nonstop for at least three hours. That night Jewels let Kareem have his way with her, and in return, he showed his appreciation financially in a major way.

The rough touch of Kareem's fingers between her legs brought Jewels out of her trip down memory lane.

"That hurts!" Her eyes shot open. She reached down in the bathwater and pulled Kareem's fingers out of her.

"I'm sorry, baby," Kareem said, apologizing.

She hated when he called her baby. Normally, she would say something, but she was there for a reason—to do whatever it took to get this money so she could pay Rome for what she needed to have done.

He rose up, leaned over, and grabbed a towel for Jewels off the bathroom sink. Jewels stood and stepped into the open towel he had waiting for her. He wrapped it around her and tucked it in, then kissed her on her collarbone. Jewels wanted to flinch, but she kept her composure. Whenever he started pampering her and treating her like that, it put her in an awkward place. She had expressed this to Kareem on several occasions. She always made it clear to him that there wouldn't be any relationship between them other than

the business one they had and that she didn't like for
him to treat her like there was anything more.

Tonight she would allow him to fulfill his fantasy,
as they had discussed prior to her coming over. His
request was not outlandish or anything. It was actually
something simple: feeling loved by her. Jewels began to
caress the back of his head. She faked moans as he kissed
her neck and breasts. His hands glided over her body
like he was part octopus. Jewels made circular motions
with her hands on his chiseled back. She was caught by
surprise when Kareem scooped her up by her ass cheeks
and swept her off her feet. She threw her arms around
his neck as he carried her to the bed. Jewels met his stare
as he gazed into her eyes. He guided her body over the
bed and laid Jewels down gently. His next move tested
Jewels's patience and composure. Without warning, he
forcefully kissed Jewels, slipping his tongue into her
mouth.

This nigga, she thought. She had never let any client
kiss her with an open mouth, and she'd hardly let anyone
kiss her, period. *It's for Sassy*, she had to keep telling
herself over and over in her head to keep from spazzing
out on Kareem.

Fortunately, the kiss didn't last long. Kareem slithered
down from her top lips to her bottom lips. Jewels closed
her eyes. Although the feeling was good, she didn't like it
coming from him. Still she embraced it. Kareem's tongue
felt magical. Her legs shuddered and her body quivered
as he hit the right spots and caused her to reach an
orgasm. For thirty minutes straight, Kareem made love
to Jewels's body, and she to his.

The agreement was for her to spend the night in
Kareem's arms and to wake up the next day ten grand
richer.

"Morning, honey."

Jewels woke to breakfast in bed. She covered her eyes from the brightness of the sun that hovered over downtown St. Louis. She did not return Kareem's greeting. She offered a groan instead as she yawned and stretched. She was not in the mood for pet names and lovey-dovey shit this morning. As far as she was concerned, she had had enough mushy shit with Kareem last night to last her a lifetime. The thought made her let out a light chuckle and smile; then she became sad all at the same time. She found herself sounding like Sassy.

"What's wrong, my love?" Kareem asked.

"Shut the fuck up with all that romance shit," Jewels wanted to scream. "Nothing. I always get like this when that time of the month is coming," Jewels lied instead.

"Aww," Kareem cooed. He sat beside her. Before he could get comfortable, Kareem's phone rang. He paused and retrieved it from his belt clip. "Excuse me, baby. I have to take this." He held up one finger at Jewels and stood from the bed, then made his way into the living room of his suite. That was the break Jewels needed.

Nigga, I'm outta here, anyway, she thought as she climbed out of bed.

"Shit," she cursed under her breath. She realized she hadn't gotten the money he had promised her.

She rushed to get dressed and walked into the living room, where Kareem sat at the dining table, with his head on the palm of his hand. Jewels could hear him switching back and forth from his native tongue to his broken English. He didn't notice she had entered the room. Jewels wasn't trying to listen and could barely understand what he was talking about because of his accent, but she couldn't help but hear the words *millions*, *Chicago*, and *shipment* in the same sentence. She knew she had heard more than she should have. *Motherfucka*, she cursed to herself.

All this time, she had thought Kareem was different. It didn't take a genius to figure out that he was talking about something illegal. Jewels was glad Kareem hadn't seen or heard her enter the living room. She tiptoed back into the bedroom without a sound. This time she called out to Kareem, who in return called back to give him a minute. Seconds later, he appeared with a stack of hundreds all bundled up. He handed it to Jewels with his right hand while holding his cell phone up with his left shoulder. Jewels smiled at the ten-thousand-dollar wrapper around the money. Kareem kissed her on the cheek and whispered that he'd talk to her later. Jewels happily exited the suite, but as she rode the elevator down, she couldn't help but think about Kareem's conversation on the phone.

Chapter Twenty-four

The next few days flew by, and then it was showtime. Rome had everything mapped out and hoped things would go as planned. Finding out the information they needed, including Los's hangout spots, where he liked to eat, sleep, shit, and who he was fucking, had been a piece of cake. They had decided to stage a robbery, versus risking everything they had going on. After carefully planning, they had finally figured out the best way to execute the hit.

Rome met up with Red outside the housing projects, ready to meet his mark. Rome sat patiently behind the tinted windows of a burgundy '99 Impala. His eyes were glued on Los's shadow as Los walked from room to room inside his stash house. This was where the majority of his product and profit were kept, according to Rome and Red's source. After doing his homework, Rome had Los's daily schedule down pat, like it was his own. There were no bodyguards, lookouts, cameras, or anything to keep him away from this hit.

Pulling down their masks, Rome and Red retrieved their heat and headed for their target. Rome stood guard on the left side of the front door, while Red took the right. Both men stood silently, anticipating their next move. Seconds later, on cue, the upstairs light was shut off. After another two minutes, the downstairs light went out. Then the front door lock clicked and the doorknob turned, all in one motion. As soon as the door had the tiniest crack in it, they wrestled their way inside, with their guns raised to their chests.

"Get the fuck on the floor! Get the fuck down now!"

Los was stunned. He had got caught slipping. He had been smart enough not to let anyone know where his stash was, but he'd been dumb in thinking his ass couldn't be followed. Caught up in all the pretty girls and living the life of a high roller, he had lost sight of the greed in niggas. Anybody getting money on the streets in the Lou was either hustling or getting hustled. And at that moment, Los just happened to be on the wrong side. He knew he was sucking in what would be his last breaths. Los immediately wondered where Buster was.

Using what little light was shining in from the streetlight outside, Red shoved Los down on the floor and kneeled on top of him. "Pass that shit over, or I'll take ya fuckin' dome off," he snarled. He deepened his voice as a disguise. "And where the fuck is the money?"

Los said nothing. He passed over the bag in his hand, which contained over fifty thousand dollars' worth of cocaine and high-grade marijuana. He knew either way he was dead, so why give up the money, too?

With hard eyes, Rome repeated the question. "You heard 'im. Where the fuck is the money, nigga?"

Los was quiet.

"Yo, how the hell you be getting these bitches to love you? What the fuck you be doing to them? 'Cause you ugly as shit, dawg." Rome chuckled. "Get ya ass up." Rome pulled Los up from the floor as if he were racing the speed of light.

"Fuck y'all, niggas. Kill me now, 'cause I ain't telling you shit!" Los hawked and spit in the face of the man closest to him, which was Red. The butt of Red's gun slammed against Los's two front teeth and knocked him back to the floor. Blood oozed from Los's lip. Even in pain, he wouldn't back down. "Fuck you! Either take that shit and roll out or kill me now, muthafuckas!"

Red, wiping the saliva from his eyes through the mask with his shirt, said, "It'll be ma pleasure—"

But Rome held up one hand, gesturing for Red to stop. As bad as Red wanted to send Los to meet his Maker, he had to follow Rome's lead. Still calm and cool Rome spoke. "This is your last chance to tell me where the fucking money is." His gun shifted from side to side as he spoke each word.

Los wanted to keep playing the tough guy but he was in no position to do so. He continued to spit blood on the floor every time it accumulated in his cheek. "Y'all niggas gonna kill my ass either way. You expect me to—"

Rome cut him short. "Do yourself a favor and have a fucking seat." He grabbed Los up from the floor and tossed him aside. Los landed crooked on the sectional, one leg across the arm of the sofa, the other foot on the floor, and his head between the oversize pillows. Rome pulled Los's cell phone out of his pocket and started calling out the names of his most recent flings. "Desiree . . . Shaniya . . . Kesha . . . I'ma kill every last one of these bitches if you don't stop fucking around wit' me."

Los laughed. "I don't give a fuck about them hoes."

Rome jammed the barrel of his gun down Los's throat. "But you give a fuck about this one!" Rome turned the phone around so Los could see his soon to be baby mama's name on the small screen. "First, I'ma slump her dumb ass and your unborn bastard child. Then I'ma get her to tell me where ya mama live, so I can kill her too. But not before I put hella dick up in her. Matter of fact, I'ma keep you alive to watch me fuck her before I blow her fucking brains out! Keep testing me, muthafucka!"

Los's eyes watered instantly. *Somebody has to be talking, and they have to be close to me,* he thought. He knew on his end that only he and Buster knew about the chick he had got pregnant. He hoped that maybe, just maybe, if he gave up what they were asking for, no harm would come to his loved ones. "A'ight . . . a'ight . . . I'll tell you where the money is. Just please don't hurt my family."

"So you do know how to be a good boy," Rome growled, but on the inside he was cracking up. *This shit is easier than I thought,* Rome mused. "Give that fucking money up, pussy!" Rome gripped Los by the back of his head, palming it like a basketball, and forced him back to the floor.

Los led them to a medium-size safe he had planted in the floor. He pulled back the artistic rug and punched in the seven digits to the combination. The door to the safe slowly opened.

Jackpot! Rome thought. He and Red glanced at each other.

The safe contained over two hundred thousand dollars, more to add to what they already had. Under the safe was a hidden compartment in the floor that had more coke and weed in it. Both Rome's and Red's eyes lit up. They had known Los was loaded, but not to that extent.

"Now I see why they be giving the pussy up," teased Rome.

Red began to scoop everything in the safe into a duffel bag. Rome let him handle that so he could jump to a more personal level. He stood in front of Los, who was slumped over on his knees.

"Before I let you go, I just need you to know one thing." Rome dropped a wallet-sized photo, which landed at his feet, and then slid it over with his foot for Los to pick up.

Los gazed at the face in the photo and suddenly looked like he'd seen ghost. It was Sassy.

Rome went on. "You killed somebody that has a friend that feels some type of way. And for that, it's time to die, my nigga."

An insane laugh escaped from Los's mouth. "That's what this is all about? A whore?" Los muttered. He had always thought his dick would be the death of him, but nothing like this.

"Who is it? That pretty bitch she hung out with?" He wanted to know.

"Since you a dead man, anyway, yup," Rome replied.

"Over some pussy!" Los shook his head in disgust.

His words rubbed Rome the wrong way. He couldn't hold back any longer. He refused to let a talking dead man pop shit without knowing the real reason he was dying.

"Nah, partna!" he exclaimed. "Since we the niggas that pushed your fuck boy brother, we figured we'd get your li'l dumb ass outta the way, just in case you ever smartened up."

Los couldn't believe his ears. At that moment, hearing that Rome and Red were the killers of his brother, Los decided his life meant nothing to him anymore. All he saw was red. Without warning, he made an attempt to rise up, only to be stopped in his tracks.

In the blink of an eye, Rome came out of nowhere with a hunter's knife and slit Los's throat from ear to ear. The sight of the blood gushing out sickened both Red and Rome. Red completed the job he had started, while Rome made sure there was no more money or drugs lying around.

Red wondered why his friend had held back that sensitive information. If the hit was all about a chick, then there was a strong possibility that Rome was getting too caught up. If Rome was mixing business with pleasure, then one day that could be the downfall for them both. "Why you ain't tell me he was fucking your girl?"

Rome stood there, expressionless. "You were on a 'need to know' basis. Everything you needed to know, I told you. That info, you didn't need to know. And he wasn't fucking anybody that meant something to me."

Red looked disgusted. "I don't like that trick. I don't like nothing about her gold-digging ass. You need to leave her alone, before she ends up being the death of you."

Rome shook his head. Anyone else coming at him like that would have been feeling a round from his gun in their skull.

When Rome first told Red about Jewels, Red had tried to convince him to stay away from her. He was glad that Rome had gotten up out of her place. He knew from Rome's conversations about her that Rome was feeling her, which was strange to Red, because his boy was not the type to fall for any chick, let alone a prostitute. He knew a lot more about Jewels and how she was living. She was supposed to have been a "lay low" spot until things cooled off. He had had no idea Rome had kept in contact with her.

Red continued, "I'm just telling you to be careful. You don't need to get caught up in no dumb shit over no pussy. It can't be that good. Shit, if it is, you need to let your boy over here get a little taste of that, 'cause I ain't never had no snapper like that before!"

Rome chuckled. "Get the fuck out of here, nigga. It ain't even like that. Wasn't about that," he asserted.

"Oh, I was about to say. Didn't think my boy was turning into a sucka for love, nigga."

The tension in the room eased up as both guys shared a laugh. The two men dapped each other up and got back to business. They swept the house one last time before leaving. Red exited first. He powered up the Impala and waited for Rome to join him. And, just like that, their mission was complete. They left nothing behind except for Los's headless body.

Chapter Twenty-five

A few days later . . .

Jewels followed the navigation system's directions until it said she had reached her destination. She peered up the street. She matched the destination with the address she had been texted. She grimaced. The area brought back a lot of memories. This scenery was not her cup of tea, although she was St. Louis bred. She could count on one hand how many times she had been on this side of town since she had relocated. These were her mother's stomping grounds when Jewels was growing up. Ever since her mother's incarceration, this was an area she had steered clear of.

She scanned the streets. They were infested with bodies, everyone from dealers to streetwalkers. It was business as usual. Jewels recognized two low-budget local prostitutes and frowned. It had been a long time since she'd walked the streets of the Lou, or anywhere else, for that matter. She had quickly learned a long time ago that this was indeed a business and that you had to treat it as such. She could not see herself standing on anybody's corner, trying to sell her ass for nickels and dimes.

Who the hell would spend their money on them bitches, anyway? she questioned as she eyed the two women posted up. It reminded Jewels of when her own mother and Sassy's mother used to stand on the block.

But that was a different time and a different era. Their mothers had never looked as bad as the two women she studied now. You never would have caught Jewels's or Sassy's mom with their hair looking wild, like the hair of these two women, or with the type of messy makeup these women wore. You'd never catch Jewels or Sassy looking like them, either. Even the clothes they wore were unappealing, she noticed.

Jewels pulled out her cell phone. The caller answered on the first ring.

"Yes, I'm here," she said into the receiver. Her annoyance about and disdain for their meeting place was evident. The news was filled with enough murders and shootings in this area to convince her that she needed to steer clear of it if she could help it. It wasn't that she was afraid. It was more that she knew bullets did not exit guns with instructions, and they didn't come out with names on them. The last thing she needed in her life was more negativity and violence.

But she knew she was there for a reason. She could've been told to meet in the worst part of St. Louis, and she would've been there. Her friend, her sister, meant that much to her. Jewels thoughts were broken when her attention was drawn to the blinking light to the right of her. She pulled a few feet up, toward the low-level housing apartment, and parked alongside the curb. She hesitated about getting out of her car, but she figured if it wasn't safe, she would have never been asked to meet here. She took a breath and then climbed out. She clutched her LV bag, which contained the agreed amount, and made her way to the entrance door. She was met with a half smile when she reached it.

"You straight." Rome chuckled. He could see how being in the area made her uncomfortable. "Ain't nobody gonna fuck with you. This my hood," he assured her.

His words brought her some comfort. Jewels was already aware of his capabilities in the event that there was danger around. Jewels flashed him a relieved smile as she walked past him and into the apartment. To her surprise, the small apartment was not what she had expected.

Rome closed the door behind her. "Pardon the mess," he said as he scurried over to the living-room area to straighten up. He picked up a Pizza Hut box and an empty two-liter Pepsi bottle. "Have a seat." He pointed to the couch. "I gotta go change my shirt."

Jewels noticed that although there was a little trash around and an unfolded blanket balled up on the couch, the apartment was not low budget looking or dirty. As her eyes roamed around, she realized it was actually quite tastefully decorated and neat for a man. The couch was part of a five-piece black leather sectional, which had been put together in a U shape around an area rug. An Xbox was hooked up to a seventy-inch flat-screen TV, with surround-sound speakers mounted on the walls. A picture of Malcom X peering out of a window, with an AK-47 in hand, and other black art had been strategically hung throughout the apartment.

Rome returned to the living room with no shirt on. Jewels tried to position herself so she wouldn't be staring directly at his bare chest. She was nearly eye level with his pecs.

"This is for you," she said, handing him a manila envelope.

Rome looked at the envelope oddly. "I told you, we were good. Never know when I may have to call you for a favor," he joked.

Jewels smiled lightly. "I doubt you'll ever need me," she returned. "But this isn't a payment. This is what you gave me to stay at my place."

Rome couldn't believe his ears. "I don't get it." A confused look appeared on his face.

Jewels knew he wouldn't. "I'm returning the money
you paid me to stay with me because I felt it was the least
I could do," she informed him. "Not only did you save my
life and get yourself involved in my mess, but you also
did something for me that meant a lot to me."

The more she spoke, the more Rome understood. He
was both surprised and impressed. Her gesture reminded
him of something he would do and had done on more
than one occasion. He could tell that Jewels knew about
the bartering system. He nodded and took the envelope.
He knew it would be an insult if he didn't.

"It's six, not five," she informed him. She'd included the
extra thousand dollars he had paid for the days he had
stayed past their agreed-upon date.

"That's wassup." Rome smiled.

"Well, I guess this is good-bye." Jewels stood.

"I guess it is," Rome shot back. He made a path for her.

"Thank you again," Jewels said as she made her way to
the door. She stepped outside.

Rome stood in the doorway and watched as she strutted to her vehicle, looking both ways until she had
reached it. He chuckled. Just as he was closing the door,
he caught Jewels staring in his direction. There was
something about the way she was looking at him that
made him question it. Rather than close the door, he
waved at Jewels, who was apparently still looking over at
him. He returned the smile Jewels sent his way, and then
he watched as she made her way out of the hood.

Chapter Twenty-six

Two weeks later . . .

Rome had just exited the freeway. He came to a screeching halt at the light at the intersection. He was tempted to run it, but he knew that with his luck, a patrol car would be cruising by and would pull him over. That was the last thing he needed in his life, with all that he had escaped. So instead, he took two pulls of the half a blunt he had been smoking while he rode across town. With both drugs and a loaded gun in his ride, Rome could not afford any mishaps. Besides, he was all too ready to meet up with Red and their crew and turn up for the evening at the downtown nightclub. Red had called him earlier and had told him about the mini celebration he had put together for them and the team. You didn't have to tell Rome twice. Anything Red put together, he knew would be epic, from the bottles to the chicks. Rome knew they'd be on deck if Red was behind it.

His thoughts were interrupted when his attention was drawn to a passing vehicle. It wasn't so much the car that caught Rome's attention as the person who occupied it.

I know that wasn't her, thought Rome. He peered up at the traffic light. "Come on! Come on!" he exclaimed.

As if it had heard him, the light turned green. Rather than going straight, to where Red and his crew were awaiting his arrival, Rome hooked a sharp left and sped up the block. He did sixty-eight in a thirty-five-mile speed limit zone, trying to catch up to the familiar-looking car. Once he was a safe distance away, he slowed down, thankful that there were no police in sight. Rome squinted his eyes. He was almost certain that it was her, but he needed to be sure.

Rome trailed behind the luxury car as it turned into the five-star hotel off to their right. Rome continued on down the road and then pulled over once he was sure he would be out of plain view. He threw his whip into park and then turned around to look out his back window. He watched as a chauffeur jogged around to the passenger's side of the unmistakable loud-colored car. He already knew who the man was who was about to step out of the car. But all was confirmed when he saw the extended hand of his connect help Jewels out of his red Bentley.

"You can't make this shit up," Rome said out loud. A sinister grin appeared across his face. He snatched his gearshift into drive and made a U-turn in the middle of the street. He couldn't wait to get ahold of Red to tell him what was on his mind.

Chapter Twenty-seven

The following week . . .

Jewels had already been briefed. It hadn't taken a lot of convincing by Rome. Ever since she had discovered that Kareem was not who she thought he was, she had lost the ounce of respect she had had for him. Had she known he was no different than the nigga who killed her homegirl, she never would have given him the time of day. As far as she was concerned, he had played a part in Sassy's death. Rome had told her how he had supplied the person responsible for it, so in her mind, he was partially responsible. Aside from all that, Jewels just felt obligated to help.

To most, it might sound crazy, but to her, it made sense. It was an unpaid debt she felt she needed and wanted to pay. She knew what it was like to need somebody's help and not get it. When she had needed someone the most on two occasions, both times, there had been no one there to turn to. It was Rome who had been there for her once, something she had never expected. He had saved her life and had helped her girl rest in peace. This was what Jewels had been telling herself over and over again during the whole ride over to the hotel. She had her game face on. She was just hoping that everything was on schedule and on point.

After Kareem pulled into the parking lot, she scanned the area to see if, by chance, they had been beaten there.

Realizing that they hadn't, she took a quiet breath. Normally, Kareem's driver would be chauffeuring them around, but Kareem had relieved him for the evening. He pulled into the hotel's underground parking garage and parked.

They went inside the hotel, and once they were upstairs, Jewels's mind began to race. Were Kareem not on the phone, he would've noticed her nervousness. The fact that he was engrossed in this business call created a window of opportunity for her. As soon as they arrived at the room, she got comfortable and started to undress.

Kareem had ended his first call and was dialing another number to begin a new one when he said, "I need something to drink. You want something from the machines?" he asked.

Jewels shook her head no.

"Okay. Well, be ready for me when I get back." He pushed the security lock out so the door wouldn't close all the way, stepped out, and went in the direction of the vending area.

Jewels used that time to make a call. "Hey, where are you?" she asked in a panicky voice. "He stepped out for a minute. Thought you'd be here by now. How you planning to do this?" Jewels said, rambling. She walked to the door to peek into the hall. "He ain't coming yet. Yes, same one." She paused and looked behind her. Her mind was playing games on her. "I gotta go," she whispered into the phone before abruptly disconnecting the call.

She tossed her iPhone back into her Gucci bag and hopped in the bed, pretending that she'd been there the whole time.

Kareem entered the room and locked the door. "All right. I'll get witchu when I get back to Chicago," Jewels heard him say. She watched as he placed his phone on one of the nightstands beside the king-size bed.

He looked over at Jewels seductively. His second head rose to attention immediately. "Damn, girl. Wit' a body like that, a nigga fit'na put a ring on your finger. For real," he cooed as he slithered his way over to her. The pit of Jewels's stomach knotted. She was tempted to give him a piece of her mind but then thought better of it.

For the next hour, Kareem was laying his thing down with full force. He and Jewels were getting it in. Moans and groans filled the air and could be heard clearly on the other side of the door and through the thin walls. She was sure she had never been in that many positions before. It felt so good, she was ready to change her mind. She went into character and purred like a kitten. Hearing her sweet, delicate voice and feeling the nibbling around his ear brought him to an orgasm he didn't know was possible. His eyes squeezed shut, each toe curled in a different direction, and his heart raced. Seconds later, he collapsed onto Jewels's stomach and took her sweaty breasts into his mouth.

Minutes later, he was on his feet and heading to the bathroom to wash off. With her back turned to the bathroom door, she grabbed her bag, fished out her phone, and sent a text. She then returned the phone to her bag, glanced over at the clock, and realized it had been almost an hour and a half since she'd set foot in the hotel room.

Jewels could see out of the corner of her eye that Kareem was watching her. She let half a smile come across her face. Kareem caught the smile on her face as he came out of the bathroom.

"What you grinning for?"

Jewels smiled harder. "You," she replied as she stood and scurried over to her clothes.

Kareem trailed behind her and grabbed her from behind. He gripped her ass cheeks in his palms. "You're gonna be my permanent St. Louis woman, the one that comes before all the others."

I can't believe this fool. He really got me twisted. Ya St. Louis chick, huh? I guess you the type of nigga that got many hoes in different area codes.

Jewels took offense, but she perked up her lips, like she was happy to be one of Kareem's angels. "I guess I can deal wit' that."

"Good. I was hoping you'd say that." Kareem pulled a wad of cash out of his suit jacket pocket and handed Jewels fifteen thousand dollars. Jewels took the money respectfully and put it in her bag.

Moments later they were on the elevator and headed down to the underground parking garage. They stepped out of the elevator, and Kareem hit the button to unlock the car doors when they were a few feet away from the car. When he didn't hear the usual chirp, he tried hitting the button again. Nothing happened. By the odd facial expression on his face, Jewels could see that he was trying to review his steps after parking the car.

Getting to the passenger's side of the car before he got to the driver's side, she opened the door and said, "See? You were so tied up with that phone call, you forgot to lock the doors. Or was I the one who had you slipping?" She grinned.

Kareem lost his focus. They climbed in the car at the same time. Jewels made sure she allayed any suspicions he still had. She leaned over and played with his ear. As soon as he turned the key in the ignition, he got the shock of his life.

"Don't move another fucking muscle," a voiced ordered from the backseat of the Bentley.

Although Jewels knew he was in the back, he still startled her. She almost jumped out of her seat. She held her hand across her heart and turned around. "Damn! Did you have to scare me like that?"

Kareem turned and looked at her in total disbelief.

Rome used the barrel of his gun to gently turn Kareem's face back toward the front. "Didn't I say, 'Don't move'?"

Hearing the authority in his voice sent a rush of adrenaline through Jewels's body. She had been scared at first, but now she was ready for whatever.

"Drive out of the parking lot and make a left. If you turn your head again to look at me or her, I'ma blow ya brains out," Rome growled.

Kareem did as he was told. He pulled out of the parking garage and made a left into the light ongoing traffic. The car was silent. The longer they drove, the more Jewels had mixed feelings about the whole thing. Rome, on the other hand, was furious. If the scene had been animated, steam would have been shooting from his ears.

Rome mugged Kareem with the gun and asked, "Was it worth losing your life?"

Kareem shook his head no in response. Ignoring what Rome had previously told him, he looked over at Jewels. "Fuck this trick-ass bitch. Her pussy ain't worth shit." He gathered up a mouthful of saliva and spit on her.

Feeling disgusted and violated, Jewels backhanded him with all her might. She wiped the spit from the side of her face and rubbed it on his. "I can't wait to see you die."

Rome intervened with his pistol. He clunked Kareem on the side of the face. Blood sprayed on both Rome's and Jewels's face.

"Agh!" Jewels screeched.

Rome let out a light chuckle. He had had blood splatter across his face and everywhere else on his body enough times to be immune to it. He pulled his cell out with his free hand. "We pulling up," he said before placing the phone back in his pocket. "Turn here."

Rome directed Kareem to a dirt-filled road that led to a lot with a garage. He ordered him to stop just beyond the garage. There were a lot of abandoned cars, car parts, and junk scattered throughout the dimly lit lot. Jewels's attention was focused on the sound of the garage door opening a little ways back. There was a heavy Biggie Smalls look-alike standing behind the garage door. He seemed very strange to her, but she dared not ask any questions at that moment. Jewels hopped out of the car first.

"All right, my man. Kill the engine and get out. Make sure you keep your hands where I can see them. Please don't make me use this. I really don't feel like getting no more blood on me right now."

Red stood outside the driver's side door, with his own heat at his hip. He stared the stranger down, waiting for him to make a sudden move. Kareem climbed out, eyed Jewels, then Red, then Rome as Rome emerged from the backseat. His eyes widened.

"You?" he said, recognizing Rome.

"Yeah, me, nigga," Rome shot back. "I told you I needed better prices," he added as he led the way to a room at the back of the garage. It was dark, cold, and it smelled like motor oil. He shoved Kareem over toward a wooden chair. "Sit the fuck down," Rome ordered.

Kareem sat down.

"What you gonna do wit' him?" asked Jewels.

Red looked over at her. "Baby girl, you did your job. Leave the rest of this to us." He didn't want to get her involved any more than she had to be. Red was still mad at Rome for involving her in the first place, but he didn't let it show. "Go 'head back up there to my office."

Jewels cut her eyes at Rome, who was making her feel real awkward. "We made a stop on the way to the hotel. I'm sure whatever he put in his trunk will make you happy," she told him. Then she turned, with the intention of heading to the office, as Red had instructed, but she was stopped dead in her tracks by Rome.

"Don't go anywhere," he said. Rome threw Red the keys to Kareem's car. "Go find out what's in the trunk and let me know."

Red had a bad feeling about what was about to go down. He looked curiously at Rome for answers but got none.

"Go handle that, Red." Rome aimed his weapon at Kareem. "I'm tired of being in suspense. What's in the trunk?"

Kareem answered without hesitation. "Two hundred kilos of coke and close to half a million dollars." Kareem decided to use whatever breath he had left to propose something that might get him out of his predicament. "If you play this out right, you can walk away wit' a lot more. All I ask is that you spare my life. I got over six—"

Rome cut him off with a blow to the face. Blood filled Kareem's nose and mouth and splattered all over his black ST. LOUIS VS. EVERYBODY hoodie. "I'm asking all the questions here, and I'm making all the rules. I'm not in it for the long run. I'm in it for the moment. I ain't got time to try to persuade somebody to dish out some ransom for your ass. It's a one-shot deal wit' me, so you can kiss your life good-bye."

Rome cocked his gun. He pointed it at Kareem's head and pulled the trigger. Kareem squinted his eyes to brace himself for the impact, but nothing happened. When he opened his eyes, he saw Rome pulling on the hammer. Using that moment to his advantage, Kareem gathered all the strength he could muster while sitting there and directed a powerful kick at Jewels's leg. The blow sent her crashing to the floor.

"That's for setting me up, you sheisty-ass whore." Kareem followed the kick with a mouthful of bloody saliva, which he spit on her face.

That hadn't been part of Rome's plan. He watched Jewels let out an agonizing scream. Red ran back to find out what could've possibly happened that fast. By the time he returned to the room, the chair had been flipped over and Kareem was flat on his back. Rome was over him and was beating him half to death. Red helped Jewels get up off the floor. Then he yelled for Rome to stop.

Rome was on fire as he landed each blow. Then he grabbed Kareem, lifted him from the floor, and said, "That's no way to treat a lady," as if he were a respectable white-collar gentleman. He smacked Kareem upside the head like he was his child, righted the chair with one hand, then threw him back onto it and badgered him with questions.

"Where's the rest of the shit?" was the first one.

Kareem answered with silence.

"Oh, you don't want to answer me, huh?" Rome grabbed Kareem's hand and placed it firmly on the arm of the chair. Between breaths, he pointed to a hammer that was lying on the floor. "Pass me that shit."

Red picked up the hammer and tossed it to him.

Rome flagged Jewels over. "C'mere."

Her equilibrium was still off from the kick. She got herself together and staggered to Rome's side.

Rome grabbed one of Kareem's legs, holding it steady. He looked at Jewels and asked, "Was this the leg he used to kick you wit'?"

Jewels nodded rapidly.

The shot from the hammer tore into Kareem's leg, breaking his joint in two. Kareem bit down on his lip, trying to take it like a soldier.

"Now, I'ma ask you one more time. Where's the rest of that shit you keep down here?" Rome barked.

"Fuck . . . you . . . mutherfucka," Kareem replied, slurring.

Rome snatched the hammer away from Jewels and swung it, this time at Kareem's other leg. Kareem yelled out in pain.

"Bruh, tell me something. Where it at?" Rome asked again, pulling his heat from his waist.

Kareem didn't give him anything. If there was one thing he wasn't, it was a snitch.

Rome extended his gun to Jewels and asked her if she would like to do the honors. She looked at him and grabbed hold of the gun happily.

Red stood in the corner, about to witness a point of no return. This was what he didn't want to see happen. Jewels was about to be stained with blood. "Don't make her do it," begged Red. "C'mon, man. Think about this." He knew that once Jewels pulled that trigger, it would drain all the purity left in her soul.

Rome ignored him. "If you riding wit' me, go ahead and lay this nigga to rest."

Jewels took one look at Kareem. All the bruises and blood had her shaken. She thought back to Rome holding Los's head in his hand. Then she recalled the kick from Kareem, which sent her into a rage. Without ever having any target practice, she let one shot loose. It landed smack in the side of his neck. Seeing the blood gush out made her sick to her stomach.

Kareem didn't go down right away. He grabbed the side of his neck and gasped for air. Jewels panicked. She released her grip on the gun, and it fell to the floor. Red silently shook his head, wishing she had never been involved. Rome picked the gun up from the floor and put two shots in Kareem's face, taking him out of his misery.

Showing no emotion at all about everything that had just happened, Rome turned to Red. "Call the cleanup team so we can get this faggot out of here." Then he threw his arm over Jewels's shoulder. "C'mon. I need to get you out of here and looked at," he said as he escorted her out of the garage.

Chapter Twenty-eight

It didn't take long for Rome to get Jewels to the hospital. He waited for her to be discharged. When Kareem kicked her and she fell, she had fractured two of her ribs and had bruised two more. Other than a little pain, Jewels was fine, let her tell it. The doctor prescribed her some painkillers and informed her she was in no danger from her injuries.

She looked over at Rome once they were back in his ride. "Thank you for bringing me here."

He gave a long head nod to let her know he was listening.

She quit talking and took advantage of the silence. Even though his mind was elsewhere and he had more important matters to handle than tending to her, Jewels was grateful that Rome had put everything on hold to see to it that she received the medical attention she deserved. Not that she would have expected anything less. It was because of her and the injuries she'd sustained that Rome was now in the best position he'd ever been in, in his life. She turned her body slightly toward the window and gazed out at nothing in particular.

Rome periodically turned his head to look at her. He didn't know why he had jumped to get her to the hospital. He was not a "knight in shining armor" type of guy, but he felt responsible for her condition, even though it had been her choice to put herself in the line of fire. She could've been killed—again. Still, she'd been willing to go through with the plan. It had earned her a lot of respect from him. Stomachaches, headaches, colds, fevers, and things of that nature were the usual reasons for doctor visits for normal women—not broken ribs because they set a nigga up. Jewels was not the typical around-the-way girl, he knew. There was more to her than he'd thought.

"Where are you going?" he asked.

She took a minute to think. She wanted to be by his side but didn't think it would be possible, even after her help. "Home," she answered.

There was a brief pause before he said, "Okay. Do you want me to stay wit' you?" He looked over at her.

His question caught her by surprise. Just as her immediate response did him.

"I don't mind you staying wit' me. You can stay wit' me as long as you need to."

"Cool." He nodded. "I just don't want to see anything bad happen to you. My bad for even putting you in this type of situation. I know you not about this life. Not my world, anyway," he said. "I know you're much smarter than this. Whatever you got going on in your life is on you, but I didn't bring all that extra baggage into your world. I've survived these streets for several years with this kind of drama, so I'm used to it, just like I know you used to what comes with your lifestyle."

"Thank you for that. But I'm a big girl." She smiled. "Yeah, I may not be about that life, but my mama ain't raised no punk, either. Yes, it was a messy situation, but I signed up for it. I'm stronger than you know," she offered. Jewels wanted to tell him everything so badly. It was on the tip of her tongue, but she couldn't say anything. Every time she parted her lips to speak, nothing but hot air came out. She couldn't even believe that Rome had her wanting to tell him her entire life story. She stared at Rome, who cut his eyes over at her occasionally and said nothing. She was looking for him to say something, anything.

"You can sit there all quiet if you want to, but I know you got something to say," he finally told her. He looked forward and gazed out the windshield and then glanced back over at her. "You can trust me," was all he said.

Suddenly, he cut the wheel real hard, almost sideswiping a car in the outer lane, and then sped off.

Jewels's eyes widened. Out of all of the things he could have said in response to what she had shared with him, those words were not what she had expected. She was about to say something, but when she looked up, Rome was hopping on the interstate and going in the opposite direction of her place.

"This isn't the way to my house," she announced.

"Yeah, I know. I need to go check on things with my partner before we go to your spot. It's close," he informed Jewels.

It had been a long and tiresome night, and she just wanted to go home, shower, and climb into her bed, but she understood the game and knew how it went. Like she had said, she'd signed up for it, so she had to see it all the way through.

"That's fine." She nodded.

Rome made his way across town, heading to the area where he knew Red would be. This would be the first time he had ever brought someone to their main stash spot, but Jewels was an exception, thought Rome. It was because of her that they had come up in the first place.

Jewels sat quietly, with her seat leaned back, enjoying the cool breeze. She was in her own little world, thinking about everything that was going on in her life. Rome took the opportunity to learn more about her. Jewels told him half her story. She shared things she rarely told anyone, like how her mom had told her she had the HIV virus and how her father had been killed when she was a young girl. She told him that she wanted to go to college to study business, something she had never told anyone, and that was determined to accomplish this goal.

"It sounds like you got a good head on your shoulders," Rome offered. He wanted to say more but held back.

Jewels picked up on it. She gave a weak smile before saying, "It's all about the hustle for me."

"You made it through the best way you knew how, and that's real. Some people give up, but you didn't, and that tells me a lot about you," Rome responded.

It had been a long time since a guy had spoken to Jewels in such a concerned way. Money was almost always the main topic of her discussions with anyone. Rome, on the other hand, made her realize how important school was. There was something about him, and that had her wanting to change the game.

Rome pulled into a driveway and then drove all the way to the back. "Sit tight. I'll be in and out," he told Jewels after he put the car in park.

Where the hell am I gonna go? she thought, but she shook her head as confirmation instead.

Rome jumped out. Less than ten minutes later, he hopped back in the vehicle and headed back across town. Once they were back on the highway, Rome reached into the front pocket of his black hoodie and pulled out a huge stack of bills.

"This is for you." He made sure he used the same words Jewels had uttered when she returned his money.

Jewels looked at the wad of cash. *This is at least twenty-five grand*, she thought.

"You earned that." Rome handed her the money. "Twenty-five stacks," he said.

Jewels kindly accepted her cut. Rome veered off at the intersection. A few minutes later he was pulling up to her gate. She decided to save whatever it was she intended to say for when they were inside.

He drove his SUV through Jewels's gate entrance. Once they were inside her condo, she told him to make himself comfortable and then made her way to her bedroom.

Rome found a seat in the living room. He watched as Jewels vanished down the hall and into her bedroom. For some odd reason, he had missed this place, which had been his home for nearly two weeks. *It feels good to be back in her presence and under her roof,* he thought. He picked up the remote to the stereo system and put something on. Drake's voice came blaring through the speakers. He lowered the volume and sat back.

Meanwhile, Jewels undressed, went into the bath-room, and ran a bubble bath. The doctors had told her not to strain herself or get the bandages wrapped around her too wet, so she made sure she didn't fill the tub to the rim. She took a minute to look herself over in the mirror. The reflection wasn't of the same girl from a couple of years ago. This was someone totally new. She whispered aloud to the mirror, "I lost myself." A lot had happened in the past few months. Her mind was all over the place, darting from her first meeting with Rome to Sassy's murder and to the events that followed. She felt drained. "I can't continue to live like this," she told herself out loud.

For the first time in her life, Jewels was contemplating her lifestyle. Rome had her weighing some things. She had already come to terms with the fact that she was attracted to someone she had never even thought was her type. Any person with one good eye could see that he was attracted to her too. At that moment she felt like giving up on everything. Not on life, but on death. She began to realize that if she kept living like she was, there was a big possibility that she might not make it.

"I got to do something. I can't let this control me any longer," she said aloud, referring to what she loved and had been doing to take care of herself since she was a young girl.

She climbed into the bathtub, closed her eyes, and tried to relax her mind, but instead it ran wild. She envisioned everything exactly as it had happened, from the fat white trick's attack to Sassy's disappearance, missing nothing in between. Her eyes shot open. The whole place was pretty quiet. The only thing that could be heard was the soft sound of Ashanti singing her hit song "Baby" as it drifted from the speakers mounted on the bathroom wall.

Against the doctors' orders, Jewels slid her whole body down into the water. The only thing above the water was her head. She drifted into deep thought again. Moments later, she slid down farther, letting her head join the rest of her body underneath the suds. Her count reached thirty-six before she couldn't take it anymore. She came up for air just before the water took her last breath. The drenched remains of what used to be a silky soft perm covered her face. She used both hands to brush her hair toward the back of her head and then lost herself again in deep thought.

The thought of dying alone frightened Jewels. Now that Sassy was gone, she had no one. The more she thought about it, the more she realized who and what all she really had. Jewels took a deep breath. She rose from the bathtub and wrapped the towel around her dripping body. She stuck one leg out of the water and planted her foot on the floor. The moment she planted both feet on the floor, she wanted something different and decided on taking a new direction in her life.

"Jewels? You okay?" Rome called out as he walked toward her bedroom. "Hey . . ." Rome stood at full attention when Jewels met him at the doorway of her master bath with a towel around herself. "I'm sorry. You didn't answer me, so I—"

Jewels reached for him, and her towel dropped to the floor. Rome physically didn't hold back his feelings for her, but she reminded him of her ribs, and he gently scooped her up, then laid her on the bed. There they continued revealing their feelings for each other and where they saw each other in a future together.

Chapter Twenty-nine

Eight months later . . .

Rome and Jewels arrived at Newark International Airport in New Jersey around noon that day. The layover in Chicago had been one full hour of torment for Jewels's body and mind. She had not been able to get into a comfortable resting position in the flat and wide airport chairs. It was like any other time she had flown with Rome, and still, she didn't like it. Like the other times, she'd been on edge, anxious. She still couldn't believe she had let Rome talk her into flying on their six-month anniversary as a team and a couple. In those six months, it seemed as if he had had her in the air more than on the ground. She preferred it when they drove to their destination, but this trip would have taken too long in a car and would have thrown them off schedule.

They took a car service all the way from the airport to Atlantic City, which was over an hour-and-a-half drive. That would be their home for the next two days. Rome was mixing business with pleasure on this trip, thanks to the Jersey connect he had made by using the numbers Jewels's mother had sent her. Rome had been doing business with an East Coast heavy hitter named Jameel, who was from a city called Plainfield in New Jersey. He was a major figure not only in the drug game but also in the gambling world, which was why it was nothing for him to roll out the red carpet for Rome and Jewels.

Jameel had told them to meet him in A.C. so they could enjoy themselves while they visited. Rome didn't have to put up any cash for the trip. Jameel had everything set for them. He'd told Rome he'd be offended if Rome stuck his hand in his pocket while he was in Jersey.

The driver pulled up to the entrance of the Caesars Atlantic City Hotel. Being from the Midwest, Jewels was awed by the hotel's elegance and architecture, the likes of which she had never seen. It was a world that was unknown to her back in St. Louis. Caesars was just one of the four properties owned by Harrah's that sat snugly on the boardwalk in Atlantic City. Jewels liked the hotel's crescent shape, and the layout facing the beach was divine. There were restaurants, nightclubs, a spa, a hair salon, a gym, shops, and an indoor pool. Jewels would have access to them all on the trip with Rome. She had the option to unwind at the spa, shop until she dropped, or swim in the ocean or the pool. The hotel really offered far too many activities for Jewels to partake of in just two days. Everything she could ever want to do during this trip was within walking distance, but she would have the limousine at her beck and call.

The rays of the sun streamed through the window of the oceanfront suite, which stared out at the Atlantic City beach, waking Jewels from her jet lag–induced sleep on the enormous king-size bed. Her eyes slowly opened to see who it was that had pulled the curtains back, allowing the sun to wake her.

"Rome, what are you doing?" she asked. A great yawn followed, and then she turned over, away from the window.

"Baby, it's eleven a.m. Get up, Ma!" he said, looking out one of the suite's windows that faced the boardwalk. He had just finished smoking a blunt. He stepped out onto the balcony and looked to his right and saw the mall that sat on the boardwalk. To his left was Bally's Beach Bar. He had chosen to stay at Caesars because it was centered between the other buildings and the most iconic. Rome inhaled the fresh Atlantic City air. He enjoyed the beautiful, festive atmosphere, one he could find only in Atlantic City.

This city will probably never lose its fire, he thought.

Jewels looked at him, dressed in shorts and a wife beater. She was loving the weather, and as she watched the sun bounce off his skin, she wanted to climb out of bed and join him on the balcony as he looked out over the beach and its occupants from their suite on the top level of the building.

When he came back into the suite, she said, "It's eleven out here, which means it's ten back home. *Technically,* I'm still asleep," she teased.

Rome snatched the covers off her body and laughed as she curled her body into a ball to keep warm. He got on top of her and began kissing her arms and neck. A grin appeared on her face. She turned over so that she could look at him.

"You took a shower already?" she asked.

"I sure did," Rome said. "I wanted you in there with me, but you were sleeping so peacefully. I didn't want to wake your pretty ass up."

"Well, that's too bad, 'cause I would have loved to shower with you," Jewels said, looking to her sides, at his muscular arms. "Guess I'ma have to get you dirty again."

"You wanna get dirty, eh?" Rome asked. She had read his mind. His dick was already throbbing with the desire to feel her moist vagina.

Jewels had felt his hard imprint through his jeans and wanted to do something about it. She flipped him over so that she was on top, and then moved down between his legs. She tugged his jeans off and did the same with his boxer briefs. Her hand jerked his stiff dick for a moment, and then she moved her mouth to the head and began to suck slowly. A raspy moan crept out of his mouth, letting her know that he loved the sensation. She picked up her pace and put more of him into her mouth. Jewels reached into her shorts and stuck a finger in her vagina and discovered its moistness. Once his dick was as hard as it was going to get, she pulled her shorts down and moved her panties to the side, then mounted him.

Rome ran his hands up her shirt, grabbed her full breasts, and pinched her nipples as she rode him like a champ. She used every muscle in her legs as she performed squats on his manhood and tightened her vagina with every levitation.

"God. Damn. Girl," Rome muttered as he struggled to look at her as she did the damn thing. He wanted to watch her ride him, but his eyes kept rolling to the back of his head from how good she felt and how good it felt inside her.

"Is it good to you?" Jewels cooed into his ear.

Her tongue flickered across his earlobe, and she gave him kisses from his neck to his pectorals. Rome's senses were taken to a new height when she kissed his nipples and ran her tongue down the crease in his abs. She threw her head back and decreased her speed when he gave her his answer.

"Hell, yeah, it's good," he groaned.

Trapped in sheer ecstasy, Rome grabbed her buttocks with his hands and squeezed them with everything he had. He felt the semen swelling up toward the tip of his penis, marking the onset of an ejaculation. He removed her from on top of him and told her to jack him off.

Jewels smiled seductively and placed her lips around the firm head of his dick and jerked at it until he exploded in her mouth. She grabbed the bedsheets and spit the cum out of her mouth. Rome shuddered, wishing he could have held out a bit longer.

"All right. Now we can get in the shower," Jewels said, walking into the hotel bathroom. She cut the faucet on in the shower, then removed her underwear and shirt.

Jewels peeked into the bedroom to see what was taking Rome so long. He was still lying on the bed and was now looking at his cell phone. She sighed, walked toward him, and planted her bottom on the edge of the bed.

"You all right? Did I hurt something?" she joked.

Rome smiled faintly and turned his attention away from the phone. "I'm good, baby girl. I was just texting ole boy that I'm going to be a few minutes late," he answered.

"So . . . the shower?" Jewels said, tilting her head twice in the direction of the bathroom.

"I have to pass, Jewels. I'm already a little behind," Rome said, sitting upright, then standing to his feet. He walked into the bathroom, stood at the sink, and grabbed a hand towel. He wet it with warm water and wiped Jewels's remains off his genitals.

"What time will you be back?" Jewels asked as she walked up behind him.

Rome turned around to face her and wrapped his arms around her nude body. "I should be back in a couple of hours. I'll leave some money on the table so you can have a good time out here."

"I don't need any money. I'm good," Jewels said, with the wave of her hand. She had promised herself that she would not bother him when he had business to take care of. She was certain that when it was their time to be together, Rome was going to sweep her off her feet in a new way. He always did.

For the past few months, they had been traveling from state to state, and from country to country, for both business and personal reasons, checking off the list of contacts Jewels had. Each time, she had been left alone and had had a ball in his absence, and she'd also enjoyed herself whenever he had free time. She made sure, though, that she maintained her independence, so no matter where she was, she knew how to find her own way and enjoy herself by herself.

Just then she was hit by his kiss, which sealed his departure.

"I'll call you," Rome said, before setting the promised money on the table and leaving the suite.

Jewels watched the door close behind him and then went back into the bathroom, where the steamy shower was waiting for her. After she showered, she wrapped her body in a large towel and sorted through her new wardrobe to find what she was going to wear on her first day out in Atlantic City. She held up a two-piece Victoria's Secret bathing suit.

"I know for sure I'm going to the beach," she said aloud to herself.

Jewels finished drying off and oiled her body with the new Victoria's Secret lotion she had found in her bag. She slid into the sexy swimsuit and began searching through the clothes for a top and bottoms to wear over it. She decided on a miniskirt and an Abercrombie & Fitch baby tee. A pair of gold open-toe Jimmy Choo flats topped off the look. Jewels grabbed the wrapped box of Vera Wang Glam Princess perfume and unwrapped it. She sprayed her wrists and dabbed some perfume behind her ears using her fingertips. She spritzed her hair and applied light makeup to her face.

I have too many designers on for my own good, she
joked as she put on a pair of gold diamond studs and a
matching necklace. She slid on three gold bangles, two
on her left wrist and one on her right. Once she felt
"Atlantic City approved," Jewels emptied the contents of
her purse into her new tan Prada handbag. She grabbed
the roll of money Rome had placed on the table and
counted the bills.

"One thousand eight hundred, eight-fifty, nine hundred, nine-fifty . . . two thousand." Jewels thumbed
through the cash to make sure she had enough to spend
on whatever she desired.

Ever since she had joined forces with Rome, she had
seen more money than she thought possible. She loved her
and Rome's new lifestyle. The two thousand dollars made
her realized just how far she had come. Normally, she'd already be thinking about how she was going to replace the
money she intended to spend, but nowadays, it seemed
the more she spent, the more came in, without her
having to do much. She was so far removed from her old
lifestyle that she couldn't see herself ever doing anything
other than what she was into now.

Jewels grabbed the room key, stuck it in the front
pocket of her handbag, and left the suite to see the rest
of what the hotel had to offer. She took the elevator down
to the main lobby and was greeted by the same large gold
and crystal chandeliers that had welcomed her when she
first arrived.

Jewels stepped up to the front-desk clerk. "Excuse me,
ma'am. Can you tell me where the spa is?"

"The spa is right next door, in the building with all the
black mirrors covering it," the perky clerk answered. She
pointed in the spa's direction.

Jewels thanked her and stepped out into the Atlantic
City heat, instantly telling herself that she was going to

the beach later to show off her milk chocolate figure. *I better put this bathing suit to good use in this heat,* she thought as she walked next door to the spa.

She stepped into a room that was overwhelmed by white marble tiles on the floor and the walls. A large hallway was the pathway to the front desk. A smile was all the communication that she needed.

"Hello there. Welcome! What can we do for you today?" said the woman in charge at the desk.

Jewels stared at the spa services menu and asked for a moment to decide what she wanted. After staring at the menu for a minute, she chose to get two services, the Mineral Soak and the Swedish Rubdown Therapeutic Massage. She paid the four hundred dollars up front and was instructed as to what would happen next.

"Okay, Stephanie here is going to take you to the changing room, where you can get undressed, while we start the mineral soak bath for you," the woman said after closing her cashier's drawer.

Stephanie led Jewels to the changing room. Jewels stripped out of her clothes, keeping on the bathing suit she had on underneath, and got into the robe the spa had supplied her with. She met a woman by the name of Farina outside the changing room and then followed her to the jetted bath infused with natural minerals that was waiting for her. She removed the robe, got into the bath, popped on her headphones, pressed PLAY on the iPod in the pocket of her robe so that she could listen to the Floetry Pandora station, and instantly closed her eyes. She soaked her body in the tub for the next sixty-five minutes, putting the minor aches in her muscles at ease. She could tell that her body was replenished when it was time for her massage.

Jewels put her robe back on, then walked up the stairs of the spa and into the white marble room where she would be receiving her massage. Jewels waved at the handsome Spanish masseur. He instructed her to lie down on her stomach on top of the massage table, which was covered in a brown plush towel and had a leather headrest.

"Do you want to take off your bathing suit?" he asked, knowing some customers preferred to lie naked underneath a towel while receiving their massage.

A coy Jewels clung to her robe with a tight fist. She shook her head with a smile. "No, no thank you," she answered. She sat on the edge of the massage table.

The masseur smiled, noticing her demureness. "I ask just because it's almost like a policy. You'd be surprised how many people would rather receive a massage with nothing on. Let's get started," he said.

Jewels let the robe slide off her shoulders and fall to the floor. The masseur picked it up and placed it on a spare massage table. She lay down on the table and let the Spanish masseur's fingers knead her back muscles. The masseur's hands lightly stroked her neck and shoulders, then went down her spinal column. He poured aromatherapy oil on the middle of her back and rubbed it into her backside. His hands then lowered to her thighs and legs, and he rubbed in the oil in circular motion. The massage was so ardent that Jewels almost thought the masseur was making love to her with his hands.

When her Swedish rubdown came to an end, she thanked the masseur and tipped him graciously. The curative massage immediately proved itself to Jewels. . . . It worked! She felt great. She had once been skeptical about massage therapy . . . until now. She could now attest to its

power to heal. Jewels went back to the changing room to
change into her clothes. She realized her bathing suit was
wet and decided she'd just throw on her miniskirt and
showcase the top of the two-piece bathing suit.

With her Prada bag in one hand and her shirt in the
other, Jewels stepped out of the spa and walked to
the beach, only a few minutes away. She grabbed her cell
phone to see what time it was, as she had lost track of the
hour thanks to the spa's aromatic treatment.

"Two forty-three," she read, gazing at her cell phone
screen. Then her phone buzzed. Rome flashed across
the screen. Jewels smiled and answered the phone. "Hey,
Rome! What's up, babe?"

"I just got through with this first meeting," he answered,
shaking his head. "The meeting went straight," he assured Jewels. "I'm going to meet with someone else he
wanna plug me with while we out here, and I'll meet you
back at the hotel around four thirty. Sound good?"

"Okay. Be safe," she said, coming up on the beach.

"Always." He smiled through the phone. "Sounds like
you're at the beach. Been anywhere else?" Rome said, trying to make conversation while he had her on the phone.

"The spa," she answered. "I'm thinking I might do some
shopping on the Strip, but we still have tomorrow. It's
only the first day, and I already love Atlantic City!"

"Glad you're having a good time," Rome said with a
smile on his face. He then refocused his attention on his
main objective and the primary reason they were in A.C.
in the first place. "Well, I'll let you get back to the ocean.
See you at the hotel." He honestly didn't want to let her
go and wished that he could be with her, instead of taking
care of business.

"Okay. Bye," Jewels said before hanging up the phone,
feeling the complete opposite of him. She was ready to
get off the phone and was anxious to burn the time until

she saw him.

Jewels spent some time on the beach and in the ocean. Afterward, she grabbed something to eat from a Cuban restaurant on the boardwalk, ordering the food to go because it was nearing the time she was to meet Rome back at the hotel. She wanted to be in the hotel room when Rome arrived.

Jewels opened the door to the suite with her room key and found that Rome hadn't arrived yet. Or so she thought. Then, on the bed, she spotted a blue box with a white ribbon tied around it, adding to its conspicuousness. She tiptoed over to the bed and grabbed the box.

"Tiffany & Company," she read on the box's cover. The bow unraveled with a pull on the ribbon. She popped open the box to find a eighteen-karat white gold watch with a pink face and diamond-encrusted roman numerals.

"Oh my," Jewels said, amazed at the beauty of the watch. She lifted the watch out of the box and dropped the box on the bed. She put the watch on and held her wrist out in front of her. It looked good on her wrist.

Her attention shifted suddenly to the bathroom. There on the sink countertop was a handwritten letter, along with a bouquet of alstroemeria flowers. Rome was already pleasing her, and he wasn't even in the room. She didn't think what she felt was possible. She hurried over to the bouquet and read the note he had left with it.

To My Bonnie . . . From Your Clyde! Ride or Die! See you downstairs . . .

Jewels looked at the time on her new watch and checked her cell phone to make sure the watch was right. It was. She didn't have much time left. She had twenty minutes to take a shower, do her hair and makeup, and find something to wear. She figured it would be best if she ran the shower first and picked out what she was going to wear as her shower water adjusted to her preferred temperature.

The first thing she pulled out of the suitcase was a hot pink Aidan Mattox satin cocktail dress. *This will do*, she said, holding the elegantly modern dress in front of her. She dug back into the contents of the suitcase to find a pair of shoes. She pulled a pair of soft black-leather caged heels out of the pile. She looked up toward the ceiling, mouthed the words "Thank you, Lord," and hugged the shoes.

Jewels felt like a princess. Rome was spoiling her, and she had yet to say yes to being his girlfriend. She inhaled her surroundings and then realized she had Rome waiting for her at the lounge in the lobby of Caesars. She quickly removed her clothes and accessories and took a shower, staying in just long enough to wash off the beach water and freshen up with her sweet-scented Victoria's Secret body wash. She washed her hair, deciding that she'd spritz it again and wear it loosely.

Jewels stepped out of the shower and dried off. She rubbed lotion into her skin and sprayed Michael Kors Very Hollywood perfume on her wrists and also applied the usual dabs behind her ears. She put on the one-shoulder dress, and its satin ruffles dangled at her kneecaps. The heels added four inches to her height, not that she was worried. Even in heels, Rome still had her beat height-wise. She scurried to the mirror to spritz her hair, scrunching a fistful of hair strands at one time. She picked at the hairdo and was finally satisfied with the way it framed her face. She opted not to take a purse with her and instead slipped her California driver's license, lip gloss, and two hundred dollars into the pocket of her strapless bra.

Dressed and anxious to see Rome, Jewels exited the room and took the elevator down to the lounge area. She spotted Rome and walked toward him. He was at the bar, downing a shot of Patrón. Her nerves were all over the place as she made her way to the bar and sat down in the empty chair next to him. They greeted each other with endearing smiles and a peck on the lips.

"You workin' that dress! And them heels . . . look good on you," Rome said, shaking his head as he uttered the last three words.

Jewels smiled timidly and replied, "Why, thank you, Rome. You're looking pretty good yourself. I ought to be thanking you for this outfit, since you brought it. So thank you."

Rome nodded, accepting her thank-you. So far the first outfit he had bought Jewels on his own was to his liking.

"The spa was awesome! I got a mineral bath and a Swedish massage. It was just what I needed . . . relaxation. I am having the time of my life out here. . . . Really, I am, Rome, and I haven't gone anywhere, really. I could stay here an entire weekend and not go anywhere else!" Jewels said excitedly. She was thrilled that it was only day one of the trip, and she had at least one more day to soak up the fun before it was back to St. Louis.

"Now, that's where I shoulda been today," Rome said. But he knew he had to handle business. After all, that was the purpose of the trip.

The second meeting had been equally as good as the first one. However, the leaders were not keen on him getting into the Atlantic City drug scene, being that they were trying to stay afloat with all the other territorial gangs. Rome had sensed that they weren't feeling his ideas, but he wasn't interested in the deal, either, after talking. He had made plans to cancel all the meetings for the next day and to head back to the Lou with Jewels.

If there was no business to attend to, then there was no reason to be there.

"Yeah, you should have. It was wonderful," Jewels said. "I went to the beach, too. You shoulda seen me in my cute little two-piece."

"I know it," Rome smirked. "I bet these East Coast niggas was feelin' it too."

Jewels rolled her eyes. "I don't care who was looking. I care about only one set of eyes," she reminded him. "Well, the beach was beautiful. The water was so clean and clear," she said. "Only thing that would have made it better is if you were there, Rome. Oh, my goodness, you would have been so relaxed!"

Rome smiled, feeling a slight buzz from the shot of tequila. "You ready for dinner?" he said. The grumbling of his stomach had initiated the comment.

"Starving, actually," Jewels answered, remembering the Cuban food was in the room, getting cold. "Where are we going again?"

"Bobby Flay Steak," Rome answered. "Right outside those doors. It's the best steakhouse and the best restaurant in Atlantic City."

"And how would you know?" Jewels said, taking his hand once he stood up. She followed his lead, and they made their way out of the lobby.

"Because only the best is good enough for me, baby," Rome said, scooping her into a hug as they walked to the restaurant, which was minutes away from the hotel.

"I can smell it from here, and, boy, does it smell delicious, whatever it is." Jewels laughed.

Rome opened the door for her and followed her inside the restaurant. They had to wait an agonizing hour before they were seated. Both of them had no doubt that the wait was going to be worth it. Seven o'clock rolled around, and a hostess finally led them to an intimate table on the restaurant's first level. Jewels didn't hesitate to look around at the intricate and elegant design of the restaurant. A chandelier made of handblown glass was the focal point of the room, and a glass-enclosed wine tower stretched from the first level to the second. Once they were seated at their table, they were handed their menus and given a moment to decide what they were going to eat.

"Are you comfortable?" Rome asked, making certain that she felt like a queen.

"Yes, sir," Jewels said, staring down at her menu. "You do know that I've been going to five-star restaurants nearly all my life," she reminded him. She looked up and over at him.

"My bad." Rome chuckled.

Jewels shook her head and returned to the menu. She couldn't decide whether she wanted steak or fish. Whatever she decided to have was going to be devoured as soon as the plate hit the table.

A waiter returned moments later with a pen and a pad in hand, then asked them for their choices off the menu.

"I'll take the Brandt Farms rib eye well done, with the creamed spinach and the baked potato. And a bottle of Cabernet Sauvignon," Rome answered confidently, not concerned in the slightest about the high price. "And she'll have the American Wagyu filet mignon, with the same sides as my plate, and an iced tea, please."

The waiter collected their menus and headed back to the kitchen to give the cooks the new order. He returned momentarily with Rome's wine bottle, two glasses, and Jewels's iced tea. Then he excused himself to take care of the other tables he was serving.

Rome and Jewels conversed while they waited for their entrées. They were so into each other that the thirty-minute wait for their food seemed like only half the time. The waiter returned and decorated the couples' table with two sizzling hot plates, a well-done rib eye on one and a filet mignon on the other. Both were accompanied by creamy green spinach and a fluffy baked potato with butter melting in its split center.

"Thank you," Rome said before the waiter could slip away to check on his other tables.

"Enjoy your meal," the waiter said, then proceeded to the other tables he was waiting on.

Before Rome could ask Jewels if her meal looked appetizing, she was already carving her thick boneless steak. A smile spread across his face, and he took her cue and cut into his seared rib eye.

Not much was said as the couple ate their dinner. Occasionally, they would look up at each other and grin, their way of letting the other know the meal was delectable. The food on Jewels's plate was reduced to half, while Rome managed to finish everything he'd ordered except the bottle of wine. The two made eye contact once their bellies were full and their hearts were full of anticipation for what was to come next.

"I am stuffed," Jewels said, resting her fork on the plate, sure she had had enough to eat. She waved the waiter over to get a to-go box and figured she would put it with the Cuban meal she hadn't gotten a chance to eat.

When the waiter returned with the box, Rome gave him his American Express card without even seeing the bill. The waiter took the card and walked away with a smile.

"Thank you, Rome, for dinner," Jewels said before the waiter returned to the table with Rome's card and a brown bag in which to carry the wine bottle and her to-go box.

The waiter packaged the box and the wine and thanked the couple for dining at Bobby Flay Steak. Rome set two hundred dollars on the table and rose from his seat. He and Jewels left the restaurant hand in hand, leaving the waiter very happy that he had had the honor of serving them.

"So where to now? The room?" Jewels asked with bright eyes.

"I was thinking we take advantage of the Atlantic City nightlife and hit the club later on tonight. What do you say?" Rome asked.

"I say," Jewels began, "we put this food back in our room first. I'm so down to go to the club. That way I can see if you got some real moves or not." She waved her arm in the air rhythmically and giggled at her own actions.

"I got rhythm, and I'm sure that's going to be enough for me to keep up with you," Rome said, ready to groove with her on a dance floor.

"Well, that's all you need!"

Rome and Jewels walked back into the hotel lobby. They took the elevator to the highest level of the hotel building and walked down the hall toward their room. Rome slid his card key into the door and opened it for Jewels, allowing her to enter the room first. She set her box of leftover filet mignon on the bed, next to her untouched food from earlier.

"You left the room quite a mess." Rome laughed as he looked around at her clothes, which were scattered across the foot of the bed and the floor.

Jewels hastily began to straighten up the suite and replied, "I'm sorry, Rome. I got in around four thirty and had little time to meet you downstairs. By the way, thank you for the . . ." She struggled to get the name of the flowers out.

"The al-stroe-meri-as," Rome said, sounding it out
for her. "You're welcome, babe." He unfastened the top
button of his gray Giorgio Armani dress shirt and sat
on the edge of the bed. He grabbed the remote off of the
nightstand and pointed it toward the TV.

"Yeah, they are beautiful," Jewels said, running her
fingertips over the flowers' soft petals. She then noticed
her new watch shining on her wrist. "And the watch!
Thank you for that too! You shouldn't spoil me so much."

"And why is that?" Rome asked, flipping through the
channels until he found the highlights from the basketball games he'd missed.

"Because it only makes me want you more," replied
Jewels. She went into the bathroom.

"Last I recalled, that wasn't a bad thing," was Rome's
reply.

Jewels waited until she had washed her hands and was
out of the bathroom to respond. "It's not a bad thing . . .
for you. But for me . . . It's . . . just that . . . I don't want
to be let down in the end. Then I'm left to suffer from the
misery of whether to throw away your gifts or not. And,
baby, let me tell you, I don't want to get rid of this watch
if we ever have a fallout."

Rome grinned at her response. "I wouldn't want you to.
At least it'll be something to remind you of me," he said,
half grinning.

Jewels threw her hands up and said, "Wait a minute.
Look at us! What are we talking like this for? You haven't
done anything that would make me want to avoid you.
You've been the perfect gentleman, the perfect man. I'm
really glad I made the decision I did."

Rome knew that her many thank-yous were sincere
and that Jewels's feelings for him had deepened since
they'd arrived in Atlantic City. He still had surprises

to come for Jewels. He eyed the alarm clock and noted the time. They had thirty minutes until the club doors opened.

Rome grabbed the half blunt from off the nightstand and felt the pockets of his Armani Exchange jeans for a lighter. Armed with the blunt and a light, he moved to the balcony overlooking the ocean, which was glistening from the shine of a glowing full moon. Jewels slid the balcony doors open farther and joined him.

"Pretty, isn't it?" Jewels asked. A memory of watching the sunset from the Pacific Coast Highway with Rome came into her thoughts, putting a smile on her face.

"What are you smiling about?" Rome said after blowing smoke in the direction opposite her.

"Just thinking about how I've seen some of the most beautiful scenes with you. Remember when we watched the sunset back home?" she said, folding her arms and rubbing her elbows as a breeze blew by.

"I do remember," Rome answered.

Jewels's bright eyes sparkled, and her dimple showcased her smile. "Good. I'm glad you do," she said. Her tone was firm, indicating she was serious, despite the fact that she was having a great time with him in Atlantic City.

Rome nodded his head, letting that be the end of their conversation. He finished off the blunt and placed it in the ashtray on the balcony table. "I think we can head down to the club now. They're probably just opening up."

Before they left the suite, Rome changed out of his dressy shirt into a more comfortable one. He and Jewels took the elevator back down to the now familiar lobby of Caesars, but not before stopping on six other floors for other hotel guests opting to take the elevator.

Sure enough, thumping music could be heard the moment Rome and Jewels neared the club's entrance. It was located on the lobby floor. Jewels noticed it had a mod-

ern yet plush design and attracted musical artists and celebrities from every corner of the entertainment world.
There was no telling who they'd see inside the club. They
were escorted to the VIP table Rome had reserved for
them earlier, while waiting for Jewels. The booming
music made Jewels want to dance. Rome poured her a
shot of Patrón and watched her toss it to the back of her
throat. Her face twisted from the sting of the alcohol and
then transitioned into a relaxed smile, which let him
know she was ready to party.

For the first forty-five minutes they relaxed in their
VIP section, canoodling and watching more and more
guests enter the club. Jewels took note of how Rome
shook hands, owing to the celebrities housed in the VIP
booths next to them. What was his affiliation with them?
she wondered. She wouldn't dare ask and continued to
sit pretty by his side.

The DJ catered to every kind of person's musical needs,
spinning hip-hop tracks into house music, bumping the
best pop dance hits, and throwing a rock song in every
now and then. As the night progressed, so did the couple.
Rome and Jewels made their way onto the dance floor.
Surrounded by many people, the couple felt as if they
were the only two in the room as they rocked to whatever
it was the DJ was spinning.

The vibration of his phone, which hadn't buzzed for
the past five hours, stopped Rome from dancing. "Wait a
second, baby. Let me take care of this."

Rome quietly walked toward the restroom area, where
the music wasn't so loud. He had to answer the call
because it was from his peoples who were responsible for
them being in A.C. "Hold up. I'm in the club!" he shouted
into the receiver, then walked into the restroom

Rome listened to the other caller for a minute before
saying, "Yeah. Thanks again. I'll be in touch." He ended

the call, then hurried back to Jewels on the dance floor.

For the next few hours, they popped bottles, danced, and enjoyed their night in Atlantic City. They didn't leave the club until the early morning hours. Once they were back in the hotel suite, they gathered their belongings and packed their bags. Then ordered a quick breakfast from room service, and some hours later, they were back in St. Louis.

Chapter Thirty

A few weeks later . . .

Jewels broke into a fighting stance. She was startled and had been caught off guard by the unexpected guest.

"Boy!" She walked over to Rome and punched him in the chest. "You scared the hell out of me!" she exclaimed.

Rome chuckled. He had made his way into the bedroom and had closed the door quietly behind him. He could hear the faucet handles turning as Jewels shut the shower water off when he had first entered the bedroom. He had sat down in the chair at the desk and waited. Then, upon hearing the door open, he had turned his attention toward the bathroom. Jewels had stepped out in a see-through robe. She'd still been dripping beads of water. She'd gasped loudly when she saw Rome sitting in the chair. Then she'd assumed that fighting stance.

"Um, what are you doing in here?" she asked now, trying to hide her smile.

"I just got back in town about an hour and a half ago," he answered, taking the towel off with his eyes.

Jewels clung a little tighter to the towel. "No. What are you doing *here*? I haven't heard from you in days. Days have passed without a word. Now you just show up, like it's all good." She grabbed her clothes off the door hook with one snatch and found refuge in the bathroom.

As she dressed, she calmed her raging nerves and gathered her emotions. Once her clothes were on, she unlocked the door and stepped out, a lot more comfortable now that she was dressed. Rome was still in the same spot but was now on his cell phone. Jewels wasn't surprised.

"What are you doing? Finding out where you have to be in another hour?" she asked sarcastically. She rolled her eyes once she lost his gaze.

"We have to be downtown," he answered, putting the phone in his pocket. "In another hour. We have dinner reservations." A slick grin followed.

Jewels stared at him wildly, her head tilted in disbelief. "Rome, what makes you think you can just come in here and expect me to leave with you? You haven't acknowledged the fact that you didn't call me *at all* when you were in Jersey or New York. Did you get my messages? And I know you didn't go back to Atlantic City without me, did you?" Jewels said, rambling.

Rome stared at her for a moment, absorbing how beautiful she was and how she was finally his. Whatever she was saying, he was clueless. His attention was focused on her body. He loved the fact that she could turn him on inside and outside the bedroom. Ever since she had proven herself with the connect caper, he'd been hooked. All he had ever wanted was a Bonnie to match the Clyde in him. He had found that person in Jewels. They had been rocking for months, and he had come to appreciate everything about her. Ever since he and Red had been seeing major paper, he and Jewels had grown closer. She had become his partner in crime and his ride or die.

Jewels turned around to face Rome. "I guess I'm stuck with you." She frowned, and then her expression transitioned into a bright smile, which showcased those darling dimples.

After going into the bedroom and retrieving her purse, she returned to the living room. Rome grabbed her hand and led her out the door without saying a word. Jewels followed, although she pretended to resist a little.

"You know you sexy, right?" Rome said, though it was more a statement than a question, once they were in the truck.

"Oh, stop it, Rome. You're just saying that because you know I'm supposed to be mad." She folded her arms and pushed her lips into a pout.

Rome grabbed her chin with his index finger and thumb and turned her face toward his. "That's my word on everything. I missed you, but you and I both know how things gotta be like this sometimes. I rather be safe than sorry," he said. Then, without asking, he leaned in and kissed her.

Jewels fell into the kiss. Her hands rubbed the top of his head and lowered to his neck. She pulled away after realizing she was becoming moist between her legs. She inhaled and exhaled.

"To Italian?" Rome asked, speaking with an Italian accent.

"Yes, please." Jewels lit up. "You must have remembered I'm a fan of Italian food from our first real date at your house."

"Or maybe I like Italian food," Rome said with an "all teeth showing" smile.

A short while later, they arrived at the downtown St. Louis restaurant and were immediately seated at a quiet table. After the two of them had finished their meals and enjoyed an intimate conversation, Rome called for the check.

"You ready?" Rome asked as he penned his signature on the bill, then rose from the table.

Jewels nodded, and they left the restaurant. Once they were back on the road, Rome headed northwest of the city.

"Wassup with some sex by the lake?" Rome asked, with a huge grin across his face, as he pulled into the parking area that led to the water.

Jewels rolled her eyes. Then she drew her attention to what was in front of her. She became excited as she looked dreamily at the lake, completely ignoring Rome's question. Rome parked the car just in time to catch the sunset beyond the horizon.

"Look at the sun setting," Jewels said. She watched the sun until it disappeared, reminding her of when they had first seen a sunset together.

"Isn't it beautiful?" Jewels asked.

Rome admired her as she stared in wonder, as if she had never seen a sunset before. Their eyes met. "Definitely," Rome said, peering past Jewels to check out the scene. "Is this your first time watching the sun set?"

"I think so," Jewels said, surprised. "I'm guessing this is something you've done before."

"Yeah. A few times," he answered with a grin. "I'm glad you got to see a sunset."

Jewels rolled her eyes and hung her head. "Don't say it like that. I don't care about no other bitches you brought here," she said with attitude.

Rome wrapped his arms around her and replied, "Didn't mean it like that." He was silent for a moment. "My mom used to bring me to watch this shit," he began. "I used to hate coming here as a kid. Thought it was boring and corny. But when I got older and she died, this became the place I came to by myself to clear my head."

Jewels peered over at Rome. He never ceased to amaze her. As he spoke, she realized that there were still layers to him that she had yet to peel back, despite all the

months she had known him. She knew he had lost his
mother, and she knew how he had been raised. As far as
she was concerned, he was as strong as they came. *Shit.
He has to be,* she thought, reflecting on how their lives
had come together. He had ultimately made her want
to walk away from the only life she knew. She knew it
took a strong and secure man to accept her past without
judgment.

She had never thought she'd find herself so drawn and
attracted to a street dude—and that was who he was, a
street dude—but here she was. Jewels couldn't see herself with anyone other than Rome. She just adored him,
everything about him. There was a strong magnetic pull
about him. She had felt the same force at his home on
their second date. It was wonderful to feel it again. Rome
somehow felt what she was thinking and felt the love.

Rome was thinking about Jewels at the same time she
was thinking about him. He thought back to when he
made the decision to continue their relationship.

*"So, you wanna head back to my place and watch that
movie?"*

*He grabbed Jewels's hand with his. He didn't mind
controlling the steering wheel with one hand as he navigated through the South Side as long as he could hold
her hand with the other. This increased the butterflies
Jewels already had in her stomach.*

*Instinctively, for some women, there was always
the thought that their man had something else going
on, like someone on the side. Jewels never gave the
impression that she had those concerns. She was at
ease with him, finally. He felt he could jump right into
a relationship and trust her wholeheartedly.*

*He remained quiet and in deep thought on the way
back to his house, and it seemed that Jewels was doing
the same. He sped up the hill and into his cul-de-sac. He
pulled the Range Rover into the driveway.*

He led her inside the house and helped her get comfortable by taking her coat and giving her permission to take off her shoes. Then he said, "Follow me."

Jewels didn't say a word. Instead, she followed him up the stairs, down the hall, and into his bedroom.

After Rome guided her to his bedroom, he had her sit on the bed, and then he disappeared into the bathroom. He came out with five candles and a lighter. He set the five candles on top of his dresser. He lit them one by one, then turned off the lights in his room. Rome pressed on the remote near his dresser. He didn't know that the song he chose was by Jewels's favorite male R & B group, and that, coincidentally, it was one of her favorite songs. He stood, now shirtless, by the radio with the remote in his hand.

"What's going on?" she asked.

Rome grooved toward her. With each step he took, Jewels became more and more beautiful. He placed his finger over her lips and grabbed her hands to lift her from the bed. She followed his movements. He wrapped his hands around her hips and locked his fingers together so that she could not pull away from him. She responded by throwing her hands around his neck, turned on by the fact that he wanted to slow dance in the middle of his room. They swayed back and forth silently and let their eyes do all the talking.

Jewels laid her head on his bare chest and stared down at his abs. Her breath was warm on his chest, and her hands ran down his back. Just as the music changed to the next track, she kissed his chest. "I can't believe we're here," she cooed in a low whisper.

"We are, though," Rome responded softly. He wrapped her in his arms. Without asking, all in one motion, he unfastened Jewels's jeans and began lowering them.

Rome wanted to feel his full lips kissing every part of her body, including her thighs, as they made love. It amazed him that he was moments away from having that desire fulfilled. It caused his heart to beat faster. He had never wanted to kiss any female the way he wanted to kiss Jewels.

"I don't know why you always make me feel like a schoolgirl with butterflies and shit," she cooed, running her hand along the side of his face. Her fingers outlined the shape of his lips as she examined the passionate look on his face. "I'm nervous," she admitted.

Rome smiled. He ran his hands along the curves of her legs until they were resting on her arms. "Nothin' to worry about. I got you."

Jewels answered by avoiding his eyes.

Rome ran his fingers through her hair.

Jewels nodded silently. Then their eyes met again. She was lost in them; every emotion in her body was being released. His smoldering look was overwhelming her.

"Don't hold back," he warned, then swept her off her feet and laid her on the bed. He went in for the kill and kissed her strongly.

Their kiss led to hands touching every part of the other. They stripped each other of their remaining clothes, both ready for what was going to take place in the next moments.

Jewels felt good, surprisingly, as she prepared herself to give Rome the very thing he wanted and to receive what her body had been craving since the first day they met. She was glad that she had let the intensity build up.

Rome let her sweet scent be his guide as he traveled down to the moist center between her legs. He gently kissed her inner thighs until he was face-to-face with her prized possession. He ran his tongue across her *more sensitive area, causing her legs to quiver. A sensual gasp escaped from her mouth, turning Rome on. He gripped her thighs as he continued to taste her. His tongue explored her sex, while his lips sucked on her clit.*

"Oooh," Jewels moaned. She tried to push his head out from between her legs, but he wouldn't budge. Her legs shook uncontrollably when she felt her first orgasm, a sensation she had not felt in a long time. "Aaah-weee."

Rome pulled away from her and licked his lips. Round two. He grabbed his now rock-hard dick, ready to take Jewels's body to the next level. He opened her legs wider.

"No. Wait!" She stopped him.

Rome had a confused look on his face.

"Where's your condom?" she asked.

Rome smiled. He had not intended to use one tonight. He had yet to feel himself inside of Jewels raw, but he respected Jewels for being the responsible party. He leaned over to the nightstand, opened the drawer, and pulled out one of the Magnums. He stared at her as he slid it on. She flashed half a smile.

Rome leaned down and kissed her as he placed his hand between Jewels's legs. He massaged her clit with two fingers while slipping one inside of her. His manhood stiffened even more. He knew she was ready, and so was he.

Jewels's body tensed up when Rome entered her.

"Please, Rome. Go slow. Go slow," she whispered in his ear. "I'm still sore," she said, reminding him of their last sexual encounter. No matter how much they did it, it always felt like the first time for Jewels.

"I got you," he replied.

He paused just to absorb the moment. She felt incredible. She was in a place he never wanted to leave. He wanted to make it pleasurable for her and worth it. He wanted Jewels to know that she wasn't a quick

*bang that he had been waiting to score. She was his
future, and so he would sex her as such. She had been
honest with him about the depth and extent of her lifestyle, and he had accepted that. He was not into giving
oral, but there was no doubt he enjoyed the taste
of her in his mouth and had made Jewels the exception. She was different, and he wanted her to know that.*

*He slowly slipped deeper inside her wet center.
Tender from her tight hole being reopened, Jewels bit
her bottom lip and took the pain . . . and the pleasure
that followed.*

*"You good?" he asked her as he continued his slow
grind.*

*"Yes," she moaned, in ecstasy, her nails clawing his
back.*

*It turned him on so much that with each light scratch
to his back, he thrust harder inside her. Jewels's legs
quivered with the onset of a second orgasm. She let out
a loud moan and let her juices ooze onto Rome. Even
through the condom, Rome could feel her sex muscles
contracting. Unable to hold on any longer, Rome pulled
out, snatched the condom off, and released himself on
her inner thighs. She watched, breathing heavily, as
his cream spilled onto her legs. She reached out for him,
grabbed hold of his dick, and began stroking it, to be
sure that every ounce of his juices was released. Rome
tried to resist. His dick was still sensitive, and her touch
was weakening him. His body collapsed on top of hers.
He was also winded. Jewels cuddled him in her arms
and planted a kiss on his forehead.*

"Thank you," she whispered.

*"Thank you back." Rome kissed her on her forehead
and then found the strength to get up and go into the
bathroom to grab them each a wet towel. "I needed that.*

All that grindin' had me horny," he told her from inside
the bathroom. He returned to the bed and wiped his
juices off Jewels's legs and her own from between her
legs. With the other towel, he wiped himself clean. Then
he returned the two towels to the bathroom.

"Do you want to shower?" he asked her as he stood in
the bathroom doorway.

When he didn't hear a response, he looked into the
bedroom to see why. The sight of her resting on his bed
brought a smile to his face. She looks at peace, like an
angel, *thought Rome. So much so that he decided to skip*
the shower and join her to get a piece of her heaven.

The good feelings he had had back then made his manhood rise and brought him back to the present. He spun
Jewels around and kissed her passionately as the waves
broke against the shore. He was in a place that he didn't
want to leave, and it seemed that Jewels felt the same
way. At this point he wouldn't lose her to or for anyone.

Chapter Thirty-one

The end of the weekend . . .

Rome walked through the doorway of the local barbershop on the side of town where he was from. Ever since he and Jewels had gotten together, and he and Red had been getting more paper than they ever had before, he had minimized his trips to the hood. But when it came to getting piped out, there was no other place he could see himself going. This was a popular spot to get a cut, a shape-up, a shave, and whatever else kept a man looking on point.

He shook hands and nodded as everybody in the shop greeted him.

"Yo, how many you got?" he asked his barber.

The old head barber put up two fingers.

Rome scanned the room for familiar faces. Everybody knew who he was, but he had recognized only a few of them. "Who goes next?" he asked, referring to the person who stood in the way of him being a top priority.

A man who had a young boy sitting next to him spoke up. "Me and my li'l man," he answered, pointing to his son.

"That's wassup." Rome nodded. He reached into his pocket and pulled out a wad of money. "How about I treat you and your son to lunch or something while I get a cut? Kinda in a hurry," he offered.

The man looked at the hundred-dollar bill, those in the room, and then up at Rome. "We straight, br—" He was just about to decline kindly when his son nudged him. Anyone within earshot could hear what the boy said to his dad, despite him trying to whisper.

Rome went back into his pocket and pulled out another hundred-dollar bill. He had heard the son say that his father could now afford to get him the new Jordans he had been wanting, seeing as though Rome was offering the exact amount that the man was short.

The father looked at his son, then back at Rome, who now had two crisp hundred-dollar bills in his hand. Everybody stared in envy as the man struggled with his decision.

Rome fought back his smile when the man leaned forward and reached for the money.

"You got it, my man," the father said. He dropped his head and grabbed the bills. He had an idea where the money had come from. It was no secret who Rome was. The last thing he wanted was to make it appear to his son that he was condoning what Rome stood for or represented. Still, he knew how long it would take for him to make the kind of money Rome was offering, and his son really deserved the name-brand sneakers he had been asking for, for weeks now. The fact that his son had maintained his spot on the honor roll and was a good kid appealed to the man's paternal side.

"Come on, son." He stood.

Everyone in the barbershop watched as the man and his son headed for the door.

The little boy turned and said to Rome, "Thanks, mister."

"No problem, li'l man. Stay in school," Rome said in a booming voice. Just then his phone rang. When he pulled it from his hip clip, he shook his head and smiled.

"I'll be right back. Don't give my spot away. I paid good money for that seat," Rome joked to the others in the barbershop.

He made a beeline toward the door, following right behind the man and his son. When he stepped outside, he saw the Bentley GT parked illegally across the street with its hazard lights flashing. He jogged across the street to Jewels's car, looking both ways as he went. She loved seeing him and his dimples.

"Hey, cutie," he greeted.

"Hey, handsome." She blushed.

He hopped into her car to get out of the way of a bus that was quickly approaching. They exchanged kisses.

"So wassup? What brings you to the hood?" he joked.

"Whatever." Jewels rolled her eyes. "You said you were meeting Red here, so I figured you'd be here," she said, then continued, "Just wanted to see your face since you were gone when I woke up."

Rome let out a light chuckle. "You know I be out early," he said in his own defense.

"Uh-huh," she replied.

Rome smiled. "But, yeah, Red slow ass ain't even get here yet." He checked his watch. "I just paid two hundred so I can get in and out," he told her.

"Okay. I'm on my way to get my hair done, and then I'm heading to the Cheesecake Factory. You wanna meet me there?" she said.

"Nah. I can't." He grimaced. "Got too much to do. That's why I'm trying to be in and out of here." He paused, then dug into his pocket, pulled five hundred dollars, and passed it to her. "But this should take care of your hair and everything else you get done today. Stuff like that you shouldn't have to pay for."

Jewels presented the palm of her hand to accept the money. She wasn't about to tell him "No thank you." "I'll see you tonight." She winked.

Rome leaned over and gave her one last kiss. "Yup," he said, and then he bailed out of the luxury car.

He watched and shook his head as Jewels peeled out, doing at least sixty, with the hazards still on. He had just pulled his phone out to tell her to turn them off when they abruptly shut off, right before she vanished up the street. Rome made his way back into the barbershop.

"Oh, hell, naw!" he exclaimed. "Get yo' ass up outta that seat!" he barked.

Everybody was stone-faced and quiet. Everybody except for Red. He was doubled over in the barber's chair, with the barber's smock around his neck.

"Go 'head, bruh. You next," Red stated.

"Nah, nigga. I'm now." Rome had already walked over to the chair and had begun unsnapping the smock around Red's neck. He then channeled his energy at the barber. "I paid a lot of money for this spot. How you gonna let this fool come in and jump me?"

The barber shrugged his shoulders and threw his hands up. "Come on, Rome. Don't put me in the middle of this shit," the barber said.

Red chuckled. "Nigga, you jumped the dude and his li'l man." He could see Rome was surprised he knew. "Yeah, I heard how you was in here on some ole Deebo shit," Red joked.

Rome let out a light chuckle. "Fuck all of that. Get yo' ass up 'fore I be your new barber."

The threat was enough for Red to hop out of the chair. The entire barbershop broke into laughter at the scene between the two friends.

When Red got up, his body was replaced with Rome's. "Now, if you want next, you need to break somebody off so you can get in and get out like me. Besides, I ain't got all day to be waiting on you. From here I'm out," Rome told Red.

"I'm good. Can't roll, anyway. Something came up. Gotta handle something else. We'll talk about it later," Red shot back.

"Bet."

The barber put the smock around Rome's neck and spun Rome around. "What we doing with you today?" the barber then asked.

"Just pipe me out," Rome said, looking from side to side. "My joint lookin' type rough."

"Got you." The barber laughed.

Thirty-five minutes later, Rome was staring at a new man in the mirror. "Word." He admired his fresh new cut. "This what I'm talking about."

Seeing that he was pleased, the barber poured alcohol on some of the paper he used to put around customers' necks and wiped Rome's hairline and the back of his neck. Rome flinched from the burning sensation. He closed his eyes while his barber sprayed sheen on his head and brushed it. Once the barber was done, Rome stood and let him brush the hair residue off his back.

"This pretty-ass nigga," Red teased.

He was met with a middle finger through the mirror as Rome brushed off the front of himself. Rome then pulled his money back out and handed the barber a hundred-dollar bill.

"Man, ain't nobody ballin'," the barber complained. "I can't break this. You ain't got nothing smaller?" he then said.

Rome laughed. "Nah, yo. Just keep it. I'ma pay for this joker cut, and the rest you can just pocket."

The barber's face lit up. "Sounds like a good deal to me."

Rome walked over to where Red sat. "Nigga, lift the fuck up. You sittin' on my hat."

Red chuckled. "Oh, that's what that was."

Rome joined him in the laughter.

"Yo, let me holla at you right quick outside," Red requested.

Rome popped out the dent Red had made in his hat and smacked it on his head, tilting it to the side. "A'ight, everybody," Rome called, saying his good-byes, and made his way toward the exit.

Red followed. When they reached the door, the man and his son were coming in. Rome nodded at the father, who did the same in return, only now he seemed to be in better spirits. Rome happened to look over and down at his son. Rome was sure the brand-new 12s the kid had on was the reason for the father's mood change.

"Remember what I said, li'l man. Stay in school." Rome patted the boy on the head before stepping out of the barbershop.

"Oh, that was ole boy you gave the bread to?" Red asked once they were outside.

"Yeah," Rome confirmed. "But, yo, what's good? What you gotta do that's so important you can't ride out with me?" Rome wanted to know.

"Damn, nigga!" Red laughed. "Impatient-ass nigga."

"Fuck all of that," Rome shot back. "What's up?" He was not in the mood to be joking. He and Red had planned to shoot out to Detroit to meet with some dudes who were interested in copping big. Red always had his back whenever they were breaking ground with new buyers.

Red shook his head and took a deep breath. "Remember that li'l nigga we pushed over baby girl?" he asked.

"Baby girl? Jewels?"

Red let out a laugh. "Yeah, nigga. How many shorties you killed a nigga over and for?"

"True." Rome chuckled. "Who you talkin' about? That nigga Los?"

"Yeah," Red confirmed.

"What about him? I know his ass ain't come back from the dead," he joked.

"Nah, but I hear his man that we never tracked down resurfaced and been inquiring about us."

"Word?" It was news to Rome's ears.

"Word!" Red backed him up. "But I'm on top of it," he assured his partner. "Trying to have this shit over and done with before the week out."

Rome nodded in agreement. "No question. Do that. I can handle that shit in the D."

"I'm on it, and I know you can."

"Absolutely."

They embraced each other.

"Love you, my G." Red saluted his partner.

"Love you too, my boy." Rome returned his salute, then made his way across to the street to his truck.

Chapter Thirty-two

Later that day . . .

On the other side of town, Jewels took her time exiting her car to enter the upscale penthouse she and Rome now shared on the outskirts of the city. She was getting used to driving and not having a driver, but she still hadn't gotten used to carrying all the bags she normally returned home with from her daily shopping sprees. That was why she liked when Rome went with her: it felt like she was being chauffeured around and she had her own personal bag carrier. Jewels smiled at the thought. Aside from that, she was in a zone. She sat behind the wheel, vibin' out to the latest Nicki Minaj CD. She let her head fall back against the headrest and listened to one of her favorite tracks playing on the car's system. She closed her eyes in a desperate attempt to relax her mind after making it through yet another stressful day.

The life she was living was one a woman always dreamt of as a young girl. She was living what they called the American hustler's dream. She had been managing all the properties she had set up for her and Rome's company, which was becoming more than a headache. She also washed the money he pulled in from the streets. He had made her his partner, and she in return made sure they were able to live the way they had both grown accustomed to in recent months. Rome and Red were growing stronger and stronger not only in St. Louis, but out in Indiana, Michigan, Illinois, New Jersey, and New York, as well, thanks to the plugs her mother had mailed to her before she died from pneumonia.

Jewels had rearranged her entire life since the night she conspired to kill Kareem with Rome. She had known that if she was going to be a part of his life, there were much-needed changes to be made. It was either continue on with the life of independence she had created for herself or give up mostly everything she had ever known to partner and be with him, including the hustle she had grown to love. Knowing that some of the benefits of becoming his woman were that he would never leave her wanting for or needing anything, she had chosen the latter. And in return, she was pushing a brand-new Bentley GT, lived lavishly in a three-thousand-square-foot condo overlooking the river, owned a hell of a wardrobe, and had access to more money than she could handle. *Who could be mad at that?* Jewels thought.

The song ended. Jewels killed her engine, snatched up her pocketbook from out of the passenger's seat, then opened her car door. She hit the button on her car alarm to pop her trunk. She sighed, then chuckled at the two dozen bags filled with shoes, dresses, and handbags in nearly every size, jewelry, and a few things for Rome.

You bought the shit. Now carry it, she told herself, trying to psyche herself up. "Fuck that!" she cursed aloud. She snatched up four of the twenty-four bags and slammed the trunk shut. *Rome can get the rest of this stuff*. She smiled.

Jewels activated her car alarm and made her way over to the garage elevator. As she sashayed through the garage, all of a sudden, an eerie feeling overcame her. Her eyes opened wide as she leaned forward quickly and scanned the area twice. Nothing looked out of place or out of the ordinary. Rome had schooled her on the importance of being aware of her surroundings at all times. He had her watching everything and everybody, and for good reason. With the type of money they were getting and the status he and Red had in the streets, somebody was always looking for a come up or was trying to come for the top spot. Jewels's eyes stopped and locked on a man and a woman heading in the same direction that she was, toward the elevator. They were all over one another.

"Get a room," she smirked, not intending for them to hear her. With her heels clicking rapidly against the concrete, she scanned the area a third time while heading for the elevator.

This was not the first time she had felt like someone was watching her. It had been a few months since everything had transpired, and Jewels had yet to find peace within. She had battled with herself as she wondered over and over if she'd made the right decision, but with Rome riding with her every step of the way, all her doubts had been put to rest.

Jewels searched through the clutter in her pocketbook, anxious to find her ringing cell phone. After reading the caller ID, she smiled and answered, "Hey, babe."

"Hey, love. I just left the restaurant. I'll be home shortly, all right?" said Rome.

She sighed. "I knew you weren't home yet," she whined. "What's taking you so long?"

"I was tryin'a beat you there, but something came up, so I'll be there in a few."

Jewels gave him attitude. "Whatever—"

"I ain't got time for all that, Jewels," he interrupted. "I'll see you as soon as I finish . . . up here. . . . Try . . . to wait up for—"

The phone reception began to fade in and out now that she had stepped on the elevator. She looked down at the screen, which now read call failed. Just before the elevator doors closed, she looked up and locked eyes with a man standing in the shadows among dozens of parked cars in the middle of the garage. For some reason, he seemed so familiar, but she knew she hadn't seen him anywhere before. Every nerve in her body tensed up as she watched him walk toward the elevator. The closer he got, the more anxious she became. As if on cue, the doors slammed shut just before the man had a chance to step into the light.

Jewels pounded every button on the control panel in an attempt to get the elevator doors back open, but instead the elevator ascended. She fell backward, allowing her body to rest against the wall, as her heart beat well above the normal rate. She was already strategizing her defense in her mind if he tried to attack her.

The elevator chimed when the doors opened on the second level. There were a few people waiting, and they took their time getting on. Jewels would have dragged them on quicker if she could have. The ride back down to the garage level was agonizing. The strangers beside her stared as she pushed the G button repeatedly, like it was going to get her there faster. When the elevator finally reached the ground floor, Jewels rushed out ahead of them. Her head rotated back and forth several times in an attempt to capture every angle of the lot, but the figure who had been there just minutes ago was no longer there.

Am I losing my damn mind?

"Are you okay?" asked a stranger who had walked up.

Jewels nodded her head yes.

"Are you getting on?"

Jewels ignored the woman's question and stepped onto the elevator. "Shit!" she cursed as she placed her arm in between the elevator doors. She had realized she had left her leftovers in the car. The last thing she wanted was to come out the next day to a whip smelling of salmon.

She rapidly got off the elevator and turned around. Standing in the same position she had assumed just moments ago, she looked out into the garage without thinking, blinking, or swallowing, only this time there wasn't anyone staring back at her. She contemplated leaving her bags propped up by the elevator while she ran back over to the car to retrieve the to-go box on her backseat. She decided against it, though. *Just my luck, some thirsty-ass white bitch or one of those flaming gay guys steal my shit*, she thought.

She headed back toward her vehicle. She hit the alarm button. Her lights, horn, and locks sang in unison as she approached the car. Jewels grabbed the door handle with her bags in hand, then sat them down. She didn't bother to pull the driver's seat back this time. Instead, she leaned in and over to grab the brown Cheesecake Factory paper bag. The sound of tearing could be heard as the side of her shirt got caught on the lever to lift the seat up.

"Damn it!" she swore when she saw the tear.

That's what the fuck you get for being lazy, she told herself as she backed out of her car with her food in hand. She shook her head at the mishap of the three-hundred-dollar blouse. She knew she would be going back to the store first thing in the morning to replace it. It was actually the last thought that crossed her mind right before darkness fell upon her.

Chapter Thirty-three

It was just approaching six in the evening, and the streets were alive and on full throttle. Hustlers and dope fiends filled the sidewalks in front of every open Chinese restaurant. Sisters and brothers, mothers and friends occupied their doorsteps, gossiping late into the night.

Watching the street through his rearview mirror as he cruised through his city was a habit of Rome's. He whipped his new Audi A7 as the human traffic flowed. It was back to business for him. For months, things had been smooth sailing. It had taken a lot, but he and Red had managed to tie up all loose ends, he believed, and he couldn't have been more relieved. All the talk about the murders he had been linked to, from Mike-G and Los down to Africa, had fizzled out, and the streets had moved on to the latest. Rome's name was in the streets now only because of the strong choke hold he and Red had on the streets.

Rome had never realized just how much he did in the mean streets of the Lou, but at that moment he was glad he did. He was also glad that he had followed his gut instincts and had kept Jewels in the picture. She had proven to be valuable and had become a major asset in more ways than one. It was because of her that he and Red were operating at full throttle and with an iron fist. He and Red had eliminated the competition and had the only coke around. They had nearly doubled the number of bricks of coke they had robbed both Los and Kareem

for. It was also because of Jewels, and her mother, that
Rome had gotten a new and stronger plug on the East
Coast out in New Jersey. He had grown to appreciate
what she actually brought to the table. Never in a million
years would he have believed it if somebody had said he
would end up with the type of woman who had Jewels's
past.

Before he'd met her, he would've sent anybody to
their Maker for implying that he was a trick or anything
of the sort. But these past few months, he had gotten
to know Jewels for who she was, and now he couldn't
imagine life without her. Especially after she had given
it all up for him. Rome couldn't help but smile. Jewels
words sang in his head. *I'll never let another man touch
me other than you, not for money and not for free.*
Since then that was what it had been.

His eyes suddenly caught some movement, bringing
him back to the present. He peered back into his rearview. It was one thing for the same car to turn down
two or three of the same blocks. But when the same car
turned down six or seven, that was suspicious. Rome
concluded that he had seen the BMW 745i one too many
times. *Who the fuck is this following me*? He turned
down a couple of random blocks, just to make sure he
wasn't being paranoid. The car tailed him like metal to a
magnet. *What the fuck's going on wit' this shit?*

The navy BMW 745i stayed as far back as possible
without losing sight of Rome, but it wasn't far enough.
Rome used the short time he spent at the next red light
to grab his Desert Eagle from the backseat and his nine
from the passenger's seat. He turned his radio off and
stuffed his cell phone into his pocket. *It ain't my time,
mutherfucka. It ain't my time.*

Rome focused on the small groups of people lingering
around. He was looking for a place to pull over, some-

where where there wouldn't be so many witnesses. That opportunity came about five more blocks down. He pulled over to the side, acting like he was about to park.

When Rome's taillights turned red, he could hear the engine of the unknown car and the car's screeching tires at a close distance. His adrenaline began to pump. The car came to an abrupt stop at the corner, across from where Rome had stopped. Then out jumped three gunmen. They each wasted no time emptying their whole clips before they realized that Rome was no longer in the driver's seat. Without their knowledge, Rome had slid out the passenger's side, but not before taking a bullet in the thigh.

Eyewitnesses scattered, not wanting to get caught up in the gunfire. Some ran, while others squatted as low to the ground as they could get until the battle was over. Bullets ripped through glass, storefronts, house windows, brick walls, stop signs, and flesh. Sparks flew everywhere.

Rome's Audi absorbed most of the rapid fire. He didn't let off a single shot until he saw the perfect opportunity. One of the gunmen made the mistake of stepping around to the front of the car. Rome, from the ground, put his Desert Eagle to work. The man had no chance. His life ended with several shots hitting every part of his body. He had lost his life before his body crumpled to the ground.

Rome, in pain, let off four more shots in the direction of the remaining shooters as a diversion to buy him time. The men took cover behind the doors of the BMW. That was all the time he needed. He limped to the nearest alley, escaping just seconds before the first cop car hit the scene. Bruised from the shattered glass and injured from the bullet, he didn't make it too far. He climbed a fence and hid in someone's backyard until the coast was clear. Once in a secure spot, Rome waited for a few minutes, then scurried out from behind the backyard. He got himself together before he stepped out and blended in with the light body traffic. His thigh was killing him, but he knew he had to fight the pain and keep his composure to avoid drawing any unwanted attention. He pulled out his cell phone as he inconspicuously checked his surroundings, and then he made a call.

"Fuck," he cursed.

Just like the other dozen times he had tried to reach Red, his call went straight to voice mail. *I know this nigga ain't laid up with no bitch!* he exclaimed to himself as he stuffed his phone back in his pocket.

Sirens wailed in the air. They echoed in Rome's ears, as if they were moving in on him, but he knew he was just being paranoid. He looked left, then right. There were no bodies in sight. He also noticed the body of the unidentified man he had gunned down was nowhere in sight, either. He was sure he had killed him. As luck would have it, his bullet-riddled vehicle was free and clear. He hopped over to his whip and dove in. His heart raced as he cruised past a speeding police car, which never paid him any mind. He pulled his phone back out. He knew there was only one other person he could call besides Red. The last thing he wanted to do was involve her, though. She had been through enough behind him to last two lifetimes.

Shit. Who the fuck are these motherfuckas? he wondered as he pulled up in back of his stash crib.

Chapter Thirty-four

The impact of the liquid slamming into her face brought her back to consciousness.

"Wake the fuck up!" an unfamiliar voice demanded as Jewels was doused with ice-cold water through the gate that separated the front seat from the back of the vehicle.

She had no idea how long she had been knocked out or where she was or how she had gotten there. The last thing she remembered was hitting the alarm on her Bentley and grabbing ahold of her to-go box from the backseat. After that everything else was a blur. Jewels could tell she was lying on the floor of a van. Her shoulders were sore, her stomach was cramping, and her ankles were bleeding. Her hands were tied behind her back. Her ankles were cuffed as tight as they could be. She could hear masculine voices in front of her. She struggled to open her eyes. When she finally did open them, the liquid that had been tossed in her face caused them to burn. She immediately shut them, wondering what had been thrown in her face other than water. She also wondered how many hours had gone by since she was snatched. She had been unconscious since she had taken that blow to the temple. Her head was killing her, and to top it off, she had to pee.

All types of thoughts were going through her head. She couldn't believe she had got caught slipping and had been snatched. But by whom? was the million-dollar question. Was it Kareem's peoples? The white trick's? Those of the one she had killed behind Sassy's murder? Or was it in retaliation for something Rome had done? All these questions filled Jewels discombob- ulated mind. She wondered whether Rome knew she had been snatched. And she couldn't stop wondering what was going to happen to her.

She said a quick prayer. *Please, Lord Jesus, I know that it's been a while since I've been to church, and I haven't prayed in a while, but you know my heart, so if you get me out of this fucked-up situation this one last time, I promise you that I will change my ways. Amen.*

She tensed when the vehicle came to a screeching halt. Her heart dropped to the pit of her stomach. She didn't know what was going on. All that could be heard was her heart pounding. Then Jewels heard a car door slam, and seconds later another car door slammed. She heard what sounded like two different voices, but she couldn't decipher anything they were saying. They were yelling about something. Suddenly the sliding side door of the van popped open.

"Don't fuckin' move!" one of the owners of the voices yelled as he gripped her by the head.

She squinted as he roughly wiped her face with a cloth. She opened her eyes for a second time when the kidnapper released his grip. Her eyes widened when she saw two figures standing there with pistols and masks on. She had no clue why they had kidnapped her, but from the fact that they both wore masks, she knew it had to be for something serious. Jewels paid the kidnapper's command no mind. As soon as he finished wiping her face, she instinctively went into survival mode. She instantly started kicking and bucking like a bull. One of the kidnappers grabbed her by her hair and told her to calm the fuck down and get the fuck out of the van, all the while pressing the gun firmly against her face.

Jewels climbed out of the van, searching for an opportunity. She turned to the nearest kidnapper and hog spit on the black mask he had covering his face. She was met with a backhand that sent her tumbling backward and back into the van. The next thing she heard was the sound of a cocking gun. She knew then that this wasn't a normal kidnapping. There was something missing.

"Please don't shoot!" she cried, making an attempt to beg for her life.

One kidnapper moved in closer, until he stood directly over where Jewels lay. "Bitch, you think this a fuckin' game!" the kidnapper barked. His demeanor was as cold as ice. He slapped Jewels across the mouth with the gun, then pointed it directly at her face. He had the gun's safety off and one bullet in the chamber. By the look in his eyes, she knew that he was seconds away from blowing her fucking head off. All he had to do was pull the trigger just a little to hit the nail with the hammer. Jewels was sure she was going to die. There was nothing between her, them, and her brains all over the damn pavement.

The kidnapper's next move caused Jewels's eyes to widen. She watched as he unbuckled his black denim jeans. Before she knew it, a semierect dick was dangling in front of her.

"Dick or lead! Which one you want, bitch?" he growled at her.

"Come on, Buster. We ain't here—"

"Shut the fuck up!" the kidnapper yelled, cutting his crime partner off, as he snapped his neck around. "And what the fuck you say my name for?" he added. He pulled out the extra gun he had in his waist belt and aimed it at his partner.

"Yo, what the fuck?" The other kidnapper threw his hands up in surrender mode.

Jewels watched in disbelief. *I know this motherfucka gonna kill me if he drawing on his own boy*, she concluded.

"Why the fuck you say my name?" the kidnapper named Buster asked for the second time. Little did he know, the name meant nothing to Jewels, anyway. Not that he would have cared.

"It was an accident."

If he was going to say anything else after that, he never got a chance to.

The shot tore into his skull with accuracy, ending his life instantly. The kdnapper named Buster did it without hesitation or remorse. As far as he was concerned, the other guy had served his purpose and was not needed anymore. Buster returned his attention to Jewels.

"So, which do you choose?" He gripped his gun tightly and pointed it in Jewels's face.

She stared up at him and said nothing. It had been a long time since she had touched another man, let alone performed any sexual acts on them. It was because of Rome that she had been able to walk away from that life and not look back. She had vowed never to let another man besides him ever touch her again. But this was something different. At that moment, all she could think of was Rome. *I'd rather suck this dick and live to see another than be forced to do it and still die*, she reasoned.

She moved the gun out of her face, never breaking her stare, leaned forward, and grabbed hold of his dick. He rocked up as soon as she took him into her mouth. He pressed his pistol up against her.

"You bite my shit, you die."

Jewels paid his threat no mind. She focused on performing the best oral he'd ever had in his life in order to keep herself alive. She closed her eyes and commenced making love to his entire length. The glare coming from above her caused her eyes to shoot open. When she peered up, she saw that Buster was recording her with his cell phone as she sucked his dick.

What type of shit he into? thought Jewels. *Sick bastard.*

She assumed that this was his norm and that he got a kick out of it. But his next words told her she was wrong.

"Keep sucking, bitch!" he began. "See if he gonna like this. And see how much you worth to him then!" With the gun in his hand, he grabbed the back of her head again and pushed it down onto his hard dick. Jewels gagged. Fortunately for her, she was deep throated and was able to loosen her back throat muscles before he choked her to death with his dick from fucking her face.

Jewels knew who the *he* was that he was referring to. He had answered her question. But all she could do for now was keep sucking on Buster's dick and anything else he asked of her, hoping that she remained alive long enough for Rome to figure out how to rescue her and to watch as he killed this motherfucker.

Chapter Thirty-five

Rome made it to his destination in record-breaking time. He was still trying to put the pieces together. Somebody had caught him slipping, and he needed and wanted to know who. The more he played the tapes back and thought about it, the clearer it became. And then it dawned on him. His mind traveled back to the beginning of the incident, just before the shots rang out. He realized the clothes the shooters had worn were not your average, everyday urban wear, or even American wear. *That gotta be that African motherfucka peoples*, he thought. It began to come together for Rome. He scurried into the stash crib and rapidly scrolled through his call log for Jewels's number. Before he could hit CALL, an unknown number popped up on his home screen as a text message. Rome realized there was a video attached.

"What the . . ." He grimaced as he clicked on the text message.

His blood went from lukewarm to boiling hot in a matter of seconds. It was a video of Jewels, lying on the floor of an empty van, blindfolded, gagged, and hog-tied.

His fingers couldn't move quickly enough as he texted back, Who the fuck is this? Rome knew it had to be Kareem's peoples. *Who else could it be?* he thought. *I'ma kill all of them pussies if they fuckin' hurt her*, he concluded.

He got an instant reply. You tell me, bitch made nigga!

Frustrated would be an understatement for how Rome felt. Rome had no patience when it came to people playing games. Something about the text made Rome rethink who he believed was behind the attacks on him and now Jewels.

Before he could respond, another text came through. I'm the nigga you should've killed, not my two partners. And you must not have watched the video, nigga. LOL!

Rome thought quickly. In no time, he realized who the culprit was. How the fuck could I have let this happen? he cursed silently. He was all wrong. Even though the Africans were on to him, they were not the ones who had Jewels. He was sure of that. He clenched his fists and clenched his jaw. I knew I should've tracked this motherfucka down and killed his bitch ass, Rome thought with regret as he reread the text. He now knew he was to blame for Jewels's predicament.

He never got to reply to the last two texts before a third one came in. Another video was attached to it. My bad. You never got it. The upload failed. Enjoy, pussy! I did!

Tears of anger streamed down his face as he watched the video Buster had sent him of Jewels giving him head. He couldn't bear to watch it to the end. He was enraged by the fact that Jewels had to endure what she was going through.

In his next text, Buster had made it perfectly clear that it was only going to get worse, unless Rome met his demands. You thought shit was over, nigga! You and ya man, well, ya ex-man, and this bitch? Now look at her. She my bitch now! Once a ho always a ho. Right now she just sucking my dick. Next, it might be eating my shit. Depends on how long it take you to bring me a hundred bricks of that shit and a million dollars for this dirty-ass whore.

"Fuck!" Rome cried out.

Now he knew why he couldn't reach her and why he hadn't heard from Red. A million dollars and a hundred keys were nothing for him to sacrifice for Jewels's life, if in fact Buster played fair, thought Rome. She was worth that and then some to him, but he knew Buster was a snake. The fact that he had killed Red left no doubt in Rome's mind that he was capable of crossing him and killing both him and Jewels. Rome's mind raced a million miles a minute as he snatched up his .40 cal, shoved it in his waistband, then grabbed the keys to his truck and headed back out. He needed to confirm some things before he made his next move.

Chapter Thirty-six

Buster brought two loaded pistols upstairs, into the dirty and dingy apartment. He placed them in the sink by the window. The handgun and the shotgun were locked and loaded and ready to go. Buster was ready for another round of having his way with Jewels. He looked at her body and thought she had passed out from the sedative he'd given to her. As much as he was upset at Jewels for all the shit she had caused him, it did not change the fact that she was a bad bitch. Knocked out or awake, she looked good as hell.

Initially, when he'd carried Jewels into the abandoned apartment, he was going to kill her and dump her lifeless body in a garbage can and then wait for Rome, so he could do the same to him, but seeing her in her current state had made him desire her more, and now he was about self-satisfaction before he resumed his plan. *Who says I can't enjoy myself first?* Buster thought.

Buster removed his pants and boxers. His dick was standing at attention and now was completely exposed too. The hairs on his legs and arms stood erect, like his manhood. His fingers made their way from her cheek all the way to her pelvic bone. He fondled her ass cheeks and removed her panties, exposing her inner flesh. He then removed her bra. Her naked, heaving breasts came into view. Buster's dick throbbed as his eyes honed in on her long nipples. He noticed how the areolae were darker than her skin tone and how her waist and hips were slim. Buster placed his hands on hers and proceeded to stretch her fingers and pinch her nipples, hoping subconsciously that she would awaken and would partake in the activities. His fingers pinched her nipples some more, making them longer, more rigid.

The triangle of her pussy was perfectly shaved, almost bald, but inviting. Her messy curls covered her face, making her look angelic and peaceful, but something about her still made her sensual and desirable. He started kissing her body; at first his kisses were soft, and then the pace increased. He began to grind slowly against her body as his manhood grew harder. Her petite waist gave way to her curvy yet sexy hips. Her baby-soft skin made his dick harden with each touch, until it reached its full size. Each stroke against her skin made his manhood twinge in agony. He ground his teeth to try not to release himself before even entering her.

Electric shocks pulsated through his body as he ground against her, eagerly awaiting the moment when she suddenly opened her eyes and spread her legs so he could penetrate her totally. But she never did. She remained unconscious from the blow he had delivered to her head previously. Buster picked Jewels up and carried her over to where a sheetless mattress lay on the floor. The mattress bore stains that appeared to have been there for quite some time. He placed her on the filthy mattress. He let out a moan that could have awakened a bear in hibernation as he placed her hand on his manhood and proceeded to stroke himself. He closed his eyes and imagined it was her pretty little mouth wrapped around him, the way she had sucked him off earlier. This was turning him on more and more, and again he did not want to release until it was the right time. He quickly released her hand, and it dropped to her body. He then got between her legs and placed the tip of his hardness on her clit and began to flick it back and forth while gently fingering her pussy.

The sound of sex and the sweet smell of her juices mixed with Buster's musky smell filled the air. With his eyes closed once again, he pictured the two of them on a tropical island, with the sun shining. He imagined Jewels being full of life and into him. He fantasized about her mouth on his throbbing manhood. He could see her stroking and sucking it at the same time. Buster increases his pace as he envisioned her tongue brushing across his dick several times. He moaned as she ran her tongue across the tip, then pulled it hard into her mouth. The feeling was indescribable and almost surreal. The feeling of his flesh being attacked by Jewels's pretty lips seemed so real to Buster. He thrust his hips forcefully into Jewels.

Then the whole experience went from passionate and delightful to repulsive. Buster's eyes shot open. He was still between Jewels's lifeless legs, licking her pussy. Suddenly the sight and the smell disgusted him. It was like someone had flicked a switch, because he got up off the floor and looked at the body with disgust and pure rage.

"Your ass just wanna lay there, huh?" he spat. He pulled his boxers and pants up and zipped his zipper. His own guilt and shame over his actions caused him to lash out at her. But his words fell on deaf ears. That made Buster even madder. He slapped Jewels's face but got no reaction. He then gripped her nipples, squeezed them as hard as he could. He wanted to see if there would be any reaction. There wasn't.

Oh, this bitch think it's a game. Buster was pissed. He pulled his dick out and turned Jewels's on her stomach. Without any notice or warning, he rammed his rock-hard cock inside of her asshole. The penetration brought a screaming Jewels back to consciousness. Her mind told her to fight back, but her body was too weak to obey its command.

Buster was so caught up in the act of fucking her ass that he was not aware that the wetness he was feeling on his dick was not Jewels's juices but blood. He was pumping her like he had never sexed anyone before in his life. With each stroke, he turned more and more into a madman. So many things raced through his head. Buster could feel himself reaching that point of no return. His speed increased. He gripped Jewels's hips tightly. Jewels had long ago stopped screaming and crying. She refused to give him the satisfaction. Instead, she sucked it up and took it like the thorough bitch she was. Right before he was due to ejaculate, Buster quickly pulled his dick from her ass, grabbed ahold of her face, and released without warning.

"Yeah, take that, you nasty bitch!"

He grabbed his gun and proceeded to force it angrily in between Jewels's inner thighs. Jewels nearly passed out from the excruciating pain. He alternated between her ass and her pussy. The sight of her blood turned him on. Buster released her and snatched her naked body up off the mattress.

"Oh, I'm just getting started, bitch." The most insane look ever known to mankind appeared on his face.

With what ounce of strength Jewels had left, she focused her attention on Buster.

Her eyes widened when she saw what Buster pulled out after he popped open a black briefcase.

Chapter Thirty-seven

When Rome arrived, everything was confirmed. He saw that the crime scene around their neighborhood had been taped off with yellow police tape. He parked a few blocks away and walked over to mix in with the crowd. There was no need to ask who the victim was, because the body hadn't been removed yet. Looking straight through the open barbershop door, Rome couldn't believe his eyes. When he saw the familiar watch on the arm that stuck out from under the white sheet and the burgundy Tims on the feet of the dead man, he knew exactly who had been murdered. He had given Red that watch for his birthday last year.

"Motherfucka!" Rome cursed.

He inched in as close as he could get without being noticed. He was wearing a baseball cap pulled so far down, it damn near covered his eyes. He raised the brim a little to see who he could pull away from the scene and get information from. "Yo. Come holla at me," he said quietly to a fat, freckle-faced man, then proceeded to walk away.

"Is that you, Rome?" the fat, freckle-faced man asked.

"Nigga, shut ya mouth and come holla at me."

Freckle Face followed Rome back to his car.

"What the hell happened in there?" Rome quizzed.

"I don't know. I heard somebody ran up in the shop and blew Red's brains out. They don't know who it was, because he was covered up."

Rome already thought Buster was the culprit, but he refused to admit it to the man he was talking to. "I know they saying more than that. Give me the lowdown, nigga."

"Dawg, that's all I heard. They was up in there, watching a flick, and dude came out of nowhere, blasting. He never said a word. He came in, did what he had to do, and was out."

"Is that what you heard, or was your monkey ass up in there when it happened?"

The guy thought about lying for a moment but decided against it. "Yeah, man. I was up in there. That's how I know wasn't nothing said. But my ass ran to the back when I heard the first shot, so I ain't see nothing," he admitted.

"Yeah, whatever, nigga. What else happened?" Rome needed to know.

"I heard somebody say that some dude named Buster was around here."

"Buster? Been around here? Today?" Rome couldn't believe his ears.

"Earlier. That's what somebody said." Freckle Face's hands and nose began to sweat. The sound of Buster's name made him nervous. "You know him?" he then asked.

"Nigga, I'm asking the motherfuckin' questions!" Rome snapped.

"My bad." Freckle Face threw his hands up in a submissive manner.

"How long was he out here?"

Why the hell he got to be questioning me? I do not want these niggas to even think I know more than I need to know, the freckled-faced man thought before responding. "You know what? I couldn't even tell you, 'cause I bounced after I came up a couple of dollars in the crap game."

"Oh, yeah?" Rome said slyly. Before the dude knew what was happening, Rome gripped his arm and had his .40 cal up against his temple. "How about now?" he asked.

"Yo, I'm on your side, bruh." The freckle-faced dude threw his hands up. He had known Rome all his life.

Rome released him. "My bad. Shit serious right now, bruh," Rome said, apologizing. "Yo, hit me if you see that nigga anywhere." He knew it was a long shot, but he was desperate.

Rome climbed into his car and sat there meditating for a moment. He called Buster's cell several times but didn't get an answer.

"Where the fuck this dude at?" he barked aloud to no one in particular. Then he sped out of the lot. He knew he was running out of time.

There is no telling what he doing to Jewels, thought Rome.

"Fuuuck!" he yelled at the top of his lungs and banged his fists against the steering wheel.

He had no clue where to begin looking for Buster. He hated being in limbo. As it stood, he would just have to wait for Buster to return his call—if he ever did.

I gotta find this mothefucka, he told himself. *Where the fuck could he be*? he questioned.

Rome thought back to the info provided to him when he was trying to track Los down. He thought back to all the places he and Red had combed and staked out while they were trying to catch Los slipping. The more he thought, the more he envisioned all the ground they hadn't covered when they were on the hunt for Los, because they had gotten the drop on him quick.

Out of nowhere, a smile appeared on Rome's face. *I got your bitch ass*! he exclaimed as he did a doughnut in the middle of the street and headed toward the interstate.

Chapter Thirty-eight

Buster crept back down the steps to the basement with a flashlight in one hand and a brown paper bag with sandwiches and water in the other. With each step he took, the wooden steps creaked, as if they were going to give way any minute. The basement was cold, dark, and gloomy. All that could be heard was the sound of muffled sobbing and rats scurrying about. The basement was completely unfurnished and had no electricity or heat. The walls were cement, as was the floor, and the ceiling was unfinished. Electrical wires and asbestos were hanging down from every ceiling beam. As Buster cleared the last step, a foul stench could be smelled in the air. It was a mixture of body odor, urine, and feces.

In one corner of the room Jewels was laid out on her side, completely naked, handcuffed to a radiator, bruised, and badly beaten. She had a blindfold over her eyes, duct tape over her mouth, and her legs were tied together. Buster couldn't help but smile as the flashlight illuminated Jewels. She had mashed-up shit on her back and legs, and dried blood was smeared all over her face, neck, and scalp.

"Good news, bitch!" he called out. "That nigga comin' to get you."

He could hear Jewels sniffling over in the corner. He mistook it for tears.

"Don't cry now, bitch! What happened to all that tough talk?" Buster asked as, without remorse, he kicked her in the ribs.

He despised Jewels at this point. When she was getting tied up, Jewels fought back and almost disarmed him, and for that, she was beaten and raped until she was unconscious. Jewels got gun butted repeatedly in her face and sustained multiple kicks to the head and body. Buster had plans to kill her but had to hold back. It wasn't the right time, and the stage wasn't set for it yet. Rome and Jewels were going to die together.

Buster took the tape off her mouth and placed the sandwich on the floor. "Eat that shit off the floor! You ain't worth me feeding your ass."

Jewels hadn't eaten in over twenty-six hours and was so hungry that she didn't care how degraded she felt. She bent down and gobbled down the turkey sandwich in seconds.

"You was hungry, huh, bitch? You piece of shit! Don't worry. In a little while all of this will be over. You and ya boyfriend can get married in hell," Buster stated coldly.

"Fuck you!" Jewels yelled out with all the force she could muster.

"Fuck me?" Buster pointed at his chest. "No. Fuck you!" He drew his weapon from his waist belt and fired.

Jewels screamed out in agony. The bullet had torn through her leg.

"You and your boyfriend should've never fucked with me and my peoples! He made it like this. Y'all brought it on yo' motherfuckin' selves!" Buster exclaimed. He walked over to her and pointed the gun directly at her head.

Jewels looked up at him and stared him square in his eyes. "Do it, motherfucka!" she barked.

Buster chuckled. "Still wanna be tough, huh?" He applied five pounds of pressure to the trigger of his gun for a second time. This time the bullet ripped into Jewels's shoulder, pinning her up against the wall.

Buster ignored her cries. He was fed up with her cocky attitude and tough demeanor. He grabbed her by the head and brought his pistol down on the side of her face. The blow was enough to end Jewels's cries, but not before she saw the image that she had been looking for ever since she realized she had been kidnapped.

Chapter Thirty-nine

Rome had just passed the last block before his turn came up. He remembered all the spots the girl had told them they could find Los and Buster. He had checked three of the four spots and was certain this had to be it. The GPS on his phone informed him he wasn't too far from the house.

"Shit!" he cursed. It was dark. He hated the dark and really couldn't see at night.

As he drew closer, Rome spotted a white utility van parked closer to the top of the driveway than to the house. He pulled over and parked, then turned around and unzipped the duffel bag he had in his backseat. He pulled the twin .40 calibers out of the duffel. He cocked them both back and took the safety off. He then made his way over to the side of the house. He kneeled down and cupped his hands and looked through the basement's side window. He grimaced at what he saw. Jewels was sitting in a corner, tied up, naked, and bloody. Rome's nostrils flared. He couldn't tell whether she was dead or alive, because her head was slumped over.

Think, Rome. He tapped his pistol on the side of his head. He knew if he started firing shots through the window, he risked hitting Jewels. And if he missed, he knew he would get her killed, anyway. He wasn't willing to take that chance. Instead, he thought of something else.

Just as he had hoped, when he made his way around the house, he found one of the windows halfway open.

Carefully, he opened the window the rest of the way and began to climb in, only to get stuck when he was halfway through. His pants had gotten snagged on something. He struggled to get the lower half of his body through the narrow space. After making it through, he gently landed on the floor and got up, then cautiously exited the room. He made his way to the living room. As he reached it, he could hear Buster's muffled voice coming from the other side of a door by the kitchen. He put his ear to it and heard Buster say something about killing Jewels. His heart jumped. Immediately, Rome drew the conclusion that he wasn't going to let that happen, not to the woman he loved and cared about a great deal. He figured he had to do something now and do it fast.

The only thing he could come up with was to shoot first and ask questions later, but he knew that wasn't a good plan at all. But it was the only plan he had. All he could hope for was to not hit Jewels in the process. For the love of her, that was what he decided to do. Rome took a deep breath and grabbed the doorknob, then began to count to three. He snatched the door open with his guns pointed, ready for action.

The shots brought Jewels back to consciousness. Rome rushed down the steps of the basement with his smoking guns in tow. He lost his footing at the bottom of the steps, just as he tried to leap on Buster. As he stumbled to get to his feet, he noticed the blood all over his hoodie. He had broken his nose when he'd fallen. He continued to struggle to get up. Once on his feet, he staggered to the other side of the room. Buster no longer had his gun, thanks to Rome. He too was a little dazed. Rome had managed to hit him upside his head and knock his pistol out of his hand right before he plunged to the floor. Buster searched the floor for anything that he felt could be used as a weapon. He spotted a thick piece of wood and picked it up, then made his way toward Rome. When he got close enough, he drew the piece of wood back, swung at him, and hit him in the back, knocking him to his knees. He saw the .40 calibers drop out of Rome's hands as he went down, and made an attempt to retrieve one of them.

Rome quickly recovered from the blow when he saw Buster going for his gun. Buster was actually closer to the gun than Rome. Just before he was able to bend over to get the gun, Rome punched Buster right in his midsection. The punch caused him to double over. Both men were now on their knees. Rome was the first to launch another attack. He lunged at Buster. They rolled on the floor now like two female mud wrestlers in a pit. They each struggled to gain the upper hand over the other, but it was like a tug-of-war. One minute Rome was on top, and the next Buster. Remembering the other gun he had possessed, Rome made an attempt to regain possession of it, but each time he tried, Buster stopped him and tried himself to grab the gun. Finally, they both reached out for the weapon at the same time. Buster got ahold of it first.

Jewels started to kick the old radiator to loosen it from the floor so that she could slide her handcuffs off of it. She was still weak and in pain from the gunshots to her leg and shoulder, but she didn't care. Rome was here fighting for her, and now she had to fight for him.

Jewels glanced over as Rome and Buster went blow for blow. They continued to struggle, only this time it was to possess the .40 caliber. Buster managed to pull the gun over, and Rome tried to prevent him from pointing it at him. Rome somehow managed to retrieve his other gun while he continued to fight Buster off. Buster was strong, but pound for pound, Rome was stronger. All four hands were on the one gun now, as they continued to fight for the upper hand. Then, just like that, three shots echoed throughout the basement.

At the same time Jewels had succeeded in freeing herself from the radiator and was quickly removing the ties around her ankles. The shots startled her, and she didn't want to look and see who had gotten shot.

"Shit!" Buster cried out. "Yo' bitch ass shot me!" He was in pain. He had been shot once in the midsection, and he was bleeding profusely.

Rome didn't respond to him. He too had been shot. He had taken two shots to the chest at point-blank range. With what little strength she had, Jewels let out a screeching cry at the sight of Rome. Her cries could be heard throughout the neighborhood as her eyes zeroed in on him as he lay there, squirming on the floor. She was so focused on him that she never noticed Buster. He had crawled over to where Jewels was.

"Come here, bitch!" Buster struggled to stand to his feet and grabbed Jewels by her wounded shoulder. She made a failed attempt to launch an attack, throwing weak kicks and punches at Buster, only to find herself in a death-grip choke hold.

"Don't make me snap your motherfuckin' neck," he said, threatening her. His words were not worth the breath he'd used to utter them. Jewels continued fighting. Her movements caused Buster to tighten up his grip around her neck. "Calm the fuck down!" He jerked his forearms to emphasize the fact that he meant business.

Still, Jewels ignored him. At this point, she didn't care anymore, and neither did Buster. Jewels began to cough and gag from the sudden pressure being applied to her throat. She could feel herself getting weaker. She closed her eyes and could almost feel the point of no return. But something interrupted the process. The sound of a shot caused Jewels's eyes to shoot open. She could have sworn the bullet whizzed past her ear. The once tight grip around her neck loosened up, and Buster now hid behind her limber body. When she looked over, Rome was lying on his stomach, gripping his gun as tightly as he could, pointing it in her and Buster's direction.

"Nigga, I swear to God, if you don't throw your fucking piece over here, I'll blow this ho's brains out," Buster said, threatening Jewels's life again.

When Rome looked closely, he saw that Buster was hiding behind the chair that he had put down in the basement so that he could watch Jewels. Buster pulled Jewels over to the chair and sat her down, with his gun pointed at her temple.

"Kill him!" Jewels managed to yell. Just knowing Rome was still alive had given her a sudden burst of energy.

"Shut the fuck up, bitch!" Buster said, hitting Jewels upside the head with the barrel of the gun.

Rome thought quickly. He knew that Buster would kill her, just like he knew that Jewels didn't mind dying, so long as her death was avenged. But Rome didn't want it to go down like that, so he tried another route. He tried to reason with Buster. "Yo, why don't you just take all this shit, and you go your way and we go ours?"

"Nigga, you think somebody stupid? This shit'll never be over. Not until I'm dead or you and this bitch dead. Nah, fuck dat! I ain't trying to hear that shit," Buster yelled, declining the truce.

Rome had known that he wasn't going to go for that, but he had had to try. Then another thought popped into his head. "Yo, enough motherfuckas got killed already, and enough blood been spilt. I ain't trying to die, and I know you ain't, either." He hoped his words would make a difference, but somehow he knew it was a shot in the dark.

Buster couldn't help but laugh. "Nah, nigga. You wrong! I am ready to die!" Buster exclaimed in his best Biggie Smalls voice right before he let off three rounds.

Chapter Forty

Jewels was disoriented when she woke up. She had just come out of surgery. The anesthesia the doctors had given her had her body on cloud number nine. She felt light-headed, her vision was blurred, and the room seemed to be spinning. She thought she had died and had somehow made it to heaven, but she realized that wasn't the case when a sharp pain shot through her side. She had had nightmares that had seemed and had felt so real that she'd thought she might be dreaming, but the sound of someone calling her by her birth name confirmed that she was alive.

"How are you feeling?" the voice asked.

Jewels's eyes were fighting to stay open. Her body felt heavier than normal. She managed to keep her eyes open long enough to see where the voice was coming from.

"Welcome back."

Jewels was met with a Cheshire cat smile from a young-looking Caucasian woman. She checked her vitals, gave her three pills inside a small cup, and some water. Jewels stared down at the medication. The pills were three different colors and three different sizes.

"What is this I'm taking?" she asked. Her words were a little slurred.

"The white one is Motrin for the pain. The blue and green ones are antibiotics." The nurse smiled. "How are you feeling?" She went to check the heart monitor for an update.

"I feel fine," Jewels lied. The truth was, she was sore all over, and her head pounded. To top it off, her mind was flooded with images and flashes of what had taken place.

The door to Jewels's hospital room flew open for a second time. Her vision was clear enough that she could see who the new visitor was who had just entered her room. She was not surprised to see this person.

"Hello. I'm Detective Marks." A tall, dark-skinned African American man who looked more like a model or a professional bodybuilder than a policeman waved and introduced himself at the same time.

The nurse smiled and returned his hello. Jewels, on the other hand, said nothing.

"Am I interrupting?" He directed his words to the nurse.

"Just finishing up," the nurse answered. "She's all yours," she added with another smile.

Detective Marks nodded to the nurse in passing as he walked over to the side of Jewels's bed. Jewels eyed him as he approached.

"Not gonna take up too much of your time," he announced. "I know you need to get your rest so you regain your strength."

His words caused Jewels to face him. "Thanks." Her tone was low, and she sounded a little groggy. She was not in the mood to talk to Detective Marks, or to anyone else, for that matter. She just wanted to be left alone with her thoughts. She needed to figure out what all had happened and remember how she had gotten to the hospital in the first place. "I just want to be left alone," she told the detective.

"I understand," Detective Marks replied. "But first"—he pulled out his pen and pad—"I need to know who did this to you."

Jewels nodded. But the truth was, she had no intention of assisting him in any way. *What little I do know, you'll never know,* she told herself.

"Again, my name is Detective Marks." He had already reached into his inside suit jacket pocket and pulled out his card. He extended it to Jewels.

Jewels took the card, looked at it, then handed it back and turned her head the other way. Her reaction let the detective know that he was not about to get any cooperation. It was a trick, a test he had been putting people through since he was just a rookie in the crime investigation unit. If they accepted his card, most of the time they had something to say. The ones who didn't want to talk never took his card. He knew those were the ones who played by the rules. Detective Marks had already done a little background check on Jewels and had discovered she had had a life of hard knocks, so despite her beauty, there was no doubt in his mind that she was going to give him the minimum, if that. Still, it was his job.

He placed the card on the nightstand beside her. "I'll put it over here for now." He looked at the bloody gauze taped to her shoulder. "What happened to you?"

Jewels rolled her eyes and took a deep breath. She was trying to keep her composure to get through the formalities, but the detective's presence annoyed her. "I don't remember anything. Everything is a blur," she lied.

The detective studied her. He knew she was lying. "Well, an officer tells me someone dropped you off here."

His words caught Jewels by surprise. *Dropped off? By who?* The detective now had her attention. He knew things she didn't, and she needed to find out what he knew.

"Who?" she asked.

"Your guess would be better than mine," he replied.

Jewels searched his face for the truth. She had dealt with enough lying men in her profession to know when one was lying. But she concluded that he was telling her the truth.

"Was I the only one brought in?" she asked. She knew she was opening a door by asking that question.

The detective's right eyebrow rose. He thought the question was a very strange one. "Why would you think that?" he asked. "Is there something you remember?"

"Not that I'm aware of."

"Humph." He shifted positions and began to play with his beard. "You have no idea who would have or could have done this to you? Looks like whoever did this meant business, like they were angry about something."

His words caught Jewels's attention. "No! Why would I protect someone who did me like this?" Jewels became tense. The beeping on the blood pressure machine picked up speed. "I'm sure it was a case of mistaken identity or a drive-by shooting or something. Ain't nobody after me. There's no reason for them to be."

The nurse rushed in when she heard the accelerated beeping. "All right, Detective. I'm sorry, but I'm going to have to ask you to leave."

Detective Marks looked at Jewels. "You have my card. If you think of or remember anything, give me a call. Any time of the day. It doesn't matter."

Jewels rolled her eyes again and nodded her head nonchalantly, then threw her hand over her face, like she had the worst headache in the world.

"Where's my clothes? I need to get out of here," Jewels said as soon as he left.

She demanded that the nurse discharge her. She knew it was just a matter of time. The longer she stayed there, the more likely it was that the inquisitive detective would put some things together, she believed. He had said someone had dropped her off. Which meant he wouldn't stop until he found out who that someone was.

"I can't, sweetie. You need to stay here and get some rest. The doctor is the only one who can give the order to let you go," the nurse informed her.

Jewels thought back to her last hospital visit. "But you can't hold me against my will."

"That's true. But why would you want to put yourself at risk like that? They want to keep you for a couple more days, just to make sure the bleeding is under control and you're healing properly." She placed a light snack on a tray and pushed it toward the bed. "Listen, why don't you nibble on this, get a little bit of rest? Then we'll see how you feel."

Jewels thought for a moment. She was dead tired and really didn't feel like moving a muscle. "I can do that. But can you please do me a favor and tell me if by any chance my bag made it in here with me?"

The nurse twisted her lips. "It did. Let me guess. You want your cell phone." The nurse looked at her and shook her head.

Jewels tried to form a smile, but it was weak. "Can I use it please? I really do have to let some people know my whereabouts."

"Now, you know you're not supposed to use those in here." She liked Jewels. She didn't know what her situation was, but Jewels reminded her of her own daughter. "I'm going to do it for you." She walked over to where all Jewels's belongings were and grabbed the cell phone from her bag. She walked back over to the bed and placed the phone in her hand. "Promise, you won't be too long. I can get in trouble," she said.

Jewels nodded.

"I'll be back in fifteen minutes for your next vitals check," the nurse told her, then made a beeline for the door to the room.

"What's your name?" Jewels called out just before the nurse exited the room.

"Tara," the nurse turned and said.

"Thank you, Tara."

"You're welcome," replied Nurse Tara before she closed the door behind her.

Jewels wasted no time scrolling through her phone. Little by little, more of what had happened to her resurfaced. She knew Buster had kidnapped her, she remembered that Rome had come for her, and she remembered shots ringing out and being hit in the shoulder and the leg. But that was it.

He's the only person who could have dropped me off, Jewels thought as she scrolled through her phone for Rome's number. She found the number and dialed it. After the third ring, the voice she so loved came through her receiver. Jewels's heart skipped a beat.

"What's good? You know what to do," Rome's voice mail said.

Jewels cursed and hung up. She knew there was no need to leave a message, because he was bad at checking them. *Rome, where are you?* she wondered.

She understood why he would have had to drop her off. She knew he'd never leave her anywhere unless he had to. Jewels closed her eyes and tried to relax her mind. She traveled back to the chain of events from the moment Buster snatched her out of the van and forced her to give him head to when she first laid eyes on Rome after he found her. She grimaced at the images of Buster that appeared in her mind. She squeezed her eyes tightly to fast-forward the movie of the repeated rape he had inflicted on her. The horrific images were replaced with Rome's face. Jewels smiled, remembering how her heart had melted when he came rushing down the stairs of the basement where she was being held captive. His voice echoed in her head. She could hear him asking, *Babe, you okay*? She could see Rome pointing his twin cannons in Buster's direction.

Her heart sped up. She could also see Buster staring back at him, unfazed. She snarled as she relived how he had darted over to her, grabbed her up by the neck, and used her as a human shield. She could still feel the pressure he had applied to her throat. Just like in the flashback, Jewels couldn't breathe. It was as if Buster was literally choking her at that moment. Her eyes shot open. It was too painful to watch this movie. But she knew she had to continue. She braced herself, then closed her eyes and traveled back to the basement. She jerked from the sudden flash of Rome and Buster tussling over a gun. She wondered how Buster had gotten so close to Rome. *Where's his other gun*? she questioned, as it seemed Buster was gaining an advantage over him. Jewels wanted to jump in the scene and join Rome in killing Buster. The loud boom startled her. One man stood; the other dropped to the floor. Jewels's heart nearly sank into her stomach as Rome fell face-first.

"No!" she yelled out. She even let out a cry in the hospital bed as she relived the incident. The next image that appeared in her mind gave Jewels hope. As the image was displayed in her mind, the scene came back to her. Jewels watched herself scramble to get the gun, which was closer to her than it was to Buster, as he raised the one he had just used to shoot Rome. An array of shots rang out. The last thing Jewels remembered was grabbing the door handle before she passed out.

Where is Rome? Is he dead? There were so many questions still unanswered. Jewels had to get out of the hospital immediately if she wanted answers. There was no one else she could call. Again, she was on her own. She played back the conversation with the detective.

"Someone dropped you off . . . ," he'd said.

But who? There is only one person it could be. Rome.

Jewels's thoughts were interrupted by a soft knock on the door. She figured it was Nurse Tara.

"Come in, Ms. Tara."

"How are you?"

Tears formed instantly in her eyes at the sight of Rome in a wheelchair, with bandages around his chest. She tried to get out of bed, but the pain prevented her.

"I thought . . . I thought . . . What—"

"Don't worry about that now. I told you before that I always have your back." Rome wheeled himself closer to her and held her hand.

"What happens now?"

To Be Continued